WATCH OVER ME

BOOKS BY D.K. HOOD

Detectives Kane and Alton prequels
Lose Your Breath
Don't Look Back

Detectives Kane and Alton series
Don't Tell a Soul
Bring Me Flowers
Follow Me Home
The Crying Season
Where Angels Fear
Whisper in the Night
Break the Silence
Her Broken Wings
Her Shallow Grave
Promises in the Dark
Be Mine Forever
Cross My Heart
Fallen Angel
Pray for Mercy
Kiss Her Goodnight
Her Bleeding Heart
Chase Her Shadow
Now You See Me
Their Wicked Games

Where Hidden Souls Lie

A Song for the Dead

Eyes Tight Shut

Their Frozen Bones

Tears on Her Grave

Fear for Her Life

Good Girls Don't Cry

Their Haunted Hearts

DETECTIVE BETH KATZ SERIES

Wildflower Girls

Shadow Angels

Dark Hearts

Forgotten Girls

PSYCHOLOGICAL THRILLERS

The Liar I Married

D.K. HOOD

WATCH OVER ME

bookouture

Published by Bookouture in 2025

An imprint of Storyfire Ltd.
Carmelite House
50 Victoria Embankment
London EC4Y 0DZ

www.bookouture.com

The authorised representative in the EEA is Hachette Ireland
8 Castlecourt Centre
Dublin 15 D15 XTP3
Ireland
(email: info@hbgi.ie)

Copyright © D.K. Hood, 2025

D.K. Hood has asserted her right to be identified as the author of this work.

All rights reserved. No part of this publication may be reproduced, stored in any retrieval system, or transmitted, in any form or by any means, electronic, mechanical, photocopying, recording or otherwise, without the prior written permission of the publishers.

ISBN: 978-1-80550-393-4
eBook ISBN: 978-1-80550-392-7

This book is a work of fiction. Names, characters, businesses, organizations, places and events other than those clearly in the public domain, are either the product of the author's imagination or are used fictitiously. Any resemblance to actual persons, living or dead, events or locales is entirely coincidental.

To my grandchildren: Jake, Jason, Zack, Jasmine, Savannah, Cooper and great grandson, Eddie.

PROLOGUE

Friday

A shiver of fear shuddered through Ellie McBride as she peered into the darkness. Leaving the school so late had been risky, as anything might happen to a woman walking alone. She'd dashed to her vehicle and locked all the doors before driving into the night. Snow built up on the wiper blades of her SUV as she turned into the parking lot of the new convenience store on the corner of Pine and Stanton. She glanced around nervously. Going out after dark in Black Rock Falls had become a recipe for disaster but she had no choice after running out of essentials. Living alone meant she had no one to blame but herself. She'd worked late without noticing the time. Gathering her courage, she scanned the parking lot for anyone hanging around and found it empty apart from a couple of eighteen-wheelers. It was a little after eleven and her headlights picked up the rust-colored streaks of Ice Slicer in the wall of snow left from the snowplow. She parked alongside it, to avoid the arctic blast of wind buffeting the truck, and pulled her hat down over her ears.

Stepping out into the night, the drop in temperature made each breath cloud around her in steam. Glad she'd worn thermals under her clothes, her thick coat and gloves would keep her warm but didn't prevent the icy chill and snowflakes freezing her cheeks. It was so cold her eyes hurt.

The store's neon sign reflected MACK'S 24/7 in the snow in red and blue like a cop's flashing lights. She'd wondered for a time what the new store looked like inside. She'd heard the kids at the school where she taught middle grade talking about it. Moving slowly, she made her way slipping and sliding to the store, stamped her feet on the mat outside, and pushed open the door.

The tinkling of the bell on the door surprised her, as did the interior of the store as she peered around. She had expected a brand-new sparkling convenience store but this one had been built to resemble something out of the 1950s. There were the usual rows of shelves with goods for sale, glass fronted fridges with dairy products, beer, soda, and a coffee machine. The smell of coffee and burgers wafted toward her as she stepped across the black-and-white checkerboard linoleum tiles. Two men wearing trucker caps and thick coats sat in the middle of a line of red vinyl stools before a long gleaming chrome-edged counter. Her mouth watered as a soda jerk delivered plates of hamburgers and fries and looked at her. She nodded and turned toward the grocery aisles and collected the bread, milk, and other essentials she needed.

The pharmacy at one end of the store had a large sign: PAY HERE. The man behind the counter stood wearily from where he'd sat fiddling with a tablet and totaled her bill. She paid with her card and headed back to the counter and smiled at the sight of a jukebox in the corner. The owners had gone all out to make this place look genuine. No wonder the kids loved it. They'd never seen anything like it before. She wondered why it stayed open twenty-four hours a day, when the door opened in a blast of freezing air and more men walked in shaking the snow from their coats and hats. *New and popular.*

Her stomach growled at the smell of onions frying and she wished she had the courage to sit at the counter, order a burger and fries, and then just sit there eating alongside the men. Most modern women would do it without a second thought, but she had a problem communicating with any male over the age of about fourteen. Of late, she'd become more cautious than ever. So many people had gotten murdered in her town, she didn't plan on making herself an easy target. After paying for her things, she stepped out into a wall of cold and scanned the parking lot. Outside the yellow glow of the street lights, the perimeter was black, with pinpoints of light far into the distance. Steam crawled from her nostrils as she stood on the mat outside the store. Silence surrounded her. The heavy blanket of snow had dampened the usual noises. Her gaze swept the snow-covered eighteen-wheelers. The dark windows of the cabs reflected the neon sign. A couple of them steamed and made slight ticking sounds as the engines rapidly cooled.

Ellie stepped onto the icy sidewalk and walked into the eerily quiet night, keeping her head down. She crunched through the snow to her SUV. Based on the piles of snow on each side, an attempt had been made to clear the parking lot earlier, but now the latest falls had turned to a sheet of ice. The next coating of Ice Slicer wouldn't be spread until the following morning and she didn't have time to wait. The weight of the grocery bag in one hand unbalanced her slightly as she made her way back to her vehicle. She fumbled for her keys and they fell into the snow. When she picked them up, she pressed the key fob, but the hatch refused to open. Had she damaged the key just by dropping it? She tried again and sighed with relief at the familiar sound when the hatch popped open. She dropped the groceries in the back and straightened. The smell of strong cologne close by froze her to the spot. The next instant, a smelly hood dropped over her head. She cried out and turned, ready to fight. Sharp pain slammed into the side of her head. Stars danced across her vision and her legs buckled. Everything around her spun in a sickening wave of agony and she slid into oblivion.

Senses came back in a wave of pain, and cold seeped through her clothes. Ellie wanted to shout to tell someone to turn down the noise. Loud music battered her ears and her head throbbed with the beat. The hood pressed against her face sticky and wet, and the metallic taste of blood filled her mouth. *I'm bleeding.* She went to touch her face, and rough rope tore at her wrists. Using swollen fingers, she dragged off the hood, but darkness surrounded her and she couldn't stretch her legs. Heart racing, she forced herself to take deep breaths, lifted her bound hands, and touched the interior. Engine sounds and the vibrations beneath her confirmed her prison was the trunk of a vehicle. Terror gripped her as claustrophobia rose like an uncontrollable creature. The driver swerved and then the vehicle bumped along an uneven surface before stopping. A door opened and closed. Footsteps came close and Ellie panicked and pulled the stinking wet hood back on. Next came the unmistakable sounds of someone pumping gas and the odor of petroleum seeped into the trunk. She lay still and waited. The hatch opened and a light came on. A hand shook her but Ellie controlled her breathing and tried not to flinch. If they hit her again, they might kill her.

"Dammit. I've killed her." An amused but muffled voice came close to her ear. "What a shame. We'd have had such fun."

A blanket fell over her and the hatch slammed shut. Footsteps disappeared. Heart racing, Ellie removed the hood again and wiped blood from her eyes with her sleeve. She should try to escape before he returned. It had been snowing heavily for the last week, so they'd be parked undercover if she could hear his footfalls. How long had she been unconscious for? There was no way of telling. They could be anywhere in the state, but she figured they'd be at a roadhouse. From the slivers of light peeking into the trunk, she made out the inside of the vehicle. It was like her own. On closer inspection she could feel the cover above her head was the same as inside her SUV. She rolled over and ran her fingers along the inside until she found the seat release. Both back seats fell forward to make the space larger and light seeped through from the windows. Moving like a caterpillar she edged her way into the back of the vehicle and peered carefully out of the window. They were at a large roadhouse. The parking lot was filled with eighteen-wheelers. Inside the roadhouse several men in trucker hats sat around eating meals. She'd try to get out and get help. Panic came in terrifying waves. Which one of the customers kidnapped her? She couldn't trust anyone.

With difficulty, she managed to get her fingers around the door handle. She had a big problem. The moment the door opened, the interior light would come on. With luck, she might get out and shut the door before her abductor noticed, or he'd come out and hit her again. Everyone was so busy eating they wouldn't notice. She would need to move fast. Head swimming, she pushed open the door and fell onto the driveway. She hit the ground hard and kicked the door shut with her feet. On hands and knees, she scanned the area, trying to decide which way to go. She couldn't just walk into the roadhouse and start screaming. The servers would be safer, and most of them were women. Keeping the SUV between her and the roadhouse, she crawled to the end of the vehicle and, keeping down, made it to the line of dumpsters alongside the building. She looked behind her at the line of footprints in the snow, but she couldn't worry about that now. Dizzy and staggering, she headed for the back entrance and kicked at the door. It took forever before it opened. A wall of warmth and comforting aromas surrounded two wide-eyed women. One pointed a can of bear spray at her. The other let out a scream of dismay, and swaying, Ellie held out her bound hands. "Help me! Call 911! I've been kidnapped and the man is in the diner."

ONE

The insistent chiming of Sheriff Jenna Alton's phone woke her from a dream of warm sunshine and building sandcastles on the beach with her children. She stuck out her hand to grab it before it woke the entire household and stared at the caller ID.

"Who is it?" Her husband and ex-Special Forces, Deputy Dave Kane, turned on the lamp beside the bed and leaned up on his elbows.

Jenna pushed hair from her eyes. "It's Raven." She frowned. "Hi, Raven. You're on speaker with me and Dave. What's the problem?"

"I need backup at the Triple Z Roadhouse." Deputy Johnny Raven, ex-medevac chopper pilot and now K-9 trainer and one of her team, had never requested backup. At six-four and two hundred and fifty pounds of military-trained ex-soldier, he also had Ben, his K-9, as a partner. *"One of the servers at the roadhouse called 911 because a woman there insists that someone kidnapped her and is convinced her abductor is still in the building."*

Jenna dumped the phone on the bed and stood reaching for clothes. "What's your location?"

"I'm on Stanton driving toward the roadhouse from Black Rock Falls. ETA is approximately seven minutes." Raven cleared his throat. "I called Rio but he's not picking up his phone and you're closer than Rowley."

"Is the woman he kidnapped in a safe location?" Kane pulled on his jeans and pushed his feet into his boots.

"Yeah, they have her in the break room." Raven's vehicle roared as he sped along the highway. "I told them to act as normal as possible but to stay behind the counter. The woman states that she escaped from his SUV, which is parked out front. None of the servers can see the vehicle from their position. I'll take a look when I drive past and I'll try to get a plate number."

Jenna pulled on a Kevlar vest and then her jacket. She went to the gun safe to collect their weapons. Beside her, Kane was calling Raya, their nanny, to watch over their sons, Tauri and Jackson, in their absence. He gave Jenna a nod as he disconnected. Raya lived in an apartment connected by a door to their kitchen. She checked her pockets for ammo and gloves. "We're on our way. Go in by the back door. Call ahead and tell them to expect you. Don't show yourself. The roadhouse has CCTV cameras and we'll be able to identify the truck without him knowing you're there."

"*Copy.*" Raven's truck engine slowed. "*I'm going by the roadhouse now. I'll head down to the Triple Z Bar and get into the roadhouse via their parking lot so I'm not noticed.*"

Jenna nodded at Kane as he pointed toward the door. "We're leaving now." She disconnected.

A sleepy bloodhound crawled out from under the bed and shook himself.

"Go back to bed, Duke." Kane scratched the dog's head. "We'll be back soon. Watch the boys." He smiled as the dog headed along the hallway and nosed his way into the boys' bedroom. "I'm sure he understands everything I say." He followed Jenna through the house.

As they hurried to the front door, Raya came through the connecting door, gave them a wave, and headed toward the spare bedroom. Jenna followed Kane outside and reset the alarm. "Thank goodness we have Raya."

Floodlights came on as Jenna ducked icicles hanging from the front stoop and gasped as an arctic wind cut through her clothes. The previous evening, Kane had liberally coated the walkways to the garage and barn with an ice retardant, yet snow still coated everything. She ran past a winter rose, its pink petals frozen solid and looking as if it were made of sugar. All the windows of the ranch house were covered with swirling ice patterns. She grabbed Kane's arm to steady herself as they ran to the garage and climbed into Kane's tricked-out black truck, affectionately known as the Beast. The truck took off with a roar and the snow tires gripped the road as the snowplow attachment in front cut through the driveway snow with ease. It was fortunate that the snowplow driver lived next door and kept clear the road that connected Jenna's ranch to the main highway into Black Rock Falls. Apart from the town needing their sheriff, they also needed a snowplow. Ahead, the road's rusty appearance showed evidence of a recent coating of Ice Slicer, made from a mineral mined locally.

Pushed back in the seat as Kane lifted the snowplow attachment from the road and accelerated, Jenna stared at her phone. "Why do you figure Rio isn't answering his phone?"

"It's Friday night, Jenna." Kane's lips curled into a smile. "Maybe he has a hot date? He wasn't on duty tonight, was he? It was Raven's turn to man the 911 calls." He sighed. "The single guys need a life. They work all the hours you ask of them, so don't be too hard on him."

Jenna hadn't even considered that Rio might have a date. Her concern was for his safety. The high snowfall and low temperatures caused accidents and house fires. "I have no interest in his social life, but I don't expect him to have his phone turned off for any reason whatsoever. He is the member of our team living closest to town. In an emergency, I need him to get on scene as soon as possible. That's why I made him chief deputy." She sighed. "Tonight is a perfect example. We're twenty minutes away from the Triple Z Roadhouse, and Raven could be in a life-threatening situation. Living in town, Rio could have been there in five minutes."

"I can see your point." Kane slowed as they went through town. Main was practically deserted, with only vehicles parked outside Antlers, the steakhouse and entertainment hub of the town. "He's been immersed in the footage from the BW Ranch. If you recall, you asked him to check the trail cam footage for the comings and goings of suspicious deliveries of pelleted horse feed. He is convinced that Bryce Withers is doing something illegal. No one uses armed guards for deliveries of horse pellets. Something is sure going on there."

Jenna did recall Bryce Withers, the wealthy horse breeder who traveled extensively around the state. He'd become a suspect in a previous murder investigation, and her deputies had witnessed the strange behavior around the delivery of supposed sacks of horse pellets. At the time, they had a serial killer on the loose and had found no evidence for a search warrant or for any other reason to check the delivery. During the investigation, they'd been watching the movements of all the suspects by using trail cams alongside the roads to their properties or where they worked. It was perfectly legal for law enforcement to record movement on any highway. Because of Rio's concern about the delivery, they decided to leave the cameras outside Withers' property to check if he received regular deliveries of horse pellets. This was because, in Rio's opinion, the delivery they'd witnessed was large enough to last even the biggest ranch at least three months. She nodded. "Yeah, we'll need to follow up on that. I'll be interested to see what data Rio has collected. It might be enough to convince a judge for a warrant."

As they headed along Stanton, Jenna reflected on her unconventional team. She'd arrived in town like Kane, with a new face and name. He was an active asset to the government and could be called back into service at any time, but she started her law career as DEA Special Agent Avril Parker, who, after taking down a drug cartel, was placed in witness protection. Rio was a gold shield detective from LA with a retentive memory, and Raven a superb doctor, chopper pilot, and dog handler who hid himself in the forest to deal with PTSD. The only person who hadn't suffered some kind of trauma was Deputy Jake Rowley. He'd been the most helpful and loyal rookie a sheriff could dream of. Now after seven years, he was indeed a valued member of the team. She chuckled and Kane glanced at her, one eyebrow raised. "I was just thinking how we're surrounded by damaged people. Apart from Rowley, even our FBI contacts have been through the mill of problems."

"That's what keeps them edgy." Kane turned into the Triple Z Roadhouse. "How do you want to play this?"

Scanning the parking lot and not seeing an SUV parked by the pumps, Jenna shrugged. "I figure we walk in the front door and see who runs."

TWO

Nobody ran when Jenna stepped inside the Triple Z Roadhouse and inhaled the smell of hamburgers and fries. She scanned the room with Kane close behind her. Having his six-five two-hundred-and-seventy-pound wall of muscle behind her was very reassuring, plus he could draw and shoot with accuracy most people could only dream of. Most of the drivers tipped their cowboy hats or nodded in their direction. Not one avoided their gaze. She walked up to the counter, ordered two cups of coffee to go, and casually asked about the woman. The server behind the counter waved them through a locked door and into a back room. Jenna looked at her. "We still want that coffee, make it four cups, please, and bring the fixings." She handed the woman some bills. "I need to talk to her in private. Can you keep everyone away for a time? We won't be long."

"That's fine. I'll bring it right along." The server smiled and turned back to the diner.

Jenna opened the door. Inside, Raven stood barring the door. Beside him, Ben, his K-9, growled and showed a line of white teeth. She stopped dead and looked at her deputy. From his expression, no one was getting past him. As he stood down and smiled at her, she nodded to him. "What have you got for me?"

"This is Ellie McBride. She is the middle school teacher from our local school. Someone tried to kidnap her tonight." Raven's brow furrowed. "She received a nasty blow to the head. I've applied ice but she needs sutures. Now you're here, I'll get my medical kit from my truck. It's just outside in the alleyway."

"I'm Deputy Kane and this is Sheriff Alton. You're safe now. No one is getting in here." Kane pulled out a seat.

The woman said nothing and just stared into space.

"Ellie." Jenna sat opposite her. "Can you tell me what happened?"

Nothing.

"Concussion?" Kane looked at the woman and then at Raven. "Has she spoken to you?"

"My head hurts but I'm thinking straight. I'll be okay." Ellie scrubbed her hands down her face and looked at Kane. "You're both so big and intimidating, the dog keeps growling, and I'm too afraid to move."

"We're here to protect you." Raven frowned. "I'll fix your head, but I'd like you to have a CT scan." He looked at Jenna. "She needs to spend the night in the secure ward at the hospital so I can run more tests."

Seeing the woman's sheet-white face under the bloodstains, Jenna nodded. "Yeah, I'll make that happen. Grab your kit. We'll take it from here."

As Raven left, the server arrived with a tray of coffee in to-go cups. Jenna waited for her to set them down and leave before looking at the blood-soaked woman. "Can you remember what happened?"

"Yes, I remember everything." Ellie blinked. Under her eyes, bruising was spreading. "My head hurts."

Placing her phone between them, Jenna activated the recording app and took out her notebook. Allowing Ellie to tell her story in her own time, and then asking questions, worked well with traumatized victims. The concern on Ellie's face as she stared at the blood on her fingers meant that she needed to take a softer approach. The woman needed reassurance. "Deputy Raven is a doctor. He'll have you feeling better in no time. Just tell me what you remember. Let's start with just before the attack. Where were you and what time was it?"

Ellie told her story, but important information was missing. Jenna pushed a cup of coffee toward her. "Take a few minutes to gather yourself." She glanced up as Raven came through the door. "Do you mind if we ask you questions while Deputy Raven is tending to your head?"

"No, it will take my mind off it." Ellie spooned sugar into her to-go cup and drank the coffee black. "I believe I've told you everything I can remember."

As Raven went to work cleaning and suturing the cut on Ellie's head, Jenna looked at Kane and gave him a slight nod. He had an interviewing technique that assisted people to remember small details and was the best person to take the interview from here.

"Did you notice any vehicles in the parking lot when you arrived at the convenience store?" Kane held his hand loosely around his to-go cup on the table.

"Yes, two eighteen-wheelers." Ellie flinched as Raven injected a local anesthetic into her head. "I figure they belonged to the two men sitting at the counter eating hamburgers and fries."

"What made you believe they were drivers?" Kane sipped his coffee.

"One of them had a jacket with TAYLORS written across the back and I noticed the same name on one of the trucks." Ellie picked at the blood on her fingers. "The other man just looked like one—the ball cap, the work boots, and the conversation about where they were heading in a potential blizzard."

"That's great." Kane smiled at her. "So as you left, more men came into the store. Could you describe them?"

"Not really." Ellie stared into her to-go cup. "I kept my eyes averted and left as soon as they'd headed toward the counter. They arrived in eighteen-wheelers, so I imagine they were drivers like the others."

"When you walked back to the parking lot, did you see anyone else or any other vehicles?" Kane leaned forward slightly when Ellie shook her head. "Okay, now close your eyes and imagine you're walking out into the snow. Look around. What do you see?"

"Only the line of eighteen-wheelers and footprints in the snow leading to the store." Ellie kept her eyes shut tight, a small frown creasing her blood-smeared brow.

"Now go back to when you were placing your groceries in the SUV. Did you hear or see anything?"

"Not at first, but then I heard heavy breathing close by." Ellie's hands shook. "It happened so fast. The smelly hood went over my head and I panicked."

"Okay." Kane exchanged a look with Jenna. "Keep your eyes closed. You mention smell. Did you smell anything before the hood went over your eyes, or hear anything at all?"

"Why?" Ellie opened her eyes and frowned and then winced.

"When we're looking for suspects we need all the information we can gather." Kane turned the cup in his fingertips. "If the attacker smells like oil or gas, he might work in the automotive industry or with machinery, and if he smells like cows or horses, we'd look for him at one of the ranches. Smell can be a very important tool to finding someone and identifying them as your attacker. Cast your mind back. What can you smell?"

"Onions, frying." Ellie's eyes popped open. "Cologne. Cologne, it was strong. Not nice, cheap and nasty."

A solid clue. Jenna smiled. "Could you recognize it again?"

"Yes." Ellie looked up at Raven as he gently cleaned the blood from her face and neck.

"Can you recall anything about the vehicle?" Kane pushed the packet of wipes Raven was using toward her to clean her hands. "Make, color, license plate?"

Concerned by Ellie's pale complexion and trembling fingers, Jenna gave Kane's arm a squeeze. She looked at the young woman. "Are you okay to keep going? We can do this tomorrow."

"I want to keep going. I know how important it is for you to get information so you can catch this person before they hurt someone else." Ellie looked up as Raven checked her eyes again. "I feel better than I did before."

"I don't believe you have a concussion, but there's excessive bruising." Raven took two pills from a bottle and handed them to her. "These will help with the pain. When the local wears off, it will hurt again, I'm afraid."

"Thank you for helping me." Ellie's lips quivered into a smile. She turned her attention back to Jenna. "The vehicle was an SUV hatchback. I have one and I'm familiar with the inside. That's how I knew to get out through the back." Ellie swallowed the meds with the remainder of her coffee. "Not a new one, maybe seven years old, it looked just like mine. It had a blue or gray interior, same with the outside. It was either gray, silver, or light blue. I didn't see the plate, I told you. I climbed out of the side door and ran."

"Great." Kane sipped his coffee. "Now, the person who grabbed you spoke to you—man or woman? Size? Height? Did you see any part of them?"

"I'm only small, so everyone seems big to me." Ellie fingered the dry blood in her hair and shuddered. "Not tall like you but wider than me. I fought them and they were strong and took control really fast. I'm not sure if they were male or female. Their voice was muffled but I made out what they said." She swayed a little. "That's all I can remember. I really need to lie down."

"I'll take her to the hospital." Raven gathered up his things and removed his gloves. He looked at Jenna. "I've already called ahead and they're waiting for us."

Jenna stopped recording and folded her notebook. "I know you're anxious to run tests, but she is likely covered in evidence. You'll need to cover your seat with a foil blanket and make sure there's no cross-contamination from your vehicle. I'll call Wolfe to meet you at the hospital. He'll get things done fast and she'll be able to take a shower and wash off the blood." She looked at Ellie. "Rest up. You'll be perfectly safe. We have a secure ward. No one gets in or out without permission."

"Who is Wolfe?" Ellie looked at Jenna with eyes like saucers.

"Dr. Shane Wolfe, the medical examiner." Kane smiled at her. "He's a very nice guy."

"I have left groceries in my SUV." Ellie sighed. "The groceries will likely be frozen solid by now."

"We'll go and check your vehicle at the convenience store." Kane smiled at her. "Don't worry."

"What happens in the morning?" Ellie looked from one to the other. "I need to feed my cat and I need to be at work on Monday."

"I'll be by to see you in the morning." Raven helped her to her feet. "We'll make plans then and I'll make sure your cat is fine. If the tests come back clear and you feel okay, you might be able to return to work."

"What if they try to grab me again?" Ellie looked wildly around.

The woman was echoing Jenna's thoughts. "I'll make sure you're okay. For now, stay at the hospital because it's safe. I'll arrange security for you when you're ready to leave."

"I don't have my purse, my keys, or my phone. They could

be in the back of my SUV." Ellie bit her bottom lip. "I need my phone."

"We'll go and look for your vehicle." Kane stood. "I'll make sure you have your things."

Jenna watched as the poor woman left with Raven. "What did they hit her with? Not a knife, a sharp metal object?"

"I think so, maybe a car jack?" Kane headed for the door. "If we can find her vehicle, we might find some answers."

Jenna glanced toward the servers moving around outside the break room. "I need to speak to the staff and take a look at the CCTV footage before it's wiped." She searched her pocket and pulled out a thumb drive. "We need a copy of the footage for an hour before we arrived. I figure whoever did this will be on the tape. You go and see the night manager and I'll speak to the servers."

THREE

No one stopped Kane as he shouldered his way through servers carrying dirty dishes and found the night manager's office. The door was open, and behind a desk, a stick-thin man stared at a computer screen. Kane knocked on the door. "Sheriff's department. May I have a moment of your time?"

"I guess so. Did you find out what happened to that woman?" The man looked up at him and frowned.

Kane checked his watch as he moved into the office. "A woman was viciously attacked and kidnapped. She says she was thrown into the trunk of an SUV and then the perpetrator stopped here for gas and a meal. The woman managed to escape. So I need to look at your CCTV footage between eleven and twelve to identify the vehicle and who did this."

When the manager flashed him an indignant stare and his mouth set in a thin line, Kane raised one eyebrow. "You're not breaking anyone's privacy laws by showing me. This person could be in the diner right now. Do you want to risk one of your customers or staff being injured?"

"I guess not." The manager tapped on his keyboard and then beckoned Kane around the other side of his desk.

Bending to peer over the man's shoulder, Kane watched the footage. The camera was aimed at the pumps and only a few vehicles stopped for gas. As a light-colored SUV stopped in front of the pumps, but on the opposite side to the entrance to the roadhouse, Kane laid a hand on the manager's shoulder. "Go back and then stop when the license plate comes into view." He nodded. "Now zoom in."

Mud splattered the plate and covered the details. Sighing, Kane straightened. Snow covered the vehicle, making it difficult to identify. He asked the manager to zoom in again as a figure opened the hatch and bent inside before heading for the restaurant. He'd need the FBI IT specialist Bobby Kalo to look at the footage to get a closer idea of the size of them. The person's face was hidden by a ball cap worn under a hoodie. "Go ahead slowly. I want to see when the woman escapes."

He watched slowly but saw nothing. The woman could have used the vehicle for cover and slipped into the dark perimeter of the lights. He handed the manager the thumb drive. "Can you give me a copy? I'll get the FBI to clean it up for me."

The manager obliged and Kane pushed his cooperation a little more. "We know the exact time the driver used his card at the pumps. I need to know his name. It will be easier to do this now than have my team come in here with a search warrant."

"Okay, okay." The manager held up both hands in mock surrender. "Give me a minute." He tapped away on his computer and then handed the thumb drive back to Kane. "The name on the card was Ellie McBride." He shook his head. "Seems to me your kidnapper was a woman and not a very smart one either."

Kane bit down hard on his cheek, tempering the need to swear. What the heck was happening? He straightened and handed the manager his card. "If you hear anything relating to this matter, please call me. Thank you for your cooperation."

He turned to leave and found Jenna standing at the counter speaking to one of the servers. He waited for her to finish and went to her side. "I have the footage and the credit card details and guess what? Our victim paid for her abductor's gas." He shook his head. "There's nothing, not a shred of usable evidence."

"I found nothing either." Jenna frowned. "It doesn't sound right, does it? I figure we sleep on it and look at it again in the morning." She shook her head. "I was expecting a nice relaxing weekend in front of the fire playing with our kids."

Kane walked beside her to the door. "Me too."

As they stepped out into a blizzard, ice smacked his cheeks and bit into his flesh. He grabbed Jenna's hand and they slid their way to the Beast and jumped inside. In the short time they'd been away, snow had packed the windshield. He started the engine and then grabbed a snow brush and the de-icing spray from the back. The snow wasn't packed, so he brushed it away and then sprayed a good amount of de-icing spray over it. His lips and cheeks numb, he slid back behind the wheel. "Man, it's cold out there. The convenience store isn't far from here. We'll see if we can find Ellie's SUV." He went along the ramp to the highway.

Snow packed against the windshield and built up on the wipers. Visibility had dropped by the minute by the time the lights of the convenience store came into view. Kane drove into the parking lot and spotted an SUV coated in white parked beside a wall of snow. "That looks like her vehicle."

"I've got a flashlight. Let's go." Jenna pulled up her hood and jumped down from the truck. "The hatch isn't secured. I can see a gap."

Kane pushed open the hatch. The interior light came on. "There's no purse here but there's a car jack. I bet this is what he used to hit her and there's blood all over. I see the groceries but no purse."

"We'll bag the car jack." Jenna handed him an evidence bag. She searched the interior and then went to the driver's door and opened it. "No keys in here."

Kane searched the snow at the back of the SUV and bent to look underneath. "Found them. She likely dropped them in the struggle. I'll lock the vehicle, and Wolfe can look at the items in the morning." He looked at Jenna's blue lips. "We need to get out of the cold."

"Yeah, we do." Jenna rubbed her arms. "I'm freezing."

Sliding behind the wheel, Kane stared at the blanket of snowfall. Conditions had worsened in the last few minutes. "I hope the snowplows have been out since we left home. The snowplow attachment can only do so much."

"Yeah, it's bad right now. I hope Raven gets home okay." Jenna frowned. "He needs to get through the forest."

Kane brushed snow from his face and turned the truck toward home. "His road is on the snowplow priority list and he has his own attachment on his truck. He should be fine."

"I like him." Jenna flicked him a glance. "As you knew him in your past life, I know he's a danger to you, but he kind of fits in, as if he's meant to be here. Another misfit that's found a home. Do you figure I'm crazy?"

Biting back a grin, Kane gave her a long look. "He is a handsome guy. Should I be worried?"

"Oh, heavens, no." Jenna giggled. "I mean, he could be your brother. It's as if you have two, Raven and Carter, and Carter is the black sheep of the family, but Raven is like you, a big teddy bear at heart but will turn into a grizzly if provoked."

Shaking his head, Kane eased back onto the highway, peering through the blanket of snow. "You sayin' I've got a hump on my back?"

"No, but you get... Well I was going to say mad but you never get mad." Jenna tapped her bottom lip. "He doesn't get mad either. Oh, you know what I mean. You can be nice as pie one second and lethal the next."

Kane shook his head. "Raven isn't and has never been lethal." He slowed to a crawl and then stopped. He dropped the snowplow attachment and took off slowly. "He's nothing like me. He was trained to help men in the field. My training was specific. I was trained to infiltrate enemy lines, either to get intelligence or eradicate a target. I'm sure he can take care of himself in a fight but he's a doctor. I like him too but never confuse our abilities."

"So, what happened when you met him?" Jenna looked at him as they crawled along the highway. "I know you fought in the desert somewhere—you don't need to be specific."

Hating to relive the missions he'd rather forget, Kane blew out a long breath. "It was bad. I'd completed a mission, and Wolfe was trying to get me to an evacuation point. The problem was, somehow the enemy knew we were coming, so someone leaked the information. A ground team had been evacuated miles from my position, but I was getting swarmed and time was running out. The only chopper that hadn't been shot down was Raven's medevac ride. He was overloaded but risked dropping a rope for me. I'd grabbed the rope ready to be hauled up when the chopper was hit. I fell but rolled and got to cover as the chopper went down."

Images flashed across Kane's mind. Bodies on fire, blackened limbs, men crying out in pain before taking their last breath, and the smell of burning flesh and hair. "It was a nightmare. I checked everyone, all but Raven died in seconds. We were taking fire and there was nothing I could do. He was out cold with a cut on his head. I tossed him over one shoulder and ran for cover before the vultures arrived."

"The enemy was on the ground coming for you?" Jenna blinked at him and gripped his arm. "Oh, Dave, that would have been terrifying."

Kane shook his head. He hoped Jenna would never understand the horrors of war. "Getting captured is terrifying, being under fire means that you're still alive. It was like that twenty-four-seven. It was easier for me than some because I knew the terrain. Remember, I'd been alone there for a long time. I ran for about five miles and found cover in the sand dunes."

"You ran with Raven on your back for five miles?" Jenna stared at him, disbelief on her face.

Shrugging, Kane nodded. "Yeah, we were expected to be able to do that before we left on a mission. We never left a man behind, and if there'd been a team with me, we'd have carried out the bodies as well and taken them back to their families."

"From what Raven told me, he suffered PTSD after that mission." Jenna hadn't taken her eyes off him. "I can't imagine what you went through."

Glad to see the lights of town come into view, Kane nodded. "Yeah, it was bad. We almost didn't make it. This is where we're different, Raven and me. My specific job was to take out targets. I'm able to switch off the horror of killing someone but he can't. I do have empathy but not for threats to our country. I don't enjoy taking a life but sometimes to keep our country free, it's necessary and someone has to do it." He looked at her. "We were in the desert under fire for a long time, weeks. He was a soldier and we worked together well, but I did all the killing. I did what was necessary for us to survive." He cleared his throat. "Like now, with serial killers. I'll disable them before I'll kill them, but if they're coming at us shooting, I don't think twice about taking them down and I don't dwell on it afterward either. I know in my heart I made the right decision."

"That's good to know." Jenna peered out the windshield and then took a deep breath. "So how did you get out?"

Not surprised she wanted the full story, Kane nodded slowly. "I had Wolfe in my ear. As you know, then like now, I was chipped. He could track me and now he still can, since the new chip was installed. He gave us intel on the run. I'd taken Raven miles away from a friendly border because it was crawling with militants. I needed to get him mobile and safe, which I did. We were both tanned. His brown eyes and beard made him easy to disguise but some questioned my blue eyes so I wore shades. Once we'd acquired robes and headgear, I had enough language skills to deal with any factions we met along the way. We needed food and met friendlies who helped out. Everyone carried weapons, so we fit right in, apart from being bigger than most of them. Long story short, and without the grisly details, we managed to make our way along the border until Wolfe could get us a ride out of Dodge."

"Raven remembers Junior, so you gave him your name." Jenna turned in her seat to look at him. "Why would you do that, when you used a codename? What if he were captured and tortured?"

Raising his eyebrows in disbelief, Kane glanced at her. "Junior was safe. My codename would give them access to my command. Heck, every time I spoke to Wolfe, I needed to leave Raven alone. Speaking to Wolfe, I needed to use my codename." He sighed. "Once I'd gotten him to safety, I was taken out of the zone and reassigned. Wolfe told me he'd been asking after me. When it was reported I died, my name was given as Junior. He heard about it and still believes I'm dead. Yeah, there is a resemblance to my old self, but I had wrinkles from being out in the desert, many scars and tattoos. I had a jagged scar down one cheek." He pointed to his face. "The surgeon performed a miracle; they even took out the cleft in my chin. I look like I did back in college. You have the me I'd have been if I hadn't joined the military but with all the skills." He grinned. "They took skin from my backside for skin grafts. Think about that next time you're kissing my cheek."

"Oh, stop it." Jenna grinned back. "They changed my eye shape and it's amazing how different my eyes look. The rest of me is much the same apart from long blonde hair. Back then, I'd fit nicely into Wolfe's family. Although I look ten years younger than I did after living with the Carlos cartel. It was a nightmare living there. I didn't have one wrinkle when I met you."

He smiled at her. "You don't have any now." He waited for their gates to struggle open against the snowdrifts and drove through. "You're as beautiful as when I met you." He looked at the ranch house, lights blazing a welcome. "Thank goodness, we're home."

FOUR

Saturday

After completing a hard workout and tending the horses with Kane, Jenna jumped into the shower. She dried her hair and dressed rapidly even though the house was toasty. She wanted to spend as much time as possible with her boys before going into the office this morning. As she stepped out into the hallway and made her way to the family room, giggling and loud shouts came from the front yard. She went to the window and peered outside. Her yard was a winter wonderland. Snow piled up all over and long icicles hung around the porch like ancient swords. She reached for her phone smiling and, walking outside, started filming. Kane and Tauri were in the middle of a snowball fight, and Jackson was doing his best to throw snow at both of them. Steam rose in the air around all of them until they finally fell laughing in a heap and became snow angels. Giggling, Jackson climbed slowly to his feet and ran to her. Big for his age, he had started walking at ten months and, now at seventeen months, was getting around everywhere without any problems and also had a good vocabulary.

"Mommy, look, snow." Jackson pointed to the ground. His red nose and pink cheeks damp with snowflakes.

She put away her phone. "Yes, it's lovely. Are you cold?"

"No!" Jackson giggled and pointed to his feet. "Boots on."

"Diamond days." Kane brushed snow from his clothes and then helped Tauri. He smiled at her. "Our time with the kids will go so fast. We need to make the most of every second. You should have seen Jackson's face when I opened the door and told him we could play outside."

Nodding, Jenna took in the scene and sighed. "Yeah, I wish we could stay home today but maybe working out what happened last night will only be a few hours. I took a video of the snowball fight. We have that for our files."

"Snow, cold." Jackson grinned at Jenna. "Yummy." He licked snow from his red gloves.

Scooping him up, Jenna brushed the snow from his clothes and blew raspberries on his cold cheeks until he giggled. "Come on, you lot. Let's get you dried off so Mommy and Daddy can go to work."

She left the boys playing trains on the family room rug, with Raya watching over them. There were never any long tearful goodbyes, the children had gotten used to them leaving. It was normal for her to tell them when she needed to go to work. She always added what they'd be doing when she returned or planned something for them to look forward to if she and Kane needed to work a weekend. Most times at work, Rio would take over to give them family time. Like Kane had said, the diamond days with the kids flew by so fast—every second was precious. They would have welcomed another baby or two, but they were thankful for the two healthy boys they had. Having a big family had been a dream, but when she looked at her team, all like close family, maybe she'd gotten her wish after all.

"You look wistful." Kane glanced at her as they headed for

the office. "I know it's difficult to leave the kids, but we knew this going into having them, didn't we?" He squeezed her hand. "I turned out okay, well I believe I did, and I rarely saw my father. Although, I did have my mom and my sister."

Dragging her gaze away from the snow-covered lowlands, flat and brilliant white stretching out for miles, Jenna smiled at him. "It's not leaving them I was thinking about. I was just wishing that we could have had more. Adopting Tauri was a big step and he's added so much joy to our lives. Having Jackson was so special. For me having him, it was like giving you back everything you'd given up for me. I know you wanted a ton of kids, I—"

"Whoa! Hold up." Kane pulled the Beast to the side of the road and turned in his seat and stared at her. "I figure you have our relationship a little skewed. You took me, a broken damaged man, and made me whole again. I gave up nothing to be with you, but you took on a whole lot of trouble when you married me. I figure I'm the luckiest man in the world. Our boys make life perfect—don't they? Two or ten kids makes no difference to me. I'm content." He bent and kissed her. "Now about Ellie McBride. We're going to speak to her now, right?" He pulled back onto the highway.

Noting how Kane skillfully changed the subject, Jenna nodded. "Yeah, there's something about her that just doesn't sit right with me. I've interviewed many people in the same situation and they all seem a little confused, and yet her story was so slick. If she had been knocked unconscious as she claims, I would imagine she'd be a little disoriented, but she didn't come across like that to me." She pulled her black cap down over her ears, tucking in her hair. "Maybe she didn't have a purse with her, and leaving the keys under the back of the SUV would make it appear as if she'd been attacked and dropped them."

"I have a few questions on the logic of this idea." Kane

flicked her a glance. "Why would she do that? Why would anyone hit themselves in the head, and how did she get to the Triple Z Roadhouse afterward? The SUV parked at the pumps in the CCTV footage wasn't there when we arrived, so if she is trying some type of scam on us, for whatever reason, there has to be more than one person involved. The other driver who pumped the gas and stopped for a meal"—he sighed—"it couldn't have been her, because at the time, she was hammering on the back door of the roadhouse to get help."

Jenna shook her head. "There's no footage of the person going into the roadhouse, is there?"

"No, but she did have a nasty cut on her head." He glanced at her. "Sure, she could have run around the back from there, but if she did, who drove her SUV back to the convenience store?"

What Kane was saying made sense, but Jenna still had a niggling feeling that something was not right. She'd witnessed so many strange behaviors in her lifetime that anything was possible. "What if she's setting up some type of alibi? I mean, what if she and her boyfriend are planning on kidnapping women and maybe murdering them—or have already? If she pretended she'd been kidnapped, and women start showing up dead, we wouldn't consider her as a suspect."

"I figure that's a little farfetched but nothing people do surprises me these days." Kane blew out a long sigh. "I just can't imagine how anyone would consider that a grade-school teacher would be considered a suspect in a kidnapping murder. For me, it doesn't make sense. I guess we talk to her again this morning and see if we can work out what's going on." He glanced at her as they took the turn toward the hospital. "I've always told you to trust your gut instinct, and if you figure there's something wrong with this woman's story, we'll make sure we put her on the suspects list if anything else happens. In the meantime, if she is telling the truth, she might be in danger of being kidnapped again. We don't know why she was abducted in the first place and why the perp has her purse, her credit cards, and her phone."

FIVE

Jenna climbed out of the Beast and stared at Raven's sheriff's department vehicle, parked in their allocated area out front of the hospital. She turned to Kane. "I hope he hasn't been here all night."

"I don't think so. There isn't that much snow on his vehicle." Kane followed her up the steps to the entrance. "She is his patient, so he's probably following up on the scans they did last night. He is a really good doctor."

The smell of antiseptic surrounded Jenna as she smiled at him. "Maybe so, but I'm sticking with Shane, even though people have questioned me about having the medical examiner delivering our baby. I had quite a discussion with Wendy at Aunt Betty's the other day. She had discovered that Rowley's wife, Sandy, had delivered her twins in the morgue and Shane had delivered their little girl as well."

"What did you tell her?" Kane pushed the buttons on the elevator and they walked inside.

Shrugging, she met his gaze. "A little white lie. I told her he'd been my doctor when I lived in Texas and I'd recommended him to Sandy."

"Good enough." Kane led the way to the secure ward and flashed his card on the entrance scanner.

The doors opened and they walked inside. The hum of machines greeted them and nurses moved around, their rubber-soled shoes squeaking on the tile, along with people pushing carts laden with dirty dishes. At the nurses station they asked for Ellie's room and then made their way along the hallway and scanned their way through another locked door into the secure area. They found Raven chatting to another doctor outside her room and waited for him to finish. Jenna raised her eyebrows expectantly. "How is Ellie?"

"All her scans came back fine." Raven frowned. "She does have a slight concussion. Wolfe came by last night and checked her over as well. He took swabs and collected her clothes to scan them for evidence. She looks a little worse for wear this morning, two black eyes and bruising."

"She seemed to be lucid last night when we interviewed her." Kane's brow creased. "She didn't appear to be that badly damaged."

"I've seen guys injured in the field with half their brain missing and still talking as if nothing had happened." Raven rubbed his chin. "She was running for her life and pumped full of adrenaline. Sometimes it gives incredible clarity of mind." He narrowed his gaze at them. "Do you have concerns about her story?"

The suspicion would not go away and Jenna nodded. "Something about it doesn't sit right with me and I can't put my finger on it. I'll do everything I can to assist her. The abductor has her purse and phone, and that might cause a problem. We already know they used her credit card for gas and a meal at the roadhouse last night. They could try to take her again."

"We'll speak to her and when she's ready to leave the hospital maybe move her to the Her Broken Wings Foundation apartments, where she'll be secure until we apprehend this person." Kane glanced at Jenna. "We can arrange for someone to drive her to work and collect her. She'll be safe at the school during the day."

"If she gives her permission, you will be able to trace her credit card." Raven leaned casually against the wall. "Whoever abducted her might not know that we're onto them and use the credit card."

Glad Raven was on the same wavelength as them, Jenna nodded. "You must have read my mind. I guess we'd better go in and speak to her now." She walked along the hallway glancing at the room numbers.

"Do you know if she's had any visitors?" Kane glanced at Raven. "I don't recall asking if she had any relatives in town."

"No, no visitors, and I asked her if there was anyone I could call for her last evening and she said she was all alone in the world." Raven sighed. "She has friends from work, but that's about it, and she didn't want to bother them at midnight. She's anxious to get back to work."

Jenna nodded. "She did mention something about going home to feed her cat. We have her house keys, and her vehicle is still at the convenience store on the corner of Stanton and Pine. Do you consider that she's fit to leave the hospital?"

"I'd release her on Sunday afternoon." Raven rubbed the back of his neck. "Although her injury required stitches, it was a glancing blow, because apart from the two black eyes, there doesn't appear to be any other damage. She had Tylenol for the headache and seems to be functioning just fine. If she feels okay, she can go back to work on Monday."

"What about her cat?" Kane frowned. "She can't leave it at home until we catch this person."

Jenna looked at him. "She can keep it in her room at the foundation. People have had pets there before and they don't seem to cause a problem."

"If you give me her house keys, I'll go and feed her cat." Raven smiled at Jenna. "I'll come by on Sunday afternoon and collect her. We can go by and get her vehicle. She can go home and pack a bag, grab the cat, and I'll follow her to Her Broken Wings."

Nodding, Jenna liked his plan. "I'll get Rio to follow her to the school on Monday. She can give us a call when she's leaving and we'll send someone to follow her back to the foundation."

"I don't figure anyone is going to grab her off the street and we don't have the manpower to act as personal bodyguards." Kane frowned. "Or in the school grounds. There's CCTV cameras very prominent outside the foundation and trained on the teachers parking lot. You'll need to insist that she leaves and returns in daylight when there's plenty of people around."

Jenna nodded. "Okay, but Raven stick to your plan but collect her vehicle last. If there's anyone hanging about watching her, they might change their mind about abducting her if they see her arrive and leave in a police vehicle. I can always ask one of the social workers at the foundation to make sure she gets to her vehicle okay and to watch out for her return. They do the same for many of the occupants living there."

They came to her room and Jenna pushed inside. She smiled at Ellie sitting in bed watching TV. "How are you this morning?"

"I'm okay." Ellie switched off the TV and looked at them as they walked to her bedside. "Strangely, I slept well last night. I didn't have any bad dreams and I'm not having any flashbacks. It was a terrifying experience, but it seemed as if it were not happening to me at the time. I felt like I was outside my body watching what was happening like in a movie. Does that mean I'm crazy?"

"A knock on the head would do that." Raven glanced at the vital signs on the beeping machinery beside the bed. "Everything looks okay, and no, you're not crazy. The sheriff has found your keys, so I'll drop by your house and feed your cat, if that's okay? I figure you should stay here for another night and maybe go home tomorrow afternoon."

"Okay." Ellie smiled at him. "Everything you need for Precious is in the mudroom."

Jenna pulled up a chair and sat beside the bed. She pulled out a pen and her notebook and opened it to a clean page. "Do you have anything to add to what you told us last night? Can you remember any details of the person who abducted you?"

"Nothing I haven't already told you." Ellie frowned and stared at her hands. "That's all I've been doing since I arrived here. I've run what happened in my head over and over again. I closed my eyes and tried to see the parking lot again and if there was anyone there, but I don't recall seeing anyone at all. Although the vehicle he put me into would have been close by, I don't recall seeing it. It's all very confusing as if that small chunk of my memory has been erased." She looked up at Jenna. "I don't remember how they got me into the car. I woke inside the hatch and I was bleeding. There'll be blood all over the seats. I remember seeing it smeared on the door as I tried to climb out."

"Run through that again." Kane moved closer. "I've watched the CCTV footage. How did you get out of the SUV?"

"I climbed from the back into the back seats and managed to get the door open. I knew they would be close by, so I had to wait to make sure that they had their back turned in case the interior light came on when I opened the door." Ellie gingerly touched the bandage on her head. "The vehicle was on the opposite side of the pumps to the roadhouse, so the vehicle shielded me from sight once I was out. I ran toward an eighteen-wheeler parked opposite in the dark and ran alongside it and then headed along the back of the roadhouse until I found a door. I hammered on the door until someone opened it."

Jenna needed something to go on, anything at all to pinpoint a suspect. "Has anyone been hanging around lately or has anything unusual happened in your day? Have you upset anyone? Perhaps one of the parents of the children that you teach? Can you think of any reason why someone would want to kidnap you?"

"No to all of your questions." Ellie sighed. "I believe living alone makes me more cautious than normal. I live a very quiet life and don't upset anyone. I can't imagine why anyone would want to kidnap me, it's not as if I have any money for a ransom, or any family that would pay one."

At a loss to know which way to take the investigation, Jenna folded her notebook and stood. "As we have no idea who the perpetrator is or why they did this, I would like you to stay at the Her Broken Wings Foundation for a few days until we can be sure that you're safe. Hopefully this was just an isolated incident. It's very nice at the foundation—and modern. You'll be able to take your cat and we'll make sure someone escorts you to and from your vehicle, if you want to go back to work."

"Okay, I'd like that, thank you." Ellie smiled. "I'm a little afraid of going home in case they follow me."

"There is one other problem." Kane scratched his cheek. "Your purse and phone are missing. We have to assume whoever abducted you has them. They've already used your credit card to buy gas and a meal at the roadhouse. We'd like your permission to track your phone and any purchases on your credit card, so we can find this person." He took a notebook from his inside pocket and placed it on the overbed table beside her bed and maneuvered it into place. "If you wouldn't mind writing two notes—saying you give the sheriff's department permission to trace your phone and, on the second note, saying you give the sheriff's department permission to trace the purchases on your credit card, and sign both of them—we'll get to work. I suggest you cancel your credit card without delay. I'll also need your phone number."

Ellie gave him the details and then wrote the notes and signed them. She handed the book back to Kane. He smiled at her. "Thanks." He took a smartphone from his pocket and handed it to her. "This is a sheriff's department phone you can use until we find yours. I'm sure there will be people you need to call."

"Thank you, but I don't have any contacts." Ellie frowned. "I guess I can find the number of the school on the internet and I'm sure Ms. Bell will help me. She's the office administrator."

Jenna stood. "That's good to know. I believe we have enough to work with for now. Get some rest and call if you remember anything. The number is in the contacts."

"I will. Thank you, Sheriff."

Jenna headed out the door and paused in the hallway. "I guess we follow this up and take precautions to make sure she's safe." She pulled a woolen cap from out of her pocket and pushed it on her head. "She seems like a very nice person, but her story doesn't add up. The vehicle resembles her own, no one saw her abductor, and her credit card was used to pay for gas. I just can't get it out of my head that she's doing this to deflect our attention away from another crime—or she craves attention. How she managed to do it, is a complete mystery to me—unless she had an accomplice."

"Maybe it's because she's not hysterical or acting the same way as people usually do when they've been kidnapped." Kane shrugged. "She's almost clinical as if she was expecting it to happen to her one day. She reacted very well to her fight-or-flee response and ran for her life. She made rational and clear decisions when injured. We're used to interviewing terrified women who are losing it. I personally can't see any way she could get from the convenience store to the roadhouse in a blizzard with a head injury." He glanced at his watch. "If we ask Kalo to follow up on the phone and credit card, we can go home."

Jenna turned to Raven. "I figure we should go with Raven to her house. We have permission to be inside. We'll check it out and make sure no one is lurking about while he feeds the cat."

"Sure, let's go now and then we'll be home for lunch with the boys." Kane headed for the elevator. "Maybe our weekend won't be ruined after all."

SIX

Constantly wondering if her imagination was playing tricks on her, Laney Prescott peered out of the window of her two-bedroom log cabin on the outskirts of Black Rock Falls. It had seemed like a good idea to live here in summer, but now in winter, it seemed more isolated than ever. The problem was she'd seen headlights behind her on her way home from work on Friday. No one had passed her and it was as if someone had parked along the highway, and when she'd taken the track to her house, they'd stopped to watch her. Her job as a social worker meant she came in contact with many different people, and some were more hostile than others. Although she tried to help everyone, it wasn't always possible to produce the outcome they expected.

The feeling of being watched had started over a week ago when she'd heard footsteps behind her on the walk to the coffee shop and turned to see nobody there. Once inside and drinking her coffee, something brushed or touched her hair. There had been a man close by, but when she turned around, he just looked at her and smiled. Was she paranoid? Maybe, but she'd arranged for a contractor to drop by and see her about installing a security system. Now sure that someone had followed her home, insecurity about the safety of her new home concerned her. Maybe it was all in her mind, but the strange noises all night like someone dragging fingernails over a chalkboard had scared her. She'd gotten up and walked around, peering out of windows, and seen nothing but snow falling hard. She'd found herself living in a snow globe.

Laney tossed and turned, unable to sleep. Eventually she got up and made herself a cup of hot chocolate. The house should be warm, but steam escaped from her lips as she breathed on her way back to the bedroom. Confused, she went to the thermostat on the wall in the hallway and discovered it had been turned down. At this temperature, she couldn't survive—not with her asthma. She readjusted the thermostat and tried to recall when she'd first set it. She remembered that it had been at the beginning of winter when the temperature changed suddenly and the little cabin was very cold inside. Her stomach dropped considering the implications of a broken furnace. Her savings had gone to the house and it would cost a fortune to replace the furnace. Even repairs could be costly and she had only one wage coming in at the moment. Maybe she'd need to take on a second job.

By the time she'd finished the beverage, her head was aching with worry. She took two Tylenol from the bottle beside her bed and closed her eyes. Trying to push away the worry of the furnace and the insistent strange noises that continued to rattle through the house, she eventually went to sleep.

In the morning, she woke to a warm house and sighed with relief. She sat up in bed and checked her watch. She'd slept through to ten. It was just as well she didn't have to go to work today. Laney pushed her feet into her slippers, turned to pull the blankets up over the bed, and froze. Across the pillow on the other side of the queen-size bed were written the words *I've been watching you sleep.*

Terrified, she took a few steps backward and then peered around the bedroom. Someone had gotten into her house and her phone was in the kitchen on the table with her purse. She searched for anything she could use as a weapon. She didn't own a gun and the only thing she had in her bedroom was either a bedside table lamp or a hairbrush. She pulled the plug from the power outlet and carrying the lamp in front of her with both hands, edged her way through the door and along the hallway looking both ways. With trembling legs, she kept her back to the wall until she reached the kitchen. It was empty and she could see her phone sitting exactly where she'd left it.

She ran the last few steps into the kitchen, put down the lamp, and grabbed up her phone. She turned it on and her thumb went to dial 911 when a sound came from the mudroom. A shadow filled the doorway, the phone slipped from her fingers, spun across the table out of reach, and then clattered to the floor. Terrified and heart racing, Laney grabbed up the lamp and ran back along the hallway. She could lock herself in the bathroom. Why had she closed her door? Her sweaty palms slipped on the doorknob as she fought to open the door. *Hurry, hurry, he's coming.*

Footsteps, slow and deliberate, came along the hallway. A scream caught in her throat at the sight of a dark figure. The door flew open and she staggered inside and ran around the bed. Too late. In seconds, something dropped over her head. The lamp slipped from her fingers as a cord tightened around her neck. She tore at the cord squeezing the breath out of her, and her fingernails dug into leather gloves. Black spots danced in front of her eyes and her lungs screamed for lack of air. The room blurred and the bed came up fast as she tumbled over it. Something hard pressed into her back and the pressure on her throat increased. She tore at her neck as the room around her darkened. There was no escape.

SEVEN

Sunday

Outside Jenna's ranch house, the snow had been falling continuously all night. Patterns of swirling leaves covered the windows in ice, each one different from the next, much like snowflakes. It was a phenomenon that Jenna found extremely interesting. It was cozy inside the family room with the blazing fire and the crackle of pine cones filling the air with the smell of the forest. She sat on the rug in front of the fire with Kane, Jackson, and Tauri, wrapping Christmas gifts for their friends. The children had enjoyed trimming the tree but Pumpkin her black cat had stolen many of the decorations from the lower branches and turned them into toys. The kids had screamed with laughter watching her rush from room to room with a sparkling bow in her mouth growling like a leopard.

The family tradition of sitting down in front of the fire and wrapping the gifts had started when they had adopted Tauri. They wanted to immerse their sons in every aspect of the holiday festivities. Of course, personal family gifts would be wrapped in secret and would arrive by Santa on Christmas Eve.

Jenna held out a wrapped gift for Jackson to press a bow on top. His handsome face was creased in concentration as he pressed the bow to the wrapping paper. When it had attached successfully, even though a little off center, he gave Jenna a smile like an angel.

They had quite a production line going. Kane would cut the wrapping paper, wrap the gift, and hold it out to Tauri for the tape. Jenna attached a label and held it out for Jackson. They had quite a large pile of gifts under the tree. Each Christmas they would host lunch for all the team members who could make it. During the day, most people would drop by on their way to family commitments. For Jenna, it was one of the best days of the year. When her phone chimed, she looked at Kane and they exchanged a meaningful look. Weekends were precious times with their children and phone calls usually meant they would be called into the office. The call came from Rio, her chief deputy. "Morning, Rio."

"Morning, Sheriff. Do you recall the surveillance I've been doing on Bryce Withers out at the BW Ranch?" Rio's boots tapped on tile and she assumed he was in the office.

Jenna stood and headed to the kitchen. She collected her notepad and pen. "Yeah, you mentioned you've been logging all the comings and goings at the ranch, looking for the horse pellet deliveries that you considered suspicious. If he is distributing drugs, it's not happening here. There haven't been any reports of overdoses or deaths. If there had been any increase in drug dealers in town, I'd have heard about it. Have you come to any conclusions?"

"I figure he is a distributor, as in a big-scale interstate consortium. He gets the drugs sent here because we really don't have a drug problem here. It's a place no one would look for an operating cartel. It fits, the armed guards and the huge amount of horse pellets delivered regularly. There are other deliveries during the week as well, but it's easy to see the sacks of horse

pellets as they come in on a flatbed truck. I find it strange that they get a delivery on a Sunday." Rio's chair squeaked as he sat in front of his desk. "Now that we know what days the deliveries are arriving, we might be able to get enough information to the judge for a search warrant. Right now, we can't prove Withers is doing anything illegal."

Jenna looked up as Kane walked into the kitchen and she put her phone on speaker. "Does the surveillance you've been doing show that Withers has armed guards around the shipment when the pellets are being delivered? I'm assuming this doesn't happen with any of the other shipments he receives?"

"That's correct. I've been scanning his farm from a spot on the mountain. Now that we know the delivery times, it makes it easier. It's either been me or Rowley, but Raven is out there today. Raven is going to try to get closer and get some clearer images than the ones we've taken previously."

"He's not in any danger is he?" Kane looked at Jenna and raised both eyebrows. "No matter what the case, I really don't like anyone out doing surveillance on their own."

Nodding, Jenna checked her watch. "Do you know exactly where he is?"

"He's not on the ranch. He's probably up a tree somewhere with his ultra-zoom camera." Rio chuckled. "He has Ben with him and I don't figure he'll run into trouble. He knows how to survive in the forest. I doubt very much he'll encounter a bear at this time of year with the snow on the ground."

Unhappy with his lack of protocol, Jenna shook her head. "I like to know where deputies are at all times when they're in the field. We don't know what might happen, and knowing where they are means we can get to them faster if they happen to get into danger." She sighed. "Next time, make sure you have his coordinates. If you do get proof these horse pellet deliveries are covering shipments of illegal substances, which certainly looks the case if they have armed guards around them, we need to get a search warrant ASAP. When is the next delivery due after today?"

"Wednesday at seven in the evening." Rio tapped on his computer. "*If Raven has collected enough evidence, we'll add it to what we have and maybe get a search warrant on Monday.*"

It was obvious that some solid work had gone into the case Rio had insisted on investigating. Jenna watched as Kane refilled the coffee pot. It was coming up to lunchtime and the children would be hungry. "That sounds like a plan, but please check on Raven and make sure that everything is okay."

"*Yes, ma'am. I'll call him and then head home.*" Rio disconnected.

Jenna drummed her fingers on the counter and looked at Kane. "I was hoping by now that Bobby Kalo had found time to look over the CCTV camera footage of Ellie McBride's abduction. He has all types of gizmos in the FBI office to enhance the image."

"Maybe, as it isn't a murder case, he figured asking for overtime might be a problem?" He took a casserole out of the refrigerator and slid it into the microwave. "I figured we might need a hearty lunch today. I warmed bread rolls in the oven as well. I'm starving. Cold weather always does this to me."

Jenna laughed. "I don't think the weather has anything to do with it. You're always starving hungry." She glanced over one shoulder as giggling came from the family room. "I hope you didn't leave any scissors or anything dangerous for the boys when you left them."

"No, I put away everything apart from the ribbons and bows. I don't figure they will hurt themselves with them." Kane turned as the kids' footsteps echoed in the hallway. He laughed. "What have you been doing, Jackson?"

Jackson and Tauri, grinning broadly, walked into the kitchen. Each had a blue sparkly bow stuck in their hair.

"We are your Christmas presents but we don't want to sit

under the tree because we're hungry." Tauri hugged Jackson and laughed. "Do you like your gifts, Mommy and Daddy?"

Misty, Jenna bent and hugged them, wondering how she'd get the sticky bows out of their thick hair. "That's wonderful, thank you." She took Jackson's hand. "Why don't we wash up for lunch?"

EIGHT

Raven had been keeping the BW Ranch under surveillance for many weeks. The unusual activity around the delivery of horse pellets had made him suspicious. Six armed men had surrounded the previous delivery, and as one was due within the next hour, he wanted to get as much information as possible. The deliveries came in regular intervals and were easily distinguished by the sacks of horse pellets piled up on a pallet in the back of a flatbed truck. On all the other deliveries he'd witnessed over the last few weeks, everything that arrived on a pallet had been unloaded using a forklift. The horse pellets received different attention. Two men would jump onto the back of the flatbed wearing protective gear and carrying plastic bins. Horse pellets would be moved with care. From what he could make out, the men on the back of the flatbed would count the bags, so many in and so many down in the pile, before removing the top sacks and dragging out two and placing them on the back of the flatbed.

The next stage of the procedure was precisely the same each time. The sack of pellets was opened to reveal bags of what resembled rainbow-colored pills. These bags of pills were placed in the plastic containers, the lids sealed and handed to other men dressed in protective gear. Using his zoom-lens camera, Raven had taken many shots of the procedure. After speaking to Special Agent Beth Katz at the Rattlesnake Creek field office, he'd discovered the pills were most likely to be street fentanyl or a concoction of oxycodone, fentanyl, and other opioids mixed with talcum powder or powdered sugar. The number of pills in each bag could potentially kill thousands of people. He didn't need to be reminded that an amount of fentanyl the size of two grains of salt could kill a man.

He'd obtained more shots of the delivery, mainly to prove they were frequent and happened on different days. All his photographs were date-stamped and would be conclusive evidence of the unusual delivery. The records that he, Rio, and Rowley had collected over the last three months would show just cause for a warrant to be issued to search the property. He'd spoken to Kane about the difficulty of approaching a drug syndicate with only a few men when all of guards were carrying AK-47s. It would be a bloodbath. When he'd spoken to Agent Katz, she'd mentioned her partner Agent Styles' experience in busting drug distributors. Due to the isolation of Black Rock Falls, the weather alone would pose a problem for the DEA to become involved, especially when FBI agents were within a chopper ride. Kane's advice was to bring in FBI agents to assist in the takedown.

Raven parked alongside the fire road. He climbed out and the rush of cold air chilled his face. Snowflakes landed on his eyelashes and he brushed them away and pulled on his sunglasses. Once he walked away from the fire road, the brightness from the forest floor would be blinding. As a precaution, he'd been wearing his Kevlar vest since he left home and now he pulled on his backpack. Inside he had a few supplies and his zoom camera. He checked his watch. The delivery would come by in the next ten minutes or so unless it had been delayed by the blizzard. He let Ben down from the back seat and rubbed the dog's ears. Ben had a thick winter coat, but Raven had added his K-9 coat with the police logo written in yellow along each side. Being alone in the forest, anything might happen and sometimes having a trained dog by his side gave anyone planning to attack him pause for thought.

He headed through the trees to the location where he'd taken all the previous images, but this time, this new camera would give him close-up shots of the men's faces and a better look at what was hidden in the sacks of horse pellets. These images would clinch the deal with the judge when they went for a search warrant. After walking for approximately ten minutes, he found the tree beside a huge boulder. He removed his backpack, took out his camera, and slung it around his neck. "Stay, Ben."

The tree was easy to climb. It was an older pine with thick lower branches, which made great footholds. He climbed easily and made himself comfortable in the Y-shaped trunk. After attaching the zoom lens to the camera, he waited for the flatbed truck to roll along the driveway of the BW Ranch. The flatbed turned around and backed into the opening of a large barn. Men surrounded it in seconds, with their AK-47s slung over their shoulders. They stood around scanning the area in different directions as if expecting a raid. Uneasy, Raven frowned at the sight of them. The money involved in drug distribution was extremely high and these men would be paid a fortune to keep the delivery safe. They would stop at nothing to protect the man who employed them. Being up a tree, he had no cover or backup, and if he got into trouble, those men looked the type to shoot first and ask questions later.

He sucked in a deep breath. He had a job to do. Taking his

time, Raven zoomed in on each of the faces of the men as they moved around, taking as many shots per man as possible. Next, he moved his attention to the truck. The driver had gotten out and was away talking to the man he knew as Bryce Withers. Usually, the driver went into the office and then came out a few moments later and climbed back in his truck. This time, Withers handed him a manila envelope, slapped him on the back, and followed him back to his truck.

Snow piled up on Raven and covered his beard, but intrigued by the new development, he took as many photographs as possible. He zoomed in on everyone's face and detailed the complete process of the counting of sacks and removing the bags of rainbow pills. He'd also captured the license plate of the truck, which was a bonus as the last photographs he'd taken hadn't been clear enough, but this time when he scanned through the digital photographs on the camera, he could make out the license plate as clear as day. After removing the lens from the camera and placing it carefully inside his pocket, the branch beside his head exploded and he lost his balance and slid down the tree. He grabbed at branches as shots rang out all around him. Bark and twigs pelted him as he descended the tree. Sliding down the last few feet, he fell flat into the snow.

He needed to get out of here now and find cover. The thick underbrush all around the clearing would hide his camouflage gear. Legs stiff from the freezing cold, he grabbed his backpack and belly-crawled into the musty darkness. Shots cracked in the silence above him. How had they seen him? Maybe the tree had moved and given away his position, but he could have easily been a bear. Even this late in the year, some still foraged for food. He grimaced. Some fools would shoot at anything. He waited, considering his options. Remain here, and if they sent anyone to check, they'd find him. He needed to move. He whistled for Ben, who was close by, sniffing under bushes and doing doggy things.

The dog returned with cobwebs and burrs stuck in his fur. He crawled on his belly beside him, tail wagging. Keeping the dog calm and not allowing him to alert to danger was a priority, so Raven rubbed Ben's ears and stood slowly, keeping his back to a large pine tree. "What on earth have you been doing?"

Been sneezed and shook his head, blinking up at him with big brown eyes and a doggy smile that no one could resist. Raven bent to pluck out the burrs and brushed the snow from the dog's thick fur. The shooting had stopped and he peeked around the tree, seeing nothing through the dense forest. Cold had crept into Raven's bones. In this weather it would be easy to be overcome by exposure. He sipped from his water bottle. Under his jacket it had taken the heat from his body and water went down his throat in a tepid slide. "I figure we should jog back to the fire road."

From high in the tree, he'd noticed an animal track that led in a more direct route than the one he'd taken this afternoon. He headed in that direction with Ben close on his heels. They weaved in and out of the trees, trying to avoid the large clumps of snow dropping down all around them. Raven's heart raced as loud cracks pierced the silence like gunshot. Close by, frozen branches broke and tumbled down through the trees leaving great puffs of snow in their wake. When the temperature dropped this low, the forest became dangerous, not only for the risk of being caught in a snowstorm but also for falling branches that could break a person's neck. The next second, a tree branch exploded not far from him, the damage from a high-powered weapon evident. "Go, Ben. Go."

Having a few spare minutes to get back to his truck, Raven picked up his pace. Needing to get across a clearing to access the trail back to the fire road, he dashed from the safety of the trees and into the clearing with Ben close on his heels. A tree branch snagged his backpack, wrenching him off balance, and he staggered into the open. Without warning, the ground gave out beneath him and he fell into darkness. *A bear trap.* Time seemed to slow as he dropped. He tensed to greet the sharpened stakes set into the bottom. Above him, Ben whined and tore at the edge of the hole. The ground was coming up fast. *I'm going to die.*

NINE

At five after two, Kane's phone rang. It was the snowplow driver who lived next door. "Afternoon. Is there a problem?"

"I'm not sure." In the background Kane could hear a dog barking. *"There's a dog outside your office barking and turning round in circles. I figure it's the K-9 that works with Deputy Raven but he's nowhere in sight. A few people have gone to try and calm him down, but he ain't letting no one near him."*

Kane's stomach clenched. "Okay, I'll be right there. Tell people to leave the dog alone and we're on our way. Thanks for letting me know." He disconnected and turned to Jenna, who'd been listening. "Something's happened to Raven."

"Let's go." She ran to grab their gear.

Kane knocked on Raya's door and when she came to the door he explained and she gathered up the children and took them into her side of the house. He ruffled the boys' hair. "You be good now. We'll be back soon."

"Let's bake some cookies." Raya waved him away with a smile.

Uncertain what they might be facing after Rio's call about Raven investigating armed men receiving a delivery of horse pellets, Kane handed Jenna her Kevlar vest. "We'd better not take any chances as Raven was trying to get evidence on that delivery." He dressed quickly and pulled on his snow boots and then dressed Duke in his waterproof snow coat.

"Ben wouldn't leave his side if he'd been shot." Jenna pulled the vest over her head and tightened up the straps. "He's been trained to stay and give comfort and warmth, especially in weather like this. What is he doing in town? The BW Ranch is miles away."

Kane collected their weapons from the gun safe and secured his holster. "Raven would have given him an order. That means he's in trouble. Lock up and I'll get the Beast."

"Dave." Jenna touched his arm. "He was climbing a tree, wasn't he? Maybe we'll need some ropes or gear. What if he got stuck somewhere?"

Considering Raven's expertise in the forest, Kane shook his head. "I doubt it, but I'll take a climbing harness with us just in case. There's one in the truck." He thought for a beat. It was so cold, being stuck in the snow could be deadly. "It wouldn't hurt to take a couple of Thermoses of coffee. If he's suffering from hypothermia, he'll need something hot to drink." He headed out into the freezing snowfall.

After wading through snowdrifts, he opened the garage door, stamped the snow from his boots, and climbed into the truck. He allowed the engine to idle for a few minutes before backing out and heading toward the house. White steam billowed out from the exhaust, creating great clouds around him in the snowstorm. It would take more time than he liked to get along the driveway in the thick snow. Moments later, Jenna came out and handed him two Thermoses. She pushed Duke into the back seat and then climbed inside. Kane headed along the snow-covered driveway, using the snowplow attachment to clear the way.

The highway outside their property had been recently

scraped clean and a good coating of ice retardant had been spread, turning the white blacktop to rusty pink. He lifted the snowplow attachment and accelerated. A blinding-white landscape greeted them and they both reached for their sunglasses. Across the lowlands, snowdrifts had covered the fences, making it resemble a moonscape. In the distance he made out a herd of bison, with large clumps of ice hanging from their thick coats, making their way to higher ground. "I wonder if the bison keep moving to stay warm."

"They seem to survive okay." Jenna frowned. "They have very thick coats but it must be hard on the younger ones. The snow is so deep."

As they turned into Main, Christmas lights flashed red and green along the façades of the stores and reflected in the snowfall. Mechanical Santas rang bells or waved and as they passed the park, townsfolk bundled up in bright colors worked on a Nativity scene alongside a red-nosed Father Derry. Everything looked so peaceful and happy, but Kane had come to realize over the years that peaceful and happy never lasted very long. When they arrived at the office, Kane buzzed his siren to clear the people crowded outside. He pulled into a parking slot and jumped out with Jenna close on his heels. "Stand back. Ben is one of our team."

To his surprise the dog came right to him, grabbed his sleeve, and tried to lead him away toward the forest. "Where's Raven, boy?"

Ben dropped his arm, barked, ran in the direction of Stanton Forest, and then ran back and barked again. Kane turned to Jenna. "He wants us to follow him. It will take forever and by the look of him, he's been walking miles already." He opened the back door to the Beast, took out a bowl and filled it with water for the dog. When it had been licked dry, he snapped his fingers. "Ben, get into the truck. Seek Raven."

To his surprise the dog jumped in but clawed at the window.

"He wants the window open." Jenna frowned. "We'll freeze."

Hurrying behind the wheel, Kane backed out of the parking space. "I'll head for the forest near the BW Ranch and then open the window and we'll see what happens."

As they got closer to the ranch, Ben's excitement rose and he barked short sharp barks that Kane couldn't understand. Dogs and their handlers understood each other but it was plain that they were getting close to Raven's position. When the dog started to turn around on the seat and then tried to hurl himself out of the window, Kane pulled to the curb. He jumped out from behind the wheel and ran around to open the door. Ben took off and Kane stopped to help Duke down from the back seat. Ben stopped frequently to bark at them before bounding off again. Kane let him go ahead, Duke, his bloodhound, would follow Ben if they lost sight of him.

They grabbed their gear, and with Jenna at his side, Kane ran through the forest with Duke out in front, tail up high and big ears flopping from side to side. Heavy snow-laden branches dropped freezing clumps on them as they crunched along the ice-covered trails. The forest was eerily quiet, apart from the tinkling of icicles turned into windchimes by the breeze. Ahead, Ben would stop, and as they got closer, he'd turn around three times and then continue. "I know that signal. That means he's found something. I guess it also means, *This way. Follow me.*"

Approximately one hundred yards through the frozen forest and along twisting trails they came to a clearing. Kane rushed forward and then stopped to scan the area. In the middle, Ben dug at the edge of a huge hole partially covered by a rotting wooden cover. It had been covered with brush and pine needles. "It's an old bear trap."

"They have sharpened wooden stakes at the bottom." Jenna shuddered. "Hurry, he might still be alive."

When Ben barked, wagged his tail, and then sat down beside the hole, Kane moved closer, checking his footing with each step. "Good boy." He shone his Maglite down the hole. It was deeper than he'd imagined and on one side an old broken ladder hung in midair. Something moved at the bottom and he swept the flashlight beam back and forth. "Raven, are you down there?"

"Is that you, Dave? There's an active shooter up there—well, there was. I haven't heard anything for hours." Raven covered his eyes as the beam of light washed over him.

"There's no one around." Jenna moved closer. "It's creepy quiet."

"Thank goodness. I'm freezing down here." Raven rubbed his hands together and stamped his feet. "Did you bring a rope?"

Kane smiled at Jenna. "Yeah, we did, but Ben wasn't very specific about what had happened to you." He chuckled. "Although, he got his point across that you were in trouble. You've trained him well." He peered down the hole. "How long have you been down there? Ben made it to the office and just stood there and barked until someone came along."

"Hours. I gave him the order to get help." Raven's voice sounded a long way away. "I told him to seek Dave. I was hoping you were in the office today."

"Are you injured?" Jenna peered down the hole, her face filled with concern.

"Only my pride and maybe a few scrapes and bruises." Raven rubbed his beard. "There's an old mattress down here, and it broke my fall. I figured it was an old bear trap when I fell, and I was waiting for the stakes to go through me." He sighed. "Not a bear trap. It has an old ladder, so someone has been using it for a survival bunker, going on the trash down here. It was very well concealed and covered in snow. I didn't see it. I don't figure it's been used for a long time. The wood covering the entrance had rotted through."

Relieved at finding his friend, Kane nodded. "I've got climbing gear with me. I'll throw down a harness attached to a rope. I'll use one of the trees as a pulley and drag you up. Give me five to get organized. I'll toss down my Maglite so you can see what you're doing."

"Thanks." Raven coughed. "I hope you have water up there. I'm parched. My water bottle was crushed when I landed."

"I'll throw a bottle down to you." Jenna pulled off her backpack, took out a plastic bottle, and carefully dropped it down to him. "When you're out of here, I have coffee in the Beast. Where did you leave your truck?"

"On the fire road about fifty yards right of this position." Raven drank the water and wiped his mouth on the back of his hand. "There's an entrance into the forest that joins the fire road almost opposite the BW Ranch. I discovered it when I was fixing the trail cams. My camera is up there somewhere. It flew from my hand when I fell. I would have called for help but there are no bars down here."

After attaching the rope to a nearby pine tree, Kane went back to the hole and lowered the harness. "I've attached the rope to a tree." He waited for Raven to pull on the harness and took hold of the rope. "Jenna, grab the rope as well. We'll need both our strength to pull him out of there." He raised his voice. "Ready on the count of three?"

"Yeah." Raven's muffled voice came from a long way away.

Bracing his feet, Kane nodded to Jenna, who did the same. "One, two, three—pull."

Glad of his thick leather gloves, Kane strained on the rope as it slipped around the tree. His feet slid on the icy ground. "Wait! I need to get a better foothold." He rolled a few large rocks into the brush and pushed his feet into the indents. "Okay, Jenna. Pull."

They heaved and a twinge of pain echoed through an old injury in Kane's shoulder. He bent his knees and leaned back. The first part was the hardest, lifting a man almost the same weight as him would be a challenge, but with Jenna's help they moved him the first few feet.

"Hold! I can grab part of the old ladder." Raven's voice came from inside the hole. "Okay, pull."

The next part was easier as Raven found footholds and they managed to haul him up and over the edge. Kane slumped against the tree as Raven rolled out of the hole and lay panting on the snow, with Ben licking his face, tail wagging wildly. Raven was covered in leaves and dirt and had a scrape on one cheek, but looked okay. After taking a few minutes to catch his breath, Kane tied crime scene tape from the trees in a triangle to warn others of the hole, although it was plain to see. He turned to look at Raven. "You were lucky you didn't break your neck."

"Someone was shooting at me, so we weaved through the trees. I got caught up in the branches and didn't see the trap." Raven blew out a long breath. "I hope I haven't compromised the mission."

Kane shook his head. "No, they wouldn't have seen you. Not from the BW Ranch and there's no way they'd have spotted your camera." He glanced behind him. "They'd need a sniper to get you from that distance, so not the drug dealers. I'm guessing it's more like an illegal hunter. I'll call the forest warden and he'll check it out." He stared at the overgrown hole. "This old trap has been here for years. No wonder you didn't see it."

"I'm lucky I had Ben with me." Raven ran a hand down his face. "You would never have found me. There's absolutely no way out down there. The ladder was just out of reach, and trust me, I jumped a thousand times to catch hold of it." Raven smiled wearily as he sat up and hugged his dog. "Good boy."

"Let me look at that graze." Jenna knelt to tend the graze on Raven's cheek and checked him out for injuries. "You'll live." She pushed the first aid kit into her backpack and smiled. "Oh, look! There's your camera." She rolled to one side and reached under a clump of bushes and then held it up like a trophy. "It looks okay. Did you get any evidence?"

"Yeah, I did. More than enough for a search warrant." Raven looked at Jenna. "I watched them unload the flatbed through the camera lens. I could see right into the open barn. They dropped a pallet near the door and unpacked it. The others went to the back of the barn. Hidden in the pallets was one different bag. Small, only a few pounds maybe. The guy who handled it used gloves and a face mask. I figure it's fentanyl tablets made up ready for distribution." He rubbed the back of his neck. "Enough to kill thousands."

TEN

Monday

A blizzard in full force pelted the house when Jenna left for work on Monday morning, covering the blacktop with tall drifts of snow. The elementary school had closed the previous Friday due to the weather, and the boys would be spending their time with Raya making more decorations for the house. They'd delayed leaving until they heard the familiar sound of the snowplow and then followed it along the way into town. It was a little before eight as they drove along Main, and considering it was such a bitterly cold day with relentless snowfall, it surprised her to see so many people out clearing the sidewalk.

Christmas had always been such a festive time in Black Rock Falls. In fact, from Thanksgiving all the way through until the first week in January, the town seemed to glow in happiness and friendship. The one thing the townsfolk enjoyed the most was decorating the town. It wasn't only the stores that went all out to embrace the holiday season, but all the houses they passed as they drove into town had amazing displays of Christmas lights and decorations. Father Derry's church had a huge snowman outside and flashing red and green signs indicating the way to a new Nativity scene inside the chapel.

After her parents died, Jenna had been completely alone and decided to throw herself into her work as an undercover DEA agent. That part of her life came to an abrupt end when she testified against Viktor Carlos, a drug cartel kingpin. Forced to move into this town, she'd never believed she could be happy again. Now, even though she lived in Serial Killer Central, she couldn't imagine a happier life than living in Black Rock Falls with Kane and her children. Excitement that she'd celebrate Christmas with the best group of friends she'd ever had was so close she could touch it. It's strange how a group of people, with the exception of Rowley, who carried so much baggage from their past lives had all fit together like pieces of a jigsaw puzzle. Rowley, of course, had been there since the beginning and was the frosting on the cake. Jenna leaned back in her seat and smiled. Life was sure filled with the unexpected.

"The town looks beautiful, doesn't it?" Kane smiled at her. "It's like a Christmas card. Did you notice the huge baked turkey inside the window of Aunt Betty's Café? It has flashing eyes."

Jenna grinned at him. "Yeah, I did notice and it made me wish it were real because we're gonna need one that big to feed everyone at Christmas dinner."

"Don't worry, I've got all the meals covered. Four turkeys and three glazed baked hams. Tons of desserts planned, including apple pie and pecan pie. My famous gravy and mashed potatoes. The list goes on. Trust me, no one will go hungry, and everyone brings a plate as well." Kane glanced at her. "It seems I'm going to have some help this year in the kitchen. The FBI are coming to town. Jo and Carter are flying in from Rattlesnake Creek on the twenty-fourth, I believe, and Beth Katz and Styles are already close by in Louan. They can all fit into the cottage. There's Jo's daughter, Jaime, and Bobby

Kalo. I'm glad we added more spare bedrooms when we renovated. Jo loves to help and Beth has offered as well, although Styles helped out the last time they dropped by." He grinned at her. "I purchased more plates and silverware for this year. It seems our extended family is growing."

Sighing with happiness Jenna smiled at him. "The more the merrier. I just love that everyone gets on together."

They arrived at the office just as Maggie was hanging up her coat. Jenna leaned on the counter. "I see the deputies have arrived early this morning. It's not like them to get here before you." She waved at Rio and Rowley, but she didn't expect to see Raven at work unless she needed him. As he worked closely with dog rescue and trained K-9s, he was on call. The system worked well.

"I needed to wait for the snowplow to go by before I could get out of my driveway." Maggie stared out of the window and frowned. "Rio mentioned that Agents Katz and Styles are stuck in Louan due to the weather. Styles mentioned he could fly in the snow but not in a blizzard because of the visibility, so I guess if they're planning on going to your ranch over Christmas, they'll be hoping it stops snowing for a day or so."

Chewing on her bottom lip, Jenna let her mind go to their close friends Carter and Jo. Carter would need to fly the chopper to their ranch. She stared at the sky, hoping for a change in the weather. "I haven't checked the weather report but I hope it will clear soon. Surely it won't be snowing this heavily all through Christmas. I'll keep my fingers crossed." She turned and headed for the stairs to her office.

Inside Kane had already put on a fresh pot of coffee and was sitting studying his computer screen for any updates on the server. "Have you found anything interesting?"

"Yeah, Kalo cleaned up the images on all the files on the kidnapping case and couldn't find anything we could use." Kane twirled a pen in his fingers. "He mentions it would be impossible to make a positive identification on either the vehicle or the person leaving it. He also said he enhanced everything in the parking lot outside the convenience store and couldn't see anyone coming or going from the time Ellie McBride left the store. He says here that she walked into a shadow and vanished. After checking the footage for another hour, no vehicles similar to the one outside the roadhouse came or went."

Jenna pulled off her coat, shook it, and hung it on a peg behind the door. She removed her boots and slipped on a pair of shoes that she kept for inside the office during winter. "That case gets stranger by the second." She glanced at her watch. "Raven dropped by the Her Broken Wings Foundation women's residences yesterday to check on Ellie. Father Derry has offered to drive her to and from work until we determine it's safe enough for her to return home."

"That's very kind of him." Kane leaned back in his chair. "I asked him if he'd like to come to dinner with us this year, but he told me he prefers to spend his Christmas Day in the shelter to make sure that everyone is fed and has a bed for the night."

Jenna smiled. "He is a lovely man."

Footsteps came up the stairs and Rio and Rowley came through her office door. She glanced at them as she poured herself a cup of coffee. "Did you gather enough evidence to get a search warrant for the BW Ranch?"

"Yeah, and then some." Rio placed a folder on Jenna's desk. "Raven got some very good shots of the delivery. Along with our surveillance, I figure we can persuade a judge to give us a search warrant." He smiled. "Executing it is going to be a problem if we plan it for the day the next delivery arrives, but we don't have much choice because we have no other proof that they're handling illegal drugs."

Sifting through the photographs and noting the men armed with AK-47 rifles, Jenna closed the file and handed it to Kane.

"We would be walking into an ambush. Look at the firepower those men are carrying. Ideas?"

"I figure first you go and get the warrant." Kane stood and handed Rio the folder. "This looks big and we don't have the manpower to take down an operation like this. We'll need to call in the FBI to assist."

Jenna nodded. "It's going to take more than the five of us to take down that many men. As it happens, Maggie mentioned that Agents Katz and Styles are in Louan. You head over to speak to the judge the moment his office is open and I'll call the FBI. Once we know who is coming, we can make plans. With something this big, I would imagine the FBI will be sending in one of their DEA teams. Leave it with me." She smiled at Rio and Rowley. "Good job."

"Thank you, ma'am." Rio took the folder and led the way downstairs with Rowley on his heels.

"Dave Kane." Kane pressed his phone to his ear. "Yes, Ellie, what can I do for you?" He stood and went to Jenna's desk. "Just a second, I'll put you on speaker. The sheriff is right here." He placed his phone on her desk. "Take a few deep breaths and tell us what happened."

"When I came into the classroom this morning, there was a note written in red on the whiteboard. It says, 'I know where you live.' I immediately prevented the children from coming inside the classroom and moved them to another room. I called you right away." Ellie breathed heavily as if she'd been running. *"It's the person who kidnapped me, isn't it? They've got my purse. It has my driver's license in there, and my ATM cards. What am I going to do?"*

"Right now, stay where you are, with your students. Contact the bank and tell them about your stolen cards. Do it now." Kane flicked a glance at Jenna who nodded. "We'll be there right away."

Concerned, Jenna frowned. "This is Sheriff Alton. Are you

able to lock your classroom door until we arrive? The one that you're in at the moment, not the one where the writing is on the whiteboard."

"I'm in the classroom now and I have already locked the door. The children are safe and I've notified the principal. He'll meet you when you arrive." Children's voices hummed behind Ellie. *"I need to go. I don't want the children to get upset."*

Collecting her things, Jenna nodded. "Okay, but continue with our arrangements to keep you safe. I don't want you going home until we've caught this man. We're leaving now."

"Duke, stay." Kane rubbed the dog's head. "We'll be back soon." He grabbed his coat.

Jenna looked at Kane. "I assumed the middle school would be closed for the blizzard. They shut down for the winter break on the twenty-second. It's so close I figured they'd do the same as the elementary school." She tapped her bottom lip. "Although Raya did say the school would remain open with a skeleton staff in case students' parents couldn't find childcare if they were working."

"I'd say the less people traveling in this weather, the better." Kane headed for the door.

ELEVEN

On arrival at the school, they crunched through the ash- and salt-coated blacktop of the parking lot. Jenna brushed away the snow from her sunglasses as she walked to meet the principal, who was waiting just inside the front door. "Has anyone been inside the classroom since Ms. McBride noticed the writing on the whiteboard?"

"No." After handing them both visitor passes, the principal ran a hand through graying hair and shook his head. "I have no idea how someone just walked into the school and wrote on the whiteboard. We've implemented rigid security here. As you can see, you need to be wearing a lanyard to get inside unless you're a member of the staff. We wear ID cards and come through a separate entrance, as you will see." He led them through a side door. "The children come through in single file through the turnstiles and the scan picks up everyone. It's a new part of the AI technology that Black Rock Falls introduced for security. We have one door into the building and emergency exits all around. If someone opens one of them, an alarm sounds."

"If the pupils and the staff have photo IDs, the only possible breakdown of the system is through the visitor passes." Kane gave him a long look. "How is your security around them?"

"I keep them in the safe in my office." The principal looked from one to the other. "As you can see, anyone visiting the school who needs to talk to someone in administration has access through the lobby. We have the administration desk there so if parents need to see their kids or pick them up for some reason, they don't need a visitor pass, they only need to wait in that area until we bring the children to them. Anyone needing to speak to me receives a visitor pass and these are signed in and out. The only exception being law enforcement. I know the Black Rock Falls deputies by sight, so there's no need for them to sign in and out."

Nodding, Jenna followed the principal along a hallway lined with classrooms on each side. Through the windows, she could see the students working with their teachers. As the principal had mentioned, all of the students had lanyards around their necks. Holiday decorations in the rooms and along the hallway triggered happy recollections of her time at school. For a brief second, a memory of sitting around a Christmas tree singing carols surrounded her like a warm hug. Letting go of the past, she dragged her mind back to the case. "What about the maintenance staff and those who work in the cafeteria?"

"They have separate entrances and have to pass through a scanner like everyone else." The principal stopped outside a classroom. "I have CCTV footage of this morning. I'll go back to my office and run through the last forty-eight hours and see if I can find anything useful. If you come by my office when you're done here, I'll show you."

Jenna wanted more information and moved a little in front of him to stop him from retreating. "Can you tell me if anyone else has been in the classroom this morning? Obviously, Ms. McBride went in, but did you go and have a look as well? Was anything touched or removed from the room?"

"Ms. McBride did mention that the red pen used to write on the whiteboard is missing." The principal gave her a direct stare. "The pens are usually along the bottom of the board on that small tray. Most teachers keep three colors out: black, blue, and red. The rest they keep in a desk drawer."

Nodding, Jenna held her ground. "I'll need a complete list of all the staff and anyone else who was here today. If cleaners were working, I'll need to know their shift times. I want you to include gardeners and anyone else who works outside as well because I assume they would be coming inside at some time during the day."

"I can get that for you from the office without a problem." The principal rubbed his chin. "I don't believe that contravenes anyone's privacy issues."

"Do you send out the list of shifts with people's names on it? Or timetables for the teachers' classes?" Kane inclined his head as he looked at the man. "If so, who was here on what day is common knowledge."

"That's good to know. I'll have the office make up lists for you and have them in my office when you get there." The principal unlocked the door to the classroom and ushered them inside. "I'll leave you to it." He turned and hurried away.

Jenna followed Kane inside the classroom. They pulled on examination gloves and stood in the middle of the room turning slowly. The room smelled just as Jenna remembered from her time at school. She believed all schools had the same unusual smell. It wasn't just an old books and crayons type of smell. She'd always believed it was gym shoes and dampness from the kids after they had been playing outside. The modern schoolroom surprised her. It seemed Black Rock Falls had embraced a very modern approach to learning. Instead of rows of seats, they had the tables and chairs in an arc. Small groups of chairs were in different sections of the room, set around a single table. New equipment abounded. When she'd been at school the teacher wrote everything on the blackboard, and now it seemed that they used an interactive whiteboard. She'd noticed the kids walking around with tablets and assumed most of their work was done via a computer of some type. "Everything is computerized. I'm impressed. Although, some folk would find the expense for laptops or tablets out of reach."

"Not here." Kane examined a camera. "There's funding for laptops for kids in middle grades and upward." He indicated to the device. "This is a document camera for displaying the kids' work or other material." He waved a hand. "This is open learning. I've read all about middle school as Tauri will be here before we know it."

Jenna walked through the chairs and stood in front of the whiteboard. Slap-bang in the middle in large red writing was written: *I know where you live*. She moved her attention across the board to notes made by Ellie McBride and then back to the red writing. She turned to glance at Kane, who was standing beside her taking photographs. "Is it just me or does that writing look the same as the notes written by Ellie McBride?"

"Yeah, there are some similarities." Kane took photographs of the teacher's notes on the board. He turned to look at her and raised one eyebrow. "If this is her handwriting, is this a futile bid for attention?"

Shrugging, Jenna turned to him. "Maybe she's lonely, but she's not going to find Mr. Right in my department. Most of you are already taken." She glanced around for the missing red pen, bending to look under tables and inside a waste bin under the desk. "I can't find the missing pen and there'd be too many fingerprints in here to check. As the perp took the pen, chances are they'd be wearing gloves anyway."

"It does look suspicious." Kane removed his black Stetson and his woolen cap, scratched his head, making his hair stick up in all directions, and then smoothed it down. "I guess we hold our judgment until we see the CCTV footage. If someone did enter the classroom this morning before Ellie McBride arrived, then we'll know she's telling the truth. Although, I admit it is suspicious when we couldn't see her escaping from the SUV at the roadhouse." He pulled on his woolen cap and then replaced his Stetson. "My concern is, if she wasn't kidnapped, how did she get to the roadhouse in the first place?"

Jenna blew out a sigh. "There is only one conclusion, isn't there? There is more than one person doing this. If Ellie is lying to us, then she has someone else involved, although I have no idea why someone would try to set up something as stupid as this scheme. The only people it inconveniences are law enforcement. Maybe if we made a comment about giving a false statement to the police and the consequences, she might change her mind."

"That's an option." Kane shrugged and rested one hip on the edge of one of the desks. "My instinct is to play it out and see what happens. If we jump to conclusions that she's involved and something happens to her, we'll be stuck with egg on our face. The one thing we do need is copies of everyone's handwriting, although that script is pretty standard between teachers." He went to the whiteboard and picked up a pen. He wrote the same words and stood and looked at Jenna. "That's obviously not my handwriting but I can write almost the same as the teacher without much effort. We should also consider someone might be setting her up."

Allowing Kane's ideas to percolate through her mind, Jenna gave her head a little shake. "Okay, I guess we go and look at the CCTV footage. While we're there, I'll ask the principal if he'll arrange for every member of the staff to write that sentence on a piece of paper with their name and contact details. We'll send someone around to pick them up later. I'll email them to Kalo and he can use his magic software to see if he gets a match."

"That sounds like a plan." Kane slipped an arm around her shoulder, peered both ways through the windows into the hallway, and then pressed a kiss to her cheek. "It was great yesterday, wasn't it? I don't think I've ever enjoyed sitting down wrapping Christmas gifts so much before. Toasting marshmallows in front of the fire with the boys will stay in my heart forever." He looked deep into Jenna's eyes. "Having a family like we have has always been a dream of mine. I'd pushed it so far to the back of my mind I never thought it would be possible."

Smiling, Jenna leaned into him. "Yeah, sitting there in front of the log fire was like being in one of those holiday movies. When you say diamond days, I know exactly what you mean. We've had quite a few of them since we've had the boys, haven't we?"

"There were a few before." Kane turned toward the door. "The day I asked you to marry me and our wedding were very special." He cleared his throat and smiled at her. "I hope no one is recording us at the moment. We don't look very professional, do we?" He winked at her and headed for the door.

When they arrived at the principal's office, Jenna requested the handwriting samples. He spoke to his secretary and then took them down the hallway and into a control center, where the security guard watched the monitors. Jenna watched with interest as a man pushing a floor polisher stopped outside the classroom, went inside for less than three minutes, and then came back out again and continued along the hallway. Playback was stopped at that point and Jenna turned to the principal. "Who is that man?"

"I have no idea." The principal folded his arms across his chest and stared at the screen, his eyebrows raised. "Our janitor is in his late sixties and it's obvious that's a younger man."

"Rewind the tape and zoom in on the man's face." Kane leaned on the table and stared at the screen. "The way he has his ball cap pulled down it's hard to distinguish his features."

Jenna moved closer to the screen and shook her head. By the way the man kept his head down the entire time, he knew about the CCTV cameras. He wore gloves and a pair of coveralls, and it was impossible to even make out the color of his skin. She looked up at the principal. "Does this super AI security system use facial recognition or the barcode on the ID cards?"

"The barcode." The principal shook his head slowly. "Not one of my employees would hand over their ID card. To do so would be instant dismissal. The safety of the students is our priority in this school."

"This means that one of your employees won't be able to enter the building if the card was stolen from them." Kane straightened. "I noticed the time stamp on the footage was seven-fifty, so if you keep a record of when the staff enter the building, we should be able to pinpoint whose card has been appropriated." He turned his attention to the principal. "You do keep a record of who is entering the building and at what time, don't you?"

"Yes, and I'll ask someone in the office to do a search. They have all the software on their computers. If you'll give me a few moments, it shouldn't be too difficult to find." The principal went to leave but Kane stopped him. "Is there anything else?"

"Yeah, maybe check to see if the janitor is here today." Kane frowned at him. "If he hasn't arrived, he might be in trouble. If so, we'll need his details so we can do a welfare check on him."

The principal gave him a curt nod and headed back to his office. Jenna glanced at the security guard and indicated to the screen. "Can you follow that guy and see where he goes?"

"I already have but I can show you if you like." The security guard forwarded the tape and then jumped to another camera feed to follow the man. "He dumps the bucket in a closet and heads out of the front door. I ran the tape on a little to see if I could glimpse his vehicle leaving the parking lot." He indicated to the screen. "It's not very clear but I do believe that is a silver SUV."

"Thanks." Kane pulled a thumb drive from his pocket.

"Can you copy the vehicle footage and the part outside the classroom onto this for me? I'll get the FBI to run it through their software."

"Not a problem." The security guard went to work.

Once the copy was made, Jenna and Kane headed back to the principal's office. They waited for him to finish a call and Jenna looked at him and raised one eyebrow in question. "Have you been able to get the information we requested?"

"My secretary is putting it on a thumb drive as we speak." The principal's eyes narrowed and he leaned back in his chair staring up at them. "The janitor didn't come to work today, so I called him. He is at home and did call in this morning to say that his truck wouldn't start and he's waiting for someone from Millers' Garage to drop by to look at it. I asked him to go and look for his ID card. He usually leaves it in the glovebox of his vehicle and of course it's missing."

Jenna exchanged a glance with Kane. "So I assume whoever stole the card did something to his truck so he couldn't get here this morning."

"It sure seems that way." The principal ran a hand down his face. "I just wonder how the person who wrote the message on the whiteboard knew that the janitor kept his ID in the glovebox."

Ideas buzzed around Jenna's head. "There are a million options on how he got that information. I gather the janitor's been working here for a long time?"

"Yes, maybe fifteen years or so." The principal clasped his hands and stared at her.

Nodding, Jenna straightened. "This man might have even been employed by the school and had gotten to know the janitor and maybe seen him put his card or keys in the glovebox." She sighed. "We'll look into it. We'll need those handwriting samples. I'll send a deputy over to collect them, if you could give me a call and let me know when they're ready." She handed him her card. "Thank you for your assistance. If anything else unusual happens, call 911 right away."

Jenna led the way out of the office and waited at the secretary's desk for her to hand her a thumb drive. After thanking the woman, she turned to Kane. "I figure it's time to visit Aunt Betty's Café and we'll go over the information we've discovered and then decide what to do next. For now, we'll leave Ellie at the Her Broken Wings Foundation residences. She'll be safe there. I don't want to risk her going home until we have this sorted."

"Okay, Aunt Betty's it is." Kane pulled down the rim of his Stetson and headed out into the snow.

TWELVE

Heavy snowfall built up on the wipers as they drove back to Main. It seemed that everyone in town had decided to go to Aunt Betty's Café for lunch and parking outside was limited. Kane turned the truck around and parked on the grass alongside the park. He climbed out, his boots sinking into the deep snow, and went around the hood to assist Jenna across the road. They both stamped their feet on the mat outside the café door and stepped inside. Kane inhaled the delicious aromas of fresh-baked bread and coffee. As they walked toward the counter, the distinct smell of chili wafted toward him and his stomach growled in appreciation. Nothing better on a freezing cold day than Aunt Betty's chili along with wedges of fresh bread.

They ordered at the counter as the servers were busy. The restaurant hummed with the sound of conversation and the clinking of silverware. Kane's attention went to the fresh-baked pies in the display case and he ordered a wedge of pecan and one of peach. "I'll have them à la mode."

"I'll have the same. I'm as hungry as a wolf." Jenna grinned at him. "You can eat my leftovers if my eyes are bigger than my stomach."

Kane chuckled. "Not a problem." He took the pot of coffee Susie, the manager, had placed on the counter. "I'll take that. You're rushed off your feet."

"Thanks." Susie smiled and indicated toward another group of people coming through the door to join the line to the counter. "It's been like this since six this morning."

Kane headed toward the table reserved for the sheriff's department at the back of the room. Aunt Betty's Café had always been good to the law enforcement in town. They delivered take-out orders in record time, allowed them to jump the line when they were busy, and provided a reserved table. All these considerations made their lives better because they could dive into the café and grab a quick meal during investigations without delay. After placing the jug of coffee on the table, he removed his coat and hung it over the chair beside him and dropped his Stetson onto the seat. He sat down and rested his hands on the table as Jenna poured the coffee and added the fixings. Their table was situated up in a corner, so no one was actually sitting close by and they could talk freely without anyone overhearing them. "I noticed that you were working on your tablet on the way here. Did you happen to contact Kalo and tell him what we're up against?"

"Yeah, I did and I sent him the files on the thumb drives." Jenna pushed a cup of coffee toward him. "It's pretty quiet in Snakeskin Gully at the moment and he was glad of something to do. He's looking forward to coming to see us over Christmas. Apparently his folks have gone to Australia for twelve months for his father's work, so he'll be glad of our company."

Kane sipped his coffee, wishing that his bowl of chili would arrive soon. "This abduction case is complex, isn't it? Ellie McBride doesn't seem the type of person who would try to hoodwink law enforcement. To me, she seems like a typical teacher, but here is where I become concerned. Her abductor has her purse and phone, he knows where she lives, and almost killed her, and yet when we spoke to her this morning, her main interest was for the safety of the students in her classroom. When we mentioned taking her to the foundation to live for a few days, all she was concerned about was her cat. I've seen many abducted people and they're usually traumatized, and yet she carries on without a care in the world. It's as if it never happened. Do you find that unusual for someone who's been abducted?"

"All the people we've spoken to after a terrible tragedy or the death of someone close to them react differently." Jenna eyed him over the rim of her coffee cup. "Classrooms filled with kids can be very difficult to control and it takes a special kind of person to remain cool and calm when all about you is going crazy. She did seem upset this morning when she mentioned the writing on the whiteboard. I figured that was a normal reaction. She didn't mention anything about wanting to go home, so I believe she understands the gravity of the situation." Jenna took a long drink of her coffee and then refilled her cup from the pot on the table. "The problem is there are too many things surrounding this case that bother me. There is no proof whatsoever that she was kidnapped. We have no CCTV camera footage apart from her going into the store to buy her groceries and then heading out the door. Her purchases are still in the back of her vehicle and there were no signs of a struggle in the snow around her SUV. We have no vision of her leaving the vehicle at the roadhouse. I know it was around eleven when she left the store, but we haven't considered that she might have taken a cab to the roadhouse." She slowly added the fixings to her cup and stirred. "Then we have the writing that is almost identical to her own on the whiteboard in the classroom. My problem here is, yes, there was someone going into that classroom this morning, so she could be telling the truth, although how do we know that the man entering the classroom wrote on the whiteboard? The other thing that's bothering me is how did the man know that was her classroom?"

Kane finished his coffee pondering what she said and then poured himself another. "We'll need to check to see if the janitor finally arrived at the school this morning. If he did, we'll know he got a replacement card and there are two cards out there with his name on them. I would imagine that this person knows his way around the school, so either he's worked there before or was a past student. Teachers keep their own classrooms for many years, so it wouldn't be too far of a reach to believe that that's how he knew where Ellie McBride was teaching. It would also account for how he knows about the janitor using his glovebox for his card and keys." He smiled as Susie came over with a tray carrying their bowls of chili and a plate piled high with buttered bread still hot from the oven. "Thanks, Susie."

Kane watched her weave her way through the tables back to the counter. "The other thing I find difficult to believe is why someone would hit themselves so hard on the head that they split the skin open. When did they do it? I doubt someone would pick them up in a cab with blood all over them like that." He took a spoonful of chili, moaned with pleasure as the full flavor rushed over his taste buds, and then swallowed. "I just can't figure out a motive for why she would do such a thing."

"I've been trying to consider our next steps in this case and keep coming up empty." Jenna blew on a spoonful of chili. "We can send everything we have to Kalo but it's going to be difficult to search for suspects as we're not real sure if a crime has been committed. I'm sitting on the fence with this one." She ate the spoonful and sighed. "We'll offer her protection in the form of the foundation and I figure we wait and see what happens. I don't consider her to be in any great danger at the moment. If someone does have her purse, knows where she lives, and plans to kill her, it's not going to do him much good, if she is not staying there, is it? We'll have her escorted back and forth to work and soon it will be winter vacation and she doesn't need to leave the foundation at all. If Kalo comes up with anything we can use, we'll take it from there, but right now, I figure we should consider the case that Rio and Rowley are working on. What do you say?"

Slowly Kane buttered a slice of bread considering what Jenna had said. He shrugged. "I don't think we have any other choice. If we can determine that the handwriting doesn't belong to her, I guess we will have to believe her story, but I agree the only option we have is to wait and see if this guy makes another move. With the other case, if they do suspect that Bryce Withers is trafficking drugs, we should be bringing in the FBI. We don't have the resources to take down that many men. I *could* go in and shoot them all, but we have no proof that they're actually distributing drugs. If they are and we storm Withers' property even with a search warrant, those men are carrying AK-47s and someone is going to get hurt."

"Okay, if Rio gets the search warrant, I'll call in the FBI to assist." Jenna glanced out of the window. "Not that I believe they'll be able to fly here in this weather."

Kane nodded. "There also may be a delay with the deliveries. They come along like clockwork according to Rio, so it won't be too difficult to set up a raid on another day. I don't figure drug lords take vacations over the holidays. It will be business as usual."

"Good, that's the business out of the way." Jenna grabbed a slice of bread and placed it on her side plate. "Now let's eat before this gets cold."

THIRTEEN

On the drive back to the office Jenna's phone chimed. "Sheriff Alton."

"I'm sorry to trouble you, Sheriff. This is Mavis Kettering from the Black Rock Falls Social Security Administration. I work with a young woman by the name of Laney Prescott. Laney didn't come in to work today. She had a very important meeting and wouldn't miss it unless something was wrong. She didn't call in sick and I've been on the phone all morning and my calls go to voicemail. I'm a little concerned as, you know, being social workers we have our enemies. I'm unable to leave the office right now and as she lives alone in a little cottage on the outskirts of town, I would appreciate it if you could do a welfare check on her."

Jenna glanced at Kane and he gave her a nod and pulled to the side of the road. "I am just heading back to the office now, so yes, I will be able to do a detour and check on Laney. Give me her details, including her phone number."

Unfolding her notebook, Jenna quickly took down the details and asked the caller to repeat them. "I'll call you back on this number once I have spoken to her. The blizzard is doing strange things with the wireless signal at the moment, so maybe your calls aren't getting through. I'm on my way now." She disconnected and added the details to the GPS.

Powdery flakes swirled around them as they made their way slowly out of town and along Stanton. The snowplow had been through earlier and great mounds of dirty snow piled up along each side of the road. The pine trees' branches bent under the weight of the snow, some touching the ground. The expanse of white seemed endless apart from the stark black of the pine trees' trunks and the scattering of pine cones. The temperature had dropped rapidly and every so often a loud crack broke the silence as frozen branches shattered and fell to the ground. It was difficult to distinguish between a gunshot and a large branch exploding in the freezing temperatures. It was fortunate the town council had initiated the new program to use the red ice retardant on the highways. In the past, they often encountered many patches of black ice, causing accidents all over.

The GPS gave clear and easy-to-follow instructions, and soon heading along a snow-covered road through the forest, Jenna couldn't imagine how Laney Prescott would have been able to get into town without calling out a snowplow to clear her road. The size of the road did show an indication of recent snowplow activity, so perhaps the council cleared the road in the early morning and after five each night, which would work well for anyone trying to get to and from work. Although she hadn't noticed any other houses in the local vicinity as they drove along. They reached a small log cabin set back from the road. It resembled a gingerbread house covered in frosting. Long icicles hung down from the gutters. On one side was a garage and Jenna assumed the owner's vehicle would be inside. The snowplow attachment on the front of the Beast had cut a clear path right to her front door.

Shivering, Jenna buttoned up her coat and slipped outside. She sunk into snow up to her ankles. Wearing knee-length boots to keep her feet dry had been a good decision. She stepped in Kane's footprints on the way to the front steps and stood to one side as he hammered on the door. No sound came from within and she looked at Kane. "Hear anything?"

"Nope. She's not here." Kane peered around the side of the house. "We need to check the garage."

Jenna led the way to the garage and cupped her hands around her eyes to look inside a window. "There's a truck in here, so I assume she's home. I wonder if she's had a medical episode." They returned to the front door and knocked again. When no one answered she turned to Kane. "Can you open the door?"

"Not a problem." Kane removed his gloves and pulled out a set of lock picks. He went to work and in seconds opened the door. He replaced his gloves and pushed the door open. "Laney Prescott, this is the sheriff's department. We're coming inside to do a welfare check." He stood for a moment listening and then slowly drew his weapon. "It's cold in here and I feel a breeze. I figure one of the doors is open. We need to clear the area."

Nodding, Jenna moved to the left, keeping her back to the wall, and Kane went right. The small family room was clear, and they slowly walked toward a hallway leading to bedrooms. When she opened the first door her heart raced. A pair of feet with blue toes stuck out from around the side of the bed. She fought back the need to run as far away as possible and swallowed hard. "She's in here. Clear the rest of the house. I'll go and check her."

"Copy." Kane moved along the hallway.

Unease gripped Jenna as she eased carefully into the room, moving her weapon from side to side and up and down. If something had happened to this woman, the perpetrator could be hiding close by. As she moved around the foot of the unmade bed, she frowned at the writing on the pillow. *That's not good.* Two steps farther and the familiar smell of a voided bladder hit her full in the face. Preparing herself for a homicide, she glanced down at the woman sprawled on her chest on the floor, face turned to one side and arms spread. From the woman's torn nails and bloody fingers, she'd put up a fight. The side of her face she could make out was blue and her tongue stuck out. A cord had been tied tightly around her neck with a piece of wood through it. Jenna had no doubt the victim was deceased. With care, she stepped around the body and peered into the bathroom. She sighed with relief finding it empty.

A slight noise in the hallway spun her around and she aimed at the door. "Stop where you are. I'm armed."

"It's me, Jenna." Kane filled the doorway, his gaze moved across the room and then to her face. "The back door is wide open and the rest of the house is clear. There are signs of forced entry." He pulled on examination gloves and bent to check the pulse of the woman. "I'm assuming this is Laney Prescott?"

Horrified, Jenna pointed to the message on the pillowcase. "Can you imagine waking up and seeing that?" She indicated to a lipstick standing up on the nightstand. "Maybe this will tell us who murdered her." She pulled out her phone and took a photo of the lipstick and the top lying beside it. "Can you scan this for prints?"

"Sure." Kane moved the scanner over the lipstick and case. He looked at the screen. "There are a few nice clear prints on here." He dropped the lipstick and case into an evidence bag and wrote on it.

Moving carefully around the body, Jenna looked at Kane over one shoulder. "I don't see any signs of a struggle, apart from the mat being roughed up a bit. It appears she was out of bed and heading for the bathroom when he grabbed her from behind. I figure he took her by surprise. I wonder if she even noticed the message."

"There's a bedside lamp under the bed." Kane straightened.

"I figure when she noticed the message, she grabbed it as a weapon and ran to lock herself in the bathroom."

Nodding, Jenna bent closer to the victim. "There are scratches on her neck. She fought for her life. I'll call Wolfe. I hope he's in town today."

The medical examiner and Kane's military handler, Dr. Shane Wolfe, and his daughter Emily ran Black Rock Falls Medical Examiner's Office but they worked all over the state. His wife, Norrell, was a forensic anthropologist with her own department in the same building. Having connections with the government meant that Wolfe's equipment was state of the art. He had embraced all the available AI technology to enhance and improve the results of his work. This meant that they got their results faster, which made crime solving easier. After Jenna contacted Wolfe, she followed Kane out into the family room and they meticulously went through the house looking for evidence. They found damp patches between the mudroom and the kitchen. She turned to Kane. "I assume he got in this way."

"Yeah, she hasn't got a security alarm, and there are small scratches on the lock of the back door, so I can only assume he picked the lock the same way as I did to get in the house." Kane took photos of the lock and the damp patches on the floor. "I've scanned the door for fingerprints and found a few. Once Wolfe has finished examining the body, I'll scan the victim's prints so we can eliminate them from any I find inside the house."

Looking over the scene, Jenna determined the killer had planned the entry into the house with intent to murder. From the message on the pillow, she guessed the killer had been inside the house previously. She made a mental note to follow up on anyone who had visited the house for any type of maintenance or deliveries over the last few weeks. She would also need a warrant for Laney Prescott's office to release the details of cases involving men and to discover if she'd had disputes with anyone. She needed next-of-kin details and a list of her friends.

She walked back through the house, leaving Kane to search for fingerprints. The second bedroom had been made into an office and a laptop sat on a desk alongside a photograph of a group of three woman and a man. She copied it with her phone and walked back through the house and frowned. Apart from that one photograph, she found no other images. The calendar on the fridge door was practically empty, but Jenna bagged it, hopeful it might hold a clue to who had come by the house. She dropped the evidence bags on the kitchen table and went back to the office.

Jenna sat in the comfortable chair and opened the desk drawers, hoping to find an address book. She found a pile of invoices for work completed on the cabin. She collected them and bagged them. She took photographs of the laptop and then, using a large evidence bag, slid the laptop inside. With luck, Wolfe would be able to open the computer, and if not, Kalo would be able to guide them through the process. Having an FBI computer expert on the team was a bonus in times like this. The sound of a vehicle arriving broke the silence inside the house. Jenna stood and walked into the hallway. She could see Wolfe's van through the window. "Wolfe's here." She went to the front door and opened it.

"What have you got for me?" Wolfe stamped the snow off his boots, wiped his feet on the mat outside the door, and covered his boots with booties. His daughter Emily did the same.

Glad that Wolfe had arrived so fast, Jenna stood to one side as they came into the house. "A woman we assume is Laney Prescott appears to have been strangled. We found the back door open and signs of forced entry. Dave believes they picked the lock. We've both been inside the room without booties, I'm afraid. I removed a lipstick and separate cap as evidence. I've also taken the laptop from the office and some invoices. I've documented them all with photographs."

"I found a good set of prints on the lipstick." Kane held up his scanner. "I haven't touched the body apart from checking the pulse in the neck. I'll need the victim's prints for comparison."

"Okay, let's get this show on the road." Wolfe placed a large forensics kit on the floor and then pulled on examination gloves. "Lead the way."

FOURTEEN

Dr. Shane Wolfe scanned the bedroom, taking in the layout. He examined the pillow and frowned. "I figure he snuck in here and wrote the message while she was asleep. It's likely he sat in that chair over there and watched her sleeping. The moment she stirred, he went out into the hallway until he heard her getting up to use the bathroom. I'll examine her neck in a moment, but from the position of the garrote, he attacked from behind."

Concerned that the body might be carrying trace evidence, Wolfe moved everyone away from the door to the bedroom. "Emily, we'll wear coveralls for this one." He turned to Jenna. "Strangulation using a garrote from behind is a very personal type of murder. It also takes a deal of strength and takes four minutes minimum to asphyxiate someone. We should assume he left fibers or bodily fluids on the victim. Her nails are torn up as is her neck. She fought hard to pull the garrote away. I'll check under her nails for any foreign DNA traces, just in case she managed to claw his arms."

"She must have been terrified." Emily looked at her dad, and sadness filled her eyes. "Can you imagine waking up and finding someone in your house?" She turned to Jenna. "You gotta stop him doing this again. Do you figure it's the same person who abducted the teacher?"

"It's too early to tell, Em." Jenna met her gaze. "Find me the evidence and we'll take him down."

After covering his clothes with blue coveralls and buttoning them up, he indicated to Emily to go inside the bedroom. He turned to his assistant badge-holding deputy, Colt Webber. "Suit up. We'll need a body bag in here on the carpet so I can roll her over and into it. I also need you to vacuum the carpet all around the victim and that chair over there." He pointed to a small chair in the bedroom beside the window. "If the killer watched her sleep, that would be one of the places I would imagine he'd sit."

"I wonder how long he's been stalking her." Jenna folded her arms across her chest and looked at him. "Do you figure she noticed anyone hanging around? If so, did she mention it to anyone? This is an isolated spot. A stranger would stick out a mile."

"It's possible. Being a social worker carries a certain amount of personal risk." Kane rubbed his chin as if in deep thought. "Unfortunately, social workers are involved with a wide range of people and criminals. Most are involved in family disputes and taking children into care, which doesn't make them very popular. Others deal with substance abuse and mental health. It's not a career I would like for my daughter if I had one."

Wolfe's daughter Julie had been determined to become a children's advocate, which would make her part of the Child and Family Services division. Although she'd planned to work along with the children's court, there would always be a chance of conflict. He gave Kane a long look. "Apart from Emily, y'all in the line of fire for anyone with a grievance. Em and me, well, we don't seem to have that problem. We haven't been stalked by a corpse yet."

Once Webber laid the body bag beside the victim, Wolfe and Emily carefully rolled her over. Rigor had stiffened the body but Wolfe managed to push the arms down to the sides. They stood for a few moments looking down. Even after hundreds of crime scenes, Wolfe couldn't prevent the pang of regret when he saw a murder victim. Laney Prescott, if that was her name, had been an attractive woman but now her bloodshot brown eyes bulged and her shoulder-length chestnut-colored hair stuck to the blood around her neck. Her tongue protruded between blue swollen lips. The grotesque sight of a strangulation victim made the body unfit for viewing by relatives. In cases like this, he always advised them to remember their loved ones as they'd last seen them.

The attack had come from behind, fast and violent. The twisted rug, ripped nails, and deep gouges around her neck indicated Laney had fought for her life. She'd tried to get her fingers under the garrote and torn her neck to shreds. Wolfe scanned the room, noting the position of her slippers and bent to follow the electrical cord trailing from under the edge of the bed. He looked behind him at Webber. "Take photographs of the position of those slippers over there. I believe she might have been wearing them when the killer attacked her and she kicked them off." He turned to Jenna and Kane standing at the door watching him. "When Webber is done here, bag the lamp under the bed. I figure she used it for a weapon. Maybe she hit him."

"I hope so." Kane's eyes narrowed. "This poor woman helped people and she gets murdered. It just doesn't seem fair, does it?"

"Murder is never fair." Emily took the victim's liver temperature, pulled down her shirt, and then bent to smooth the woman's hair inside the body bag before gently zipping it up. "Can you give Webber a hand to take the body out to the van?"

"Not a problem." Kane moved inside the room.

"This house looks very spartan." Emily looked at her father.

"Do you figure she's lived here very long? It's as if she's just got the basic furniture and none of the home comforts." She followed him into the bathroom. "It's hard to believe a woman lived here. No makeup, hairbrush, cosmetics—nothing."

"I don't think she's lived here very long." Jenna leaned in the bedroom door. "I found invoices for renovation work in her desk drawer and the place hardly looks lived in. I'll find out when she purchased it. It wouldn't be a rental. I recall seeing this house in the Realtor's office window last summer."

The top of the vanity held nothing, apart from a toothbrush and toothpaste resting inside a glass. The bathroom resembled a motel room, right down to towels hanging neatly on a rung beside the shower. Wolfe opened a few drawers and discovered what he was looking for. A makeup bag sat beside a hairbrush and comb. He peered inside the bag and found foundation, eye makeup, and a pale lipstick. He collected the items and placed them inside an evidence bag. He turned to Emily. "Do you know if women have a number of colors of lipstick or do they usually wear the same color?"

"Most have a go-to color that they wear all the time." Emily peered into the shower and then bent to take swabs from the drain at the bottom. "Some, like Norrell and me, don't wear lipstick at all and just use a lip gloss or something similar. It's not unusual for others to have many different shades to match their clothes. I figure everyone is different."

Wolfe frowned. The ambiguous answer wasn't getting him anywhere. "If a woman wore makeup to work each day, would she carry a lipstick in her purse?"

"Yes, of course she would." Emily stepped out of the shower and frowned at him. "Don't you recall Mom touching up her lipstick after she'd eaten when we were out at a restaurant?"

The sudden image of his first wife, Angela, who died of cancer eight years ago, flashed into his mind and his heart twisted as it always did when he thought of her. In truth, since he'd married his beautiful young wife, Norrell, he'd tried to push the memory of Angela out of his mind. He refused to compare them as they were totally different people. Norrell didn't wear lipstick. "Now you mention it, I do. So the victim would have a lipstick in her purse?"

"I bagged the purse and phone." Jenna turned into the hallway. "Dave has it."

Wolfe stepped around Webber as he vacuumed the carpet and met Kane in the kitchen. "Do you have the victim's purse?"

"Yeah, it's here." Kane handed him an evidence bag with the purse inside. "Are you looking for anything specific?"

Wolfe opened the bag and emptied the contents onto the plastic. He found a lipstick and opened it. The lipstick in his hand had an orange hue and a different brand to the one they'd found in the bedroom. The one to write the message was deep ruby, almost blood colored. He pushed the top on and placed it back inside the purse. He went through the other contents. The purse contained a wallet with bills, some loose change, credit cards, and a card to give her access to her workplace. A hairbrush, a few feminine products, a small packet of tissues, and a set of keys." He looked at Kane. "Does this look normal to you?"

"I have no idea." Kane shrugged. "Jenna keeps most of her things in her pockets."

Wolfe met his gaze and smiled. "I've never looked inside Norrell's purse. It would seem like an invasion of privacy."

"What's an invasion of privacy, Dad?" Emily joined them in the kitchen.

He met her inquisitive gaze. "Norrell's purse. I just asked Dave if he figured anything was missing from her purse."

"It looks normal to me." Emily looked from one to the other. "I personally carry some hand sanitizer and a pair of examination gloves, but that's just me. It's not a requisite."

"Are we done here?" Jenna followed Webber into the

kitchen. "I want to get back to the office and start this investigation. We need to find her next of kin."

Wolfe turned to look at her. "I'll take the evidence bags with me for testing. I'll get the prints from the victim and upload them onto the server as soon as I get back to the office and then you can compare them with what you've found so far. Let me know when you locate the next of kin. If you speak to them personally, you might mention that viewing wouldn't be in their best interests. We will need to get a DNA sample from a relative or a copy of her dental records for the official identification."

"Okay, we'll lock up." Jenna smiled at him. "When will you have time to complete the autopsy? I need a time of death."

Wolfe handed the evidence bags to Webber and Emily. He turned to Jenna and Kane. "I'll see y'all at ten in the morning. I'll get the preliminary done this afternoon and get you as many results as possible. Going on the rigor and the liver temperature, I'd say she died in the last twelve hours."

"Okay, thanks." Jenna closed the back door and followed them from the kitchen. "See you in the morning."

FIFTEEN

Tuesday

The noise in the kitchen reached a crescendo as Jenna put her phone on speaker. "Just a minute, Emily, I'll need to put you on speaker. Jackson is fussing."

"Mommy up." Jackson tugged at Jenna's shirt. "Up, up, up." He held up his arms, and his face wrinkled into what Jenna recognized as the prequel to a frustrated wail.

She lifted him up onto her lap, tied a long bib around his neck, and then slid the plate in front of him with a dippy egg and strips of buttered toast that Kane had just prepared. She handed him the spoon. "There you go."

Jackson had come to the age where his brain had matured faster than his body. He watched what his brother Tauri did and wanted to imitate him. Not being able to climb as well or run fast enough frustrated him. Over the last few days, he completely refused to sit in his high chair, wanting to either sit on their laps to eat his food or wobble around in a booster seat up to the table. Jenna had insisted he sit between her and Kane wedged in so tight that he couldn't possibly fall off sideways. So far it had worked.

This morning, Tauri had left him behind when he went to help Kane tend the horses. She'd found him trying to pull on his socks, crying in frustration for not being ready when Kane left. She discovered that Kane hadn't known Jackson wanted to go with them. The temperature had dropped again and a freezing wind howled around the house, splattering the windows with the constant snowfall. Usually, once Kane headed to the barn, Jackson would crawl in bed with her. He enjoyed her early morning stories before she went to work. As Jackson ate, Jenna went back to her conversation with Emily. "Raven insisted that he wasn't injured."

"Well, he was." The sound of Emily's fingernails on the wooden table came through the speaker. *"He gave me a call and asked if I could X-ray his hip for him. When he fell, he landed on the water bottle and it chipped his hip bone. You should see him, Jenna. He's black and blue from that fall. I'm surprised his ribs aren't broken."*

Knowing the affection that Emily had for Raven, Jenna raised both eyebrows toward Kane. "I'm sure he's in good hands with you, Em."

"There's not much you can do for a chipped hip, is there?" Kane slid plates of food in front of Jenna and Tauri. He collected his own plate, scooped Jackson from Jenna's lap, and set him on his booster seat between them. "Did you bandage his ribs?"

"Yes, I bandaged his ribs." Emily let out a long sigh. *"Not that he wanted me to do anything to help him. He is such a stubborn man, you know?"*

"The thing is, unless the ribs are actually broken or cracked"—Kane sipped his coffee—"it hurts more getting the bandages off and on when you take a shower. Trust me, I couldn't count the times I've had bruised ribs. Wolfe just gives me some cream to rub into them. That helps better than anything."

"*Hmm, well he did mention the cream and I wrote him a prescription for it, so I assume he'll be better soon.*" Emily paused for a beat. "*There is one thing, Dave, that I'd like to mention after your comments about social workers not being safe. You do know that Julie is working very hard to get all the certificates she needs to become a children's advocate for the court. She'll be working in the department of children's services, hopefully in Black Rock Falls because apparently there are two positions available, come next May. This would mean she could literally go from graduation into employment. Dad understands the implications around such a career. We all know it carries some problems with it, because not everyone is going to agree with different verdicts or decisions made in the children's best interest. Julie insists that the best interests of the child should be taken into account and that includes what the child wants. Being on the outside looking into the team that surrounds you, Jenna, she understands that this is not always the case, and this has been her motivation to work in this field.*"

Jenna guided a piece of toast into the runny egg and smiled at Jackson. "Yeah, I know we've discussed it at length. I'm glad at last she found her vocation."

"You don't believe the boy she met at that convention has anything to do with her decision?" Kane raised one eyebrow and glanced at Jenna. "She mentioned him to your dad and he didn't seem at all impressed when he told me about him."

"*Oh, she is having a long-distance friendship with a guy by the name of Rhett.*" Emily yawned. "*They both have the same interests for their careers. He intends to move to Black Rock Falls after he graduates but he is two years older than her and has more than one degree up his sleeve.*" She cleared her throat. "*I'm betting she won't like him as much if he gets the job and she doesn't.*" She chuckled. "*Although every weekend she comes home from college she spends most of the day on FaceTime with him. I went into her room to speak to her during a call. He has the tattoo of a snake all up one arm and up his neck. He drives a Harley and looks like a typical bad boy."*

Chuckling, Jenna glanced at Kane. "Well, we have a few of them in the team. Honestly, Shane can't possibly be concerned about a tattoo, can he? It's not as if he can say anything about the Harley. He and every one of my deputies ride one now. It seems to me he'll fit right in."

"No one is good enough for Shane's girls." Kane gave her a side-eye. "You know that, right?"

"He is not so bad with Raven." Emily sighed. *"It's weird that he likes him. You know I like to keep the peace, so it makes me wonder if I'm really attracted to Raven or I'm seeking my dad's approval."*

"You sure you want me listening to girl talk." Kane shook his head. "It feels like I'm intruding."

"Me too." Tauri grinned at Kane. "Girls are silly."

"This is the problem." Emily's cup clinked on a saucer. *"When we need a male's perspective, they all run for the hills."*

"I've always been honest with you, Em." Kane ran a hand down his face. "The problem is, only you know what's in your heart. It's scary, sometimes. From a male point of view, we have two options: go in boots and all and hope the girl likes us and maybe face rejection or take the slow road, become friends, and see if the attraction is mutual. I figure Raven is much like me and your dad. We prefer the courting." He sighed. "If the pace is too slow for you, tell him."

Jenna smiled at Kane. "Yeah, well, it worked for me."

"Thanks, I appreciate your candor." A chair scraped as she stood. *"We've been dating once a week or fortnight for ages and he still drops me at the front door. I care for him and believe he would protect me with his life if need be. You're right, he's oldschool, like you, Dave. I'm just hoping I won't be thirty by the*

time he makes up his mind. Maybe I'll invite him to dinner with the family. Oh, is that the time? I gotta go or I'll be late for work. Autopsy is at ten. See you then." She disconnected.

"I don't usually give that kind of advice." Kane's lips curled into a smile. "Maybe I'll write an Agony Aunt column for the local newspaper. I'll call it 'help for dating couples—a man's perspective.'"

Pulling wipes from a packet, Jenna cleaned the egg from Jackson's hands and face and handed him a sippy cup of milk. She stared at Kane. "You know, maybe you should have told her to get involved or show interest in his dog training and rehousing program. It's a big part of his life. I don't figure he'd give that up to marry Emily. Maybe that's the reason they're only having casual dates?"

"Ha, there you go." Kane stood and collected plates. "Advice for my first column: get involved in each other's work or hobbies."

Shaking her head, Jenna stood and lifted Jackson onto one hip. "How about you concentrate your energy on finding me a few suspects?"

Laughter filled the kitchen. "Yes, ma'am." Kane looked at her over one shoulder and winked. "Gotcha."

SIXTEEN

As they headed out onto the highway, a howling wind blew the snow into great sheets that made it appear like giant wings flapping across the blacktop. Driving in a snow globe might sound like fun but it terrified Jenna. Blasts of snow smacked the windshield, slowing the fast-moving wipers. A sea of white spread out before her and even the dirty piles of snow alongside the highway had received a thick coating, making them indistinguishable from everything else. Glad of her sunglasses, Jenna peered into the brilliant white. Although the snowplow had gone through earlier this morning, the blizzard had already covered the ice retardant. By the time they reached the main highway into Black Rock Falls, the visibility had dropped to zero. The blacktop had turned into an ice rink and Jenna gripped the seat as Kane took the sharp corner onto the highway. They hit a patch of thick treacherous frozen snow and the tires spun struggling for grip. She held her breath as Kane turned the wheel and they drifted over the ice and onto the highway.

It would be slow going into town as a number of vehicles crawled along the inside lane. "That looks like patches of black ice." She pulled out her phone. "I'll send a message to the mayor. He needs to get a salt sprayer out here ASAP."

As Jenna finished the message, a rush of wind buffeted the Beast and ice shards splattered them like buckshot as an eighteen-wheeler sped past spraying them with ice.

"What an idiot." Kane's eyes flashed with anger. "He's lost control. Hang on, Jenna. It's going to get nasty."

With both hands pressed on the dashboard, Jenna gaped in horror as the eighteen-wheeler slid sideways and fishtailed as the driver tried to right it. It slid along the highway out of control, the cab and trailer bending frighteningly. Suddenly the trailer whipped around, clipping vehicles trying desperately to get out of its way, but the crushing impact tossed them into the ditch alongside the road. Brakes screamed as drivers tried to avoid the collision. Just ahead of them, the heavy trailer righted itself for a few seconds and then swung erratically back and forth, crashing into other vehicles and tossing parts of them across the hard-packed snow. Jenna held her breath as the eighteen-wheeler bounced with each sickening bang as vehicles collided. Panic gripped her as the truck screamed in a wail of metal, jackknifed, and slid toward them.

"Dammit." Kane pulled the Beast to a stop in the middle of the highway.

Shaking with fear, Jenna couldn't so much as blink and held on waiting for the impact. The Beast's engine roared as Kane reversed along the wrong side of the slippery blacktop, the truck's snow tires spinning. Behind them drivers panicked, moving in all directions to get some distance between them and the out-of-control truck. Heart pounding, Jenna stared in horror, as the eighteen-wheeler skated across the ice, completely blocking the highway. It trembled, shuddered, and in an almighty crash, the trailer came around to smash into the cab. Sparks flew and gas spilled onto the snow and then silence. Everyone around them had stopped.

"You, okay?" Kane squeezed her arm. "Take a few deep breaths. We're okay, Jenna."

Trying to breathe, Jenna swallowed hard as the shock rushed through her. She turned to look at Kane, calm and in control as usual. "That was close. My heart is beating so fast." She peered out of the window. "It looks bad. I hope everyone is okay."

"So do I. Let's go and see the damage." Beside her, Kane pulled his black woolen cap down over his ears and pushed on his Stetson. He turned to look at her. "I'll grab the first aid kit. Stay close. Duke, stay here. Good boy." He left the engine running and climbed out.

Jenna pulled out her phone, running the procedure for multiple car wrecks through her mind. She called Maggie and gave her the details. "We'll need fire trucks, tow trucks, and the paramedics, and notify the council so someone can come out and clean the debris from the road. Explain what's happening and we might get someone to push this truck over so we've got enough room to move traffic. I'll need Rio and Rowley. The driver is going down for this accident."

"I'm on it." Maggie disconnected.

Climbing out of the warm truck and into the freezing wind, Jenna pushed her hands into her pockets. The snow lashed at her face and built up on her sunglasses. She stayed close to Kane, his large frame easily recognizable in the thick snowfall. Glad of her warm snow boots, Jenna followed him to the first damaged vehicle. She peered inside, seeing a woman still gripping tight to the steering wheel with the airbag in her face. The eighteen-wheeler had badly gouged one side of her vehicle but she seemed to be okay. "Are you okay, ma'am?"

"I think so." The woman's window buzzed down an inch or so and she punched down the airbag.

Jenna nodded. "It's surface damage. Keep your engine running to keep warm. Help is on the way."

She photographed the damaged vehicle and asked the driver to show her license. She snapped a photograph of it and then followed Kane to the next vehicle. The images and licenses would be used for insurance claims. Five vehicles had been damaged on their side of the highway. The eighteen-wheeler blocked her vision of the other side. She turned to Kane. "The driver looks okay. I'm surprised. I figured the trailer had smashed his cab, but it only took out the front of it."

"I'll go and check on him but I'm more concerned about who smashed into the truck on the other side of the highway. It sounded like World War Three from here." He brushed the snow from his sunglasses and peered at her. "Please, stay close. I don't want to lose you in the blizzard. If you fell into the gully, the snow would cover your head."

Jenna snorted. "I was thinking the same thing about you. If you fell into the gully, there would be no way I'd be able to pull you out. Although I admit you'd be a bit hard to lose in the blizzard." She stared into his reflective lenses, seeing herself in miniature. Her independence still drove him crazy. "Stop worrying about me, Dave. We need to go and check for injuries. It might be some time before the paramedics get here."

"Sure." Kane held out his hand. "It's slippery and together we're stronger."

Gripping tight to each other, they made their way slowly to the truck driver and Kane climbed up to check him. Jenna kicked snow over the leaking gas. "Is he okay?"

"He has a few lacerations to his face where the windshield shattered but nothing serious. He has blankets in the back. He's going to climb in there to keep warm. We can leave him and go and look around the other side." Kane jumped down and slid over to her. "Whoa, it's slippery."

Gripping tight to Kane's hand, she followed him around the back of the truck and her mouth fell open at the sight of the carnage. One pickup trapped up to the windshield under the side of the eighteen-wheeler had been pushed forward by a number of trucks all smashed together. From the position of the vehicles, it appeared that most of them had tried to stop and ended up spinning out of control or sliding sideways into each other. Steam rose from the damaged vehicles and bits and pieces of metal stuck out from the snow across the road. With care, they picked their way through the damage, checking on the drivers of each vehicle. None of them were bleeding to death and most had superficial cuts on their face from flying glass and debris. The man in the pickup wedged under the eighteen-wheeler, possibly had broken legs. "We're going to need more doctors. I'll call Wolfe and Raven." She made the call as she followed Kane.

Jenna stood to one side as Kane wedged open the door to the pickup. He found blankets and another coat on the back seat and wrapped them around the man. It was all they could do until the paramedics and fire trucks arrived to cut him out of the damaged vehicle. She turned at the sound of a man's voice. "Please, stay in your vehicle."

"I'm Dr. Villard, an orthopedic surgeon from Black Rock Falls County Hospital." He smiled at her. "What can I do to help?"

Blowing out a sigh of relief, Jenna smiled at him. "We're currently checking victims. We haven't found anyone badly injured apart from this man so far. He's trapped and maybe has broken legs. There's not much we can do for him until a fire truck arrives. They'll be able to cut him out."

"I'll take a look." Dr. Villard held up his bag. "I have a few supplies with me. I might be able to relieve the poor man's pain until we can get him to the hospital. Give me a wave if you find anyone else who needs urgent medical attention." He frowned. "The cold is going to be the killer. Have you called the paramedics?"

"Yeah, first up." Kane gave him a long stare. "We'll leave you to it." He headed off into the snow.

Shivering, Jenna followed. The bitter cold seeped into her clothes and she couldn't feel her nose or cheeks. Concern for the pain Kane would soon suffer from the metal plate in his head was at the front of her mind. His debilitating headaches caused by the cold weather had never abated and although he bundled up, the pain would hit like a tornado. They'd been in the freezing temperatures too long. She needed to get him back into the truck. "Dave." She grabbed his arm. "If your head starts to ache, you'll be no good to anyone. I can handle the rest. Go and get warm."

"Right now, I'm okay, so keep going." Sunglasses masked Kane's expression. He'd pulled up the collar of his coat to his ears. "Move as fast as possible. There are only a few we haven't checked and help will be here soon."

Nodding and pulling her scarf up like a mask, Jenna followed him, his hand wrapped tightly around hers, strong and dependable as always. They checked three more wrecks and found no serious injuries but some of the vehicles were totaled and the occupants were in shock. She straightened from cleaning up a man with a cut on his cheek and pulled examination gloves from her freezing fingers. As she dragged on her thick leather gloves, she peered into the blizzard. Blue and red lights flashed and the wail of sirens increased. "Oh, thank goodness, the cavalry is on its way."

SEVENTEEN

It had taken over five hours to push the eighteen-wheeler to the side of the highway and clear the wrecked vehicles. The road sprayers were out in force, covering the blacktop with the pink ice retardant. Jenna had called out fire trucks and paramedics from Louan and Blackwater to deal with the people trapped inside vehicles and their injuries. It had been such a relief when Wolfe and Norrell arrived along with Raven and Emily in the same vehicle. Having four extra medical doctors on scene was a godsend. They had the injured triaged and off to the hospital in record time. None of the vehicles involved in the wreck were drivable and tow trucks arrived en masse to spirit them away to local garages. Jenna had made sure she had the information of each vehicle along with the damage sustained in the collision. There would be a chunk of paperwork to do to make sure the reports were ready for the insurance claims. The moment she got back to the office she would hand everything over to Maggie, and if necessary, she'd call someone else in to give her a hand. With two cases running parallel to each other, she didn't have time to personally do the amount of paperwork necessary.

With feet like blocks of ice, Jenna led the way into Aunt

Betty's Café. At the back of the room Wolfe and Kane pushed three tables together and everyone sat around them. It had been a long and freezing morning and everyone needed a hot meal. They all devoured plates of pumpkin soup with a dollop of sour cream in the middle and then ordered a variety of dishes, from chili to hamburgers, and of course, wedges of Aunt Betty's famous pies. They used the coffee cups as hand warmers while they waited for the meals to arrive. Jenna looked at Wolfe. "I'm sorry we missed the autopsy."

"You didn't miss anything." Wolfe sipped his coffee and sighed. "We left the moment Maggie called. Raven happened to be close by delivering a protection dog and was able to get to us within five minutes of being notified." He grimaced. "The way the weather is at the moment, that won't be the last multiple pileup we'll see this winter. I figure the snowplow drivers are doing their best but they are running twenty-four-hour shifts now."

"Have you identified the victim?" Raven leaned forward in his chair.

"Yeah, we did." Wolfe smiled at Wendy as she placed another large bowl of pumpkin soup in front of him along with a plate of hot biscuits. "It's the social worker Laney Prescott, as we assumed. Kalo called me early this morning as her prints were on file. She hasn't any priors; her prints were taken during a court case some time ago for elimination purposes." He waited for Wendy to head back to the kitchen for more food and looked at Jenna. "Something really strange showed when we ran the prints on the lipstick." His eyebrows raised. "The fingerprints on the lipstick used to write the message match the woman allegedly kidnapped. We got a match for Ellie McBride."

Everyone around the table fell silent and stared at Wolfe. Jenna put down her spoon and stared at him. "Oh, now that's really weird. What about the handwriting?"

"It's close and could have easily been written by her but we don't have conclusive evidence that she wrote the note on the whiteboard." Wolfe took a few spoonfuls of soup and met Jenna's gaze. "I've seen men shoot their toes off to get out of combat, so I don't find it unusual if Ellie McBride decided to hit herself in the head with a car jack, for whatever reason."

"My main concern about this"—Kane looked from Wolfe to Jenna and back—"is how she managed to get from the convenience store parking lot to the roadhouse at night in winter. I've watched the CCTV cameras, and no other vehicles came by to give her a ride."

Mind racing with possible scenarios, Jenna leaned back in her chair and blew out a long breath. "Unless she walked to the highway and met her accomplice there. Now we find her prints on the lipstick used to write the message. What proof have we that a man killed Laney? I'm finding it difficult to believe that she's not involved. The only thing I don't have is a motive."

"No one can just slip out of the Her Broken Wing residences without using their card, right?" Rio pushed his empty bowl away and then folded his hands on the table. "So, one call to Father Derry and you'll have the information you need. If she left the residences, which I doubt—I mean, that would be darnright stupid when she has someone hunting her down—then you'll know if she was around to murder Laney."

"Where she's staying isn't a prison is it?" Raven poured coffee into his cup from one of the pots on the table. "Its purpose is to keep people out. I'd say getting out without a card would be easy enough. There are windows low enough to climb out of and it doesn't take a genius to switch off the alarm, do the deed, and then get back inside."

"Again, how did she get to Laney's house, kill her, and get back home again?" Kane dabbed at his mouth with a napkin. "Her SUV is locked in the garage at the morgue awaiting forensic examination. She has no transport. Father Derry is driving her back and forth to work."

Every point made sense and Jenna allowed the comments to percolate through her mind as three servers arrived with the main meals. Her burger and fries looked delicious and smelled wonderful. She glanced at Kane. His section of the table surrounded him with a huge plate of barbecue ribs with all the trimmings, including corn, coleslaw, and mashed potatoes. All the men had the same meal; Norrell and Emily had chosen pulled pork bread rolls with coleslaw. Everyone had huge appetites in the cold weather. After swallowing her first delicious bite, she looked at Kane. "All that makes sense, if she worked alone. What if she has an accomplice?" Jenna took a sip of her coffee. "Maybe someone working at the school?"

"Why would she point a finger at herself by pretending to be kidnapped?" Rowley licked his fingers and then grabbed another rib from his plate. "After murdering someone, maybe, but before doesn't make much sense, does it?"

Unconvinced, Jenna conceded and sighed. "We'll follow up with Father Derry and search for any connections between her and Laney. If there's nothing, we need to find possible suspects. It's close to Christmas. I don't want any more nasty surprises." She looked at Wolfe. "What time will you be rescheduling the autopsy?"

"Same time tomorrow." Wolfe stared out of the window. "The snow isn't giving up anytime soon. If you have a problem getting to me, I'll do a video call. The time of death hasn't changed. Because of the low temperature inside the house, it's difficult to pin down. The cause of death is evident, but I won't sign off on it until I have completed the autopsy. If you want to skip it, I can also just send you my report. Right now, finding her next of kin is a priority before someone slips her name to the media. It's not fair discovering that someone murdered a loved one on the six o'clock news."

Jenna nodded. "Yeah, don't worry, we'll get right on it." She smiled at him. "Now, no more shop talk. It's been a horrific day and everyone needs a little time to gather themselves."

"Amen to that." Wolfe blew out a long sigh. "I need to switch off for a time."

Aunt Betty's had become the perfect place to push away death and disaster, even if it was only for an hour. She bit into her burger. The flavor ran over her tastebuds. She sighed in delight and noticed the smiles of everyone around the table. Great food and good company and the horrors of the morning melted away for a few precious moments.

EIGHTEEN

Ellie McBride waved goodbye to Father Derry and made her way along the snowy paths to the school entrance. It seemed strange arriving at school when the day was almost over, but being one of few who could make it to the school due to the blizzard, she assisted the other teachers' students. They'd all sent work and she would email it to the children. It was unnecessary to risk the children's lives on the slippery frozen roads, so the winter vacation had started early. Those that lived in outlying areas could be isolated for months at a time when the snowfall became so deep and treacherous. During this time if they were stuck at home, Ellie and the other teachers would prepare lessons and send them by email. They would follow this up with conference calls so all the outlying children actually had a day at school. As she headed toward her classroom, she noticed five snow angels scattered in the playground. The one in the middle had four others surrounding it. The pattern appeared oddly symmetrical. Most times if children made snow angels they would flop down anywhere.

The position of the snow angels intrigued her and as she stepped onto the walkway to the classrooms, she noticed something fluttering in the wind in the middle of the largest snow angel. Curiosity got the better of her and she went back down the steps and carefully walked across the snow. The fluttering piece of paper resembled a photograph. She bent to pick it up and gasped, stepping back in horror. A photograph of her sleeping dropped from her fingers. Was this some kind of a sick joke? She bent and snatched it up and headed back to the classroom, closing the door softly behind her and leaning against it. Her breathing sounded loud, and without the students, the eerily quiet classroom closed in on her. Heart pounding, she scanned the room, searching every corner, and then her gaze settled on the whiteboard. Red writing scrawled across the middle. *I've had my fun. Your purse is in the boiler room.*

Anger shimmered through her. How dare this person do this to her? Her life had been turned upside down since the kidnapping. The sheriff hadn't found who had taken her and told her that they had absolutely no leads whatsoever apart from the fact the vehicle was the same make and model as her own. She wanted to go home and had played enough of this person's games. Marching up to the whiteboard, she picked up the eraser and wiped out the message. Doing so made her feel powerful and in control. She went to her classroom door and walked straight to the office and got the attention of the administrator. "I need to go down to the boiler room. Apparently, someone is having a joke with me and has taken my purse there. Can you call one of the maintenance people on duty and ask them to escort me?"

"Yes, of course." The woman gave her a curious look and pressed a button on her phone. "I wonder who is acting the fool."

Ellie shrugged. "I have no idea. It's probably one of the kids."

She waited as the woman spoke to one of the maintenance people. She recalled the boiler room at the opposite side of the building, on the end of the grounds and very rarely visited by staff. A slightly familiar young man of about eighteen or twenty with a shock of red hair and a wide grin met her at the office store. She smiled at him. "Thank you for escorting me."

"It's not locked but it's so out of the way nobody goes there unless one of the boilers needs maintaining. I hear someone is playing a joke on you." He grinned. "It's not me. You lived near my family home before you worked here. I remember seeing you walking your dog. I'm Jesse Holland."

Memories slid into place of a family of red-haired kids with freckles and she smiled. "Yes, I do recall your family."

She followed him through the school and down a set of stairs to the basement. The door swung open. The dimly lit interior and the noise of the machinery made her pause. Heat spewed from the room carrying a thick miasma of oil. The smell sucked all the pristine winter air from her lungs. The young man's phone startled her with its loud ringtone and she turned to look at him as he accepted the call.

"Sorry, it's the boss." The young man listened for a few seconds and then disconnected. "I gotta go. There's another burst pipe. Will you be okay finding your way back? The light switch is on the right by the door."

As they hadn't passed a soul since they started off from the office, Ellie nodded. "I'll be fine, thank you."

As the young man hurried away, Ellie ran her hand down the inside of the wall, found the light switch, and flicked it on. Strip lighting flickered and filled the room with a yellowish glow. She scanned the room, but if someone was hiding here, she wouldn't have seen them for the huge furnaces, each making strange noises. Her gaze rested on a chair some way inside the room. She had no doubt the small lump she could see on it was her purse. She hoped her house keys, phone, and driver's license were inside. The credit cards didn't matter because she'd canceled them on the first day. Lifting her chin, she walked straight to the chair. The contents of her purse were scattered as if someone had emptied it and then pawed through it. As she got closer, lines of red writing on one of the boilers caught her attention. She stopped and gaped at the message:

You never escaped me. I released you.

Suddenly afraid, she jumped at a click behind her and turned as the door slowly closed. The heat inside the boiler room became oppressive and the pipes thumped to match her racing heartbeat. Panic gripped her and she grabbed up her things and headed for the door. The terrible feeling that someone was watching her became overwhelming and then above the noise of the furnace came the creak of leather boots on concrete. She ran for the door but as her fingers closed around the doorknob, something dropped over her head and tightened around her neck. Heavy breathing came close to her ear. Ellie tried to fight and, dropping her purse, clawed at the man's hands, breaking her short fingernails on his thick leather gloves. She couldn't breathe. The cord tightened, cutting into her flesh, and then relaxed for a second. She gasped in one precious breath of tainted air and from behind her the smell of cologne washed over her. *It's the kidnapper.*

She rocked back trying to push him away, trying to get free, but he slammed her into the metal door and the cord slid up to under her ears. He grunted and lifted her onto her toes. Pain shot through her neck but she couldn't cry out. Her mind became fuzzy and her lungs screamed in agony before everything slid into blackness.

NINETEEN

"We got the search warrant for the BW Ranch." Rio walked into the conference room waving a document. "I've already contacted the FBI and we have four agents arriving as soon as the blizzard stops." He looked at Jenna. "Do you want me to make arrangements for them to stay over in town or have you other plans for them?"

Deep in thought, Jenna looked up from the computer screen. "Everyone is coming, including Bobby Kalo?"

"Yeah, Jo is bringing her daughter Jaime with her." Rio handed her the warrant. "They mentioned something about spending Christmas at your place."

"That's right. As usual it's open house for Christmas lunch. Everyone is welcome. We stocked the kitchen in the cottage and have a ton of supplies for the house. We could hold out until the melt." Kane spun around in his office chair to look at him. "If Carter shares a room with Kalo, there'll be enough room in the cottage for Beth and Styles." He flicked a glance at Jenna. "Jo and Jaime could take one of our spare rooms. When Jo is busy working, Raya can take care of Jaime along with our kids."

Twirling a pen in her fingers Jenna nodded. "Yeah, that

sounds like a plan. Now all we need is for it to stop snowing for a while. I know the choppers can fly in the snow, but not when it's this thick. I recall Carter mentioning the visibility being treacherous at this time of year when they come through the mountains." She turned her attention to Rio. "How often are the shipments coming into the BW Ranch?"

"Lately, approximately three times a week." Rio leaned against the wall, one knee bent and his boot resting behind him. "I figure they're stepping up production over the holidays. They probably believe we all take long vacations and they are safer distributing the drugs."

"I'll need to go out and get a lay of the land." Kane turned to look at Jenna. "When this goes down, they're going to need a sniper. I'll look for a position where I can set up fast."

"I figure this can go two ways." Raven leaned back in his chair looking from one to the other. "It's all very well waving around an AK-47, but using it to kill cops is another thing. They're either going to scatter when we arrive or shoot it out and we won't know until we get there."

"They'll try and shoot it out." Kane's mouth formed a thin line. "Take a closer look at the footage we obtained from the trail cams. The guys around that truck aren't ranch hands. I figure they're mercenaries that he employs as bodyguards. I don't believe I've seen any of them in town or causing trouble at any of the bars, which means they're probably illegals and belong to the cartel Withers is working alongside." He shrugged. "Agent Styles cleared a fentanyl distribution ring from his beat and gave me a ton of intel. I'm glad he's coming. He'll have good advice."

"I can't believe they are still getting fentanyl across the border." Rowley let out a long sigh. "I guess they would need to open every bag of pellets to check if anything was inside. Why can't the dogs sniff it?"

"I know the answer to that one." Raven leaned forward,

clasping his hands before him on the desk. "If you take a look at any of the shipments with the fentanyl, they also include sacks of urea fertilizer. This is something that's commonly used for pasture treatment, and it wouldn't cause any attention, but it does give off a strong smell of ammonia and that would mask the smell of the fentanyl pills from the dogs."

Jenna raised an eyebrow. "I'm just wondering how long this has been going on, because these guys appear to have everything covered when it comes to getting the merchandise across the border, receiving the deliveries, and sending the pills out to the suppliers. I've heard absolutely nothing, not one hint about this operation before Rio tumbled into it. Although, I can be almost certain that they aren't spreading their drugs around Black Rock Falls or Louan. I haven't received reports of anyone being arrested for selling fentanyl in Blackwater either."

"Do you want to be involved in the takedown or would you prefer that I make the plans?" Rio pushed away from the wall and took a seat beside Kane at the conference table. "We'll be able to hit them on the first delivery after the agents arrive. Until they get here it's going to be a waiting game."

Jenna tapped her pen on the table considering the implications of allowing her deputies to go it alone. The idea didn't make her happy. As a team, they worked closely together and knew exactly what the next person would do in a crisis. "Make the plans, by all means. You're going to need Dave to act as your sniper backup. I would suggest you confer with him along with the others as he is an expert in takedowns. If we are not snowed under with the current case, we'll be out there in the field with you. You'll need as many boots on the ground as you can lay hands on. Keep me in the loop." She sighed. "Now I would like you to concentrate on the case at hand. We need to find Laney Prescott's next of kin. Divide the work between you. We will also be searching social media and contacting Laney Prescott's workmates for her close friends. I'll call the director of the social services department and see if I can get them to give me any information on anyone who may have put in any complaints or caused a problem for her. It will be difficult getting them to divulge any information. I'll feel them out during the phone call, and if I consider they might be withholding information, I'll get a search warrant. I don't believe the judge will withhold one, as we are talking murder here."

She glanced at the serious faces around the table. They chatted together for a few moments and as usual worked as a competent unit. Standing, she left the conference room and went to her office. Once inside, she contacted the director of the social services and spent her time refilling the coffee pots in her office while she waited on hold. She'd met Christopher Paul, the new director, when he'd arrived from Helena. As the Her Broken Wings Foundation needed to work closely with his departments, she needed to be on his good side. He agreed with her charity work and her passion for protecting anyone abused or bullied in the community. When he finally came to the phone and apologized profusely for keeping her waiting, she gave him the information about Laney Prescott. "I'm sorry to deliver this bad news over the phone but we are exceptionally busy and the weather is terrible at the moment to be driving around to see people in person."

"I understand completely." A door clicked shut and Jenna heard a scrape of a chair as Paul sat down at his desk. *"I'm extremely shocked about Laney. She was a very special person. She had a deep compassion, which after working in this profession for a long time can often become jaded. Am I allowed to ask what happened to her?"*

Jenna thought for a beat as she didn't usually give out any information prior to an autopsy or the next of kin being notified. "The cause of death is undetermined at the moment. The medical examiner will be performing an autopsy in the morning and maybe then I'll have some more information. The reason I called you is because I need the next of kin details you have in her file. I also want you to consider telling me if she had any particularly nasty cases that might have caused someone to strike out at her or if she'd been threatened in any way."

"*You believe someone murdered her, don't you?*" Paul sucked in a long breath. "*I can't believe it. Poor Laney, she certainly didn't deserve that. Do you figure it was one of her clients?*"

Not expecting any assistance whatsoever, the man took her aback with his enthusiasm to help in the case. It immediately sent up a red flag and she sat slowly in her office chair, trying very hard to compose her next sentence. "I'm sure that information would be at your fingertips. Do you recall her mentioning any problems she had?"

"*Laney had a few cases on the go. A couple of them concerned spousal abuse, and removing a woman from an abusive relationship can often cause repercussions. She worked a case where a child was taken into protective custody and both parents became very aggravated. We discovered a seriously neglected child who hadn't attended school for a long period of time. The parents made all sorts of excuses, but it was obvious when she went to view the child that he was neglected. He had bruises all over him and we had to intervene. It's not something that we enjoy doing but sometimes we don't have any choice.*" His chair squeaked as he moved around. "*I would need to access her files on her computer to see if she'd made notes about any problems with these recent clients. One thing I do know is she didn't come to me with a complaint. Sometimes we just take it on the chin and keep going.*"

Unable to believe her luck, Jenna cleared her throat. "Any information you could give us would be very helpful. One other thing. Are any of her workmates close friends?"

"*I'm not sure.*" Paul drummed his fingers on the desk. "*I'll go and speak to them and see what I can find out for you, and then if necessary, I'll be happy to arrange a time for you to come in and speak to them."* He sighed. *"That's all I can do for now. I have a client waiting."*

Making a few hurried notes, Jenna stood. "Thank you very much. I'll wait to hear from you." She disconnected, grabbed the two coffee pots and hurried back to the conference room. She smiled at Kane. "The director is going to cooperate."

TWENTY

The smell of fresh coffee wafted through the open door and Kane turned in his chair as Jenna walked into the room. She carried two coffee pots to the counter and slid them into the coffee machines. He returned her smile. At last, something had turned their way in the case. "That's good to know and I've found Laney Prescott's next of kin. She has a sister in Atlanta and her aunt lives in Helena. I've instructed the local police to inform them of Laney's death. I'm hoping they will contact us so we can make arrangements for her body when Wolfe releases her."

"The social services director has agreed to go through her files and see if he can find any problems she had with her clients. He hasn't said he will release the names to me, but if he does find anything suspicious, then our next step would be to get a search warrant so it covers him from being prosecuted for divulging the names." She filled cups with coffee and handed them around to the team.

Kane stood, collected the fixings from the counter, and put them in the middle of the table. He added cream and sugar to his cup and opened his mouth to ask for more details when

Jenna's phone chimed. He regarded her expression as she answered the call. All the color had drained from her face. Assuming something had happened to the children, he stood. "What is it?"

"It's the office administrator from the middle school. I'll put the call on speaker." Jenna placed her phone in the middle of the table. "Okay, you're on speaker and my deputies are in the room with me. Please take a deep breath and tell me exactly what happened."

"I believe someone has hurt Ms. McBride. I've called the paramedics and they're on their way. One of the maintenance team found her in the boiler room."

"That's good the paramedics are on their way. I assume you haven't gone to see if she's okay?" Jenna looked at Kane and raised one eyebrow. "Why is that?"

"The man who found her said she looked like she'd been strangled. He ran all the way back here and we locked ourselves in the office. The rest of the maintenance staff and the other two teachers who came in today have left. They wanted to get home before the blizzard got any worse."

A man's voice came through the speaker.

"I'm Jesse Holland. I escorted Ms. McBride to the boiler room. I checked it out and didn't see anyone. She noticed her purse in there and headed inside when I got a call to go and help with a burst pipe. Once we'd repaired it, I went back past Ms. McBride's classroom to see if she was okay. When I didn't find her, I went to tell Ms. Bell. She sent me back to the boiler room and I found Ms. McBride lying on the floor with a cord around her neck. Her face was blue. I didn't spend any time hanging around. I just got out of there and ran back here to tell Ms. Bell."

"You mentioned your boss." Jenna stared at the phone. "Where is he and are there any other people in the school we should know about?"

"No, once we'd sealed the pipe, the boss told us all to go

home." Jesse gasped in a deep breath. *"I saw them head for the parking lot, but I figured I should look in on Ms. McBride, considering what had happened to her."*

Kane cleared his throat. "This is Deputy Kane. I want you to tell me the reason Ms. McBride needed to go to the boiler room."

"Someone pranked Ms. McBride again this morning." Ms. Bell breathed heavily. *"She found a note on her whiteboard saying they'd left her purse in the boiler room. She wanted to go and look for it, so I sent Jesse with her to make sure she'd be okay."* She let out a small sob. *"I didn't know he'd left her there alone."*

"I've been here all day and I didn't see anyone but the normal guys working around here." Jesse's indignation came through the speaker. *"No one goes down to the boiler room unless there's a problem with the furnace. It's way down the other end of the school. The chances of anyone from the outside getting in, especially now we know someone is trying to hurt her, would be virtually impossible."*

Kane exchanged a glance with Jenna and shook his head. "And yet they did."

"When the paramedics get there, tell them to check for signs of life and that the sheriff is on the way." Jenna stood. "Tell them that it is a crime scene and to respect it as such."

Kane downed his coffee. "When you hear our siren, make sure someone is at the door to let us in. I'll be contacting the medical examiner."

"Okay, we'll be here locked in the office until you arrive." Ms. Bell disconnected.

"We'll need to clear the building." Jenna looked around the table at her deputies. "Grab your gear and Kevlar vests. We're not taking any risks with this killer. Go straight to the school. I'll call Wolfe."

TWENTY-ONE

Concern twisted in Jenna's belly as she headed for her office. She'd done everything within her power to protect Ellie McBride and she should have been safe in the school during daylight hours. The principal informed her there would be maintenance men and teachers around her all day. She took the Kevlar vest that Kane handed her and pulled it on over her head. As she tightened up the Velcro on each side, she looked at him. "This shouldn't be happening. I left her in a safe environment. No one gets in and out of that place without a card. With all the problems we have in this town, the mayor went to a great deal of trouble to ensure that the school is safe. It makes no sense at all that someone got in and strangled Ellie McBride."

"They have CCTV cameras everywhere." Kane shrugged into his coat and then pulled on his thick leather gloves. "The chances of the killer being unseen will be remote. It's snowing and hasn't stopped for days. There should be footprints or evidence he's left behind to show us how he's getting in and out of the school. I checked the place out thoroughly when we were last there and even the windows have alarms on them. Only the windows that face the playgrounds can be opened during the day. The others on the street side are protected by alarms. I'm mystified how anyone could have gotten inside without somebody knowing."

Slipping her weapon into the holster, Jenna met his gaze with a frown. "Now we have two murders, and from what they were saying, they're both strangulations. What do these two women have in common? It seems to me this is the same killer."

"Yeah, leaving notes to frighten the women and then strangling them seems to be his fantasy." Kane slid his pistol into the holster and gave her a grim look. "Ellie was murdered from behind like Laney Prescott. I figure it's the same killer. Wolfe will be able to determine that when he does his autopsy."

Jenna zipped up her coat, pulled on gloves, and headed toward the door. "Ellie didn't have anyone in town to stay with, I don't even know if she has any next of kin close by." She sighed. "When we get into the truck, I'll contact Father Derry and tell him not to go to the school this afternoon to give her a ride home. He will be very upset that something has happened to her. He went out of his way to keep her safe. I feel that I've let her down. Half of the time I suspected her involvement. That makes me feel like a heel." As they walked along the hallway, she touched his arm. "You were right all along. You never believed that she could be involved. So many things she said made me believe she'd made up stories to get attention. All this time she was telling the truth."

"You can't let this eat you up, Jenna." Kane headed for the door and an arctic breeze buffeted them as they went outside. "We couldn't find a suspect and couldn't verify anything she said. The only indication that she'd been kidnapped was when she arrived at the Triple Z Roadhouse with a head injury—and we have no proof that she didn't hit herself in the head. There's no CCTV camera footage of her arriving there and she claimed to have climbed out of the vehicle at the pumps. The person on the footage is indistinguishable in the blizzard and they used her credit card. It could have been her. She'd been bundled up and wearing similar clothes when we found her at the roadhouse. The vehicle was the same make and model as her own. I can see why you would believe that she'd been involved." He pulled down the rim of his Stetson. "Add to that the writing on the whiteboard in the classroom being similar to hers, almost had me convinced as well." He slid inside the vehicle and turned to look at her. "To be honest, I'd started coming around to your way of thinking when Wolfe discovered her fingerprints on the lipstick used to write the message on Laney Prescott's pillow." He sighed and started the engine. "My problem with her involvement in Laney Prescott's murder came down to a motive to kill her. We asked her if she knew Laney, and she'd never met her, but it wasn't that. It's very unusual for a woman to strangle another woman. It's a very personal act. There's usually a ton of emotion involved, like hate or jealousy, and I didn't see any reason for Ellie to hate someone that much. That was one of the reasons I dismissed the idea of Ellie being involved in Laney's murder."

Jenna leaned back in her seat as the truck crunched through the thick coating of ice retardant. Snow battered the windows like a swarm of angry white bees. "I found it hard to believe that she didn't know Laney Prescott. As Laney worked in children's services, she would be involved with the local teachers. Especially around the age of Ellie's students. You would figure that Laney's name would be known as she had been working there for a time." She sighed and pulled out her phone to call Father Derry. "We can talk about this 'til the sun goes down, but the fact is, it seems she's been murdered by the same person. This means we're dealing with someone who has involvement with a school and children's services. These two facts might give us a break in the case that we need. The moment we get back to the office, I'll get the search warrant for the Department of Social Services. I figure there's a connection between there and the school. If necessary, I'll ask Kalo to assist us. I might run this case through Jo as well. I can't get my head around it and as we are having a behavioral analyst dropping by for Christmas, we might as well use her knowledge."

"Don't forget you have Beth Katz coming as well." Kane turned onto Stanton and headed toward the school. "We've hit the jackpot. You'll have two of the top FBI IT specialists arriving in town shortly."

Jenna stared out at the bleak white snowscape. "That's good. We need all the help we can get."

TWENTY-TWO

Emotions jumbled through Jenna's mind as she climbed from the Beast. How could she have been so wrong about Ellie? Another thought flashed through her mind. What if Ellie had an accomplice and he or she turned on her? It would make perfect sense for Ellie to go to the boiler room to speak to them in a place no one ever went to. However, the reason she would pretend to be kidnapped still caused havoc in her mind. If she had been the second or third person to be injured after a series of murders, Jenna would have considered that Ellie did it to take the heat off her accomplice, but being the first one posed questions she didn't have the answers to.

Confusion surrounded her as she slipped her way through the parking lot and to the front doors of the school. The foyer opened up to the administration desk, concealed behind a wall of glass with only a small service counter peephole for anyone walking through the front door. She noticed the entrance into the school went via metal detectors with cameras above them. These led along a short corridor to a set of automatic doors. She guessed that if someone tried to get through without authorization they would be stopped in the middle corridor. She recalled the plan to have the security at all the schools in the area upgraded but hadn't read through all the changes. Not knowing who the next threat would be in Serial Killer Central, the council upgraded many of the local institutions to ensure the safety of the townsfolk.

The principal waited for them just inside the front door. He wore a thick winter coat over track pants. It looked as if he'd rushed to the school right away. Jenna nodded to him as she walked through the door. The principal showed them through a side door using his card and handed them both visitor lanyards. "Thanks." Jenna slipped it over her head. "Where are my deputies?"

"They're waiting in the hallway just through the next door." The principal led the way. He opened the door and waved them through. "The paramedics came and left. They confirmed she was dead and told me to keep away and wait for you."

Jenna's attention went immediately to her three deputies moving in and out of the classrooms and clearing each room as they went. She turned to the principal. "The medical examiner, Dr. Shane Wolfe, will be here shortly to take over. Have someone take him directly to the boiler room. He'll have a large team with him, so there will be four or five people carrying equipment."

"Stop people coming into the building while we are here and don't allow anyone to leave." Kane moved to Jenna's side and looked at principal. "Anyone we find will be treated as a suspect and likely arrested. Once we have seen the body, we'll come back to the office and interview Jesse Holland."

As her deputies came out of the classrooms, Jenna motioned to Rowley. "I gather you went to school here. Do you know where the boiler room is?"

"I sure do." Rowley indicated over his shoulder with his thumb. "It's at the other end of the school in the maintenance area."

Turning back to the principal, Jenna met the man's worried gaze. He appeared to have taken the death of one of his teachers badly. His graying hair stuck up all over and his coat sat uneven, with the buttons mismatched as if fastened in haste. "Why don't you go back to the office, have something hot to drink, while we do our job? We'll come and speak to you when we're done." She kept her tone calm and even. "I know this has been a terrible shock for you. You can be assured my department will be doing everything possible to discover who murdered Ellie."

"Okay, thank you." The principal let out a long sigh. "Ms. McBride has been working here for seven years or more. She is one of our most respected teachers. She goes out of her way to help the students. I can't imagine why anyone would have chosen her as a victim. It makes no sense at all. The world has lost a very beautiful, kindhearted person today."

"Murder never makes sense." Kane led him back to the door. "We'll be along shortly."

Raven and Rio walked up to Jenna and waited for her to give them orders. She looked from one to the other. "We have no idea if the perpetrator is still in the building. Rowley is going to lead the way to the boiler room, so spread out and keep your eyes peeled for anyone moving around. There are only three people that we know of in the building at the moment apart from us. They should all be in the office. Detain anyone else you come across and be on your guard. We may be dealing with a serial killer."

Jenna and Kane followed Rowley as he headed along the hallway. Walking to see a murder victim always caused a little rush of panic. If the killer still lurked in the building, they could be walking into a trap. Taking a deep breath and blowing it out to slow her racing heart, Jenna pushed her mind to another place. The smell of the school brought back memories of her childhood. Unsure how the smell of books, sweat, and gym shoes had triggered memories, she could clearly remember her teachers right from first grade through to when she graduated from high school. She'd been lucky and school had been a place she enjoyed. Many of the teachers had time to spare for the students. She'd been inquisitive and all her questions had been answered, which she believed helped her to get a scholarship to college and later join the DEA.

As she scanned the classrooms, she noticed many things had changed since she'd been at school. She recalled rigid lines of tables and a blackboard, with choking white dust from the erasers, not the interactive screens and whiteboards that they had now. It seemed that they made school days much more interesting. Her sons' time at school would be an adventure in learning.

"It's just through that walkway." Rowley used his lanyard to open the door to a short open space between the buildings.

Freezing air buffeted them as they stepped out into the cold ice-filled wind. Snow had blown across the covered walkway. "Wait!"

"What is it?" Rowley stopped midstride and turned to look at her.

Jenna paused at the open door and stared at the footprints. "Take photographs of the footprints before they're covered in snow. We'll need to get images of anyone's shoes who we know was walking through here earlier."

"Yes, ma'am." Rowley pulled out his phone and took a number of photographs moving slowly from one area to the other. "I've got them. Are you ready to move forward?"

"Yeah." Kane nodded. "Stay alert, we don't want to miss any evidence along the way."

"Copy that." Rowley continued along the walkway and used his card to swipe them into the maintenance area.

They walked past a few locked doors with signs on the outside giving various warnings until they came to the boiler room. The door stood wide open and the smell of death seeped into the hallway on a wave of heated air. Jenna glanced at Kane, who had already pulled a mask and gloves from his pocket. She turned to the other deputies. "Rio, Rowley, clear the area. I'll go inside with Kane. Raven, watch our backs but remain outside. We don't want everyone inside contaminating the crime scene."

After putting on a mask and pulling on examination gloves, Jenna waited for Kane to find the light switches. The boiler room burst into light, the overhead strip lighting buzzed and flashed for a few seconds. Jenna's breath caught in her throat at the sight of Ellie McBride. She'd seen many people murdered during her time in Black Rock Falls and they'd all shocked her. There had been other strangulations, and although she'd seen stabbings and terrible mutilations, often the faces of the victims remained untouched and didn't show the fear they'd suffered prior to their death. A victim of strangulation usually looked horrific. The faces of the victims often stayed with Jenna in a parade of terrifyingly gruesome images. Ellie McBride didn't remotely resemble the woman that she'd met previously. A wave of remorse washed over her and she reached out and touched Kane's arm. "I've let her down. This is my fault. I should have believed her."

"You followed procedure and went through the evidence—or lack of it." Kane's arm slid around her shoulder and pulled her against him. "You did everything possible to keep her safe. The person to blame is the killer. The only thing you owe her is what we owe any victim of crime in our county, and that is to find out who did this." He turned her to face him. "You're the smartest woman I know. You'll figure it out. You always do."

Nodding, Jenna pulled her professional cloak around her, took out her flashlight, and circled the body. Evidence would be everywhere, she just needed to recognize it. The cord ends at the back of the neck told her that Ellie had suffered strangulation from behind, the same as Laney Prescott. The cord, the type purchased everywhere, had been made into a garrote, left on the body, and tightened by using a small piece of wood, in this case a pencil broken in half and secured to each end. She glanced at Kane, who crouched beside the body examining the hands. She touched his shoulder. "The garrote is his signature."

"Yeah. One good thing, she has fibers under her nails. She fought very hard." Kane stood and walked slowly around the body. "I figure he attacked the other victim from behind as well. She didn't get time to run or do anything." He glanced around the boiler room. "Jesse Holland told us he'd checked out the boiler room to make sure no one was there. Someone was hiding in here where he couldn't see them." He scanned the room.

Jenna went to his side, unease creeping over her. "Maybe there's a closet here somewhere where they keep tools."

"Stay close. We'll take a look." Kane pulled his weapon and moved very slowly from furnace to furnace, checking along each wall. He led the way past an open purse, its contents scattered over the floor, and then walked along the wall at the back of the room. "There it is."

Jenna's attention moved to a yellow door with the red sign: KEEP OUT. STAFF ONLY. She followed Kane to the door. "It needs a key to open it. If someone hid in there, they could only be one of the staff. Why didn't Holland check the door?"

"Maybe he did." Kane turned to look at her. "All doors can be opened from the inside to prevent people from getting trapped. The killer could have waited here for her to come into the room. He would have taken his chances that she'd be alone, or he made the call to get Holland out of the way. We'll need to see his phone."

The smell of oil and machinery seemed to hang in the heat, and from the rancid smell, it had accelerated the decomposition of the body. "What if they're still hiding in there?"

"Doubtful, but we'll check." Kane went through his pockets and pulled out a set of lock picks and went to work. In seconds the door opened.

Pulling her weapon Jenna stood to one side of the door, as Kane opened it slowly and moved forward, leading with his M-18 pistol. A light flashed on, illuminating an almost empty room with boxes of tools lining the walls. "I guess the light has a sensor."

"Yeah, it would be for cost cutting, as people tend to leave lights on. In a room like this, maybe someone wouldn't go in there for days on end." Kane closed the door and stepped to her side. "They often use sensor lights in government buildings, especially the bathrooms."

Footsteps came down the hallway and Jenna heard Raven's voice. Wolfe had arrived with his team. Keeping to the outside of the room, they headed for the door. Having Wolfe on scene had a calming effect on everyone and Jenna's unease dropped down a level. Apart from Colt Webber, the medical examiner's office had become a family affair, and this time he brought his wife, Norrell, along, as well as his daughter, Emily. Although Norrell specialized in forensic pathology, her interest in crime solving overlapped into what she called the fresh cases. She'd taken Wolfe's name when they married, so asking for Dr. Wolfe at the medical examiner's office often caused confusion. Jenna nodded as they came into the room. "This murder is a shock to me. I'd been sure she'd be safe." She stared at Ellie's twisted blue face and swallowed hard. "We've cleared the building. You should be safe to work in here but please watch your backs."

"We're all carrying and we'll be just fine, Jenna. Did y'all record the scene?" Wolfe looked at them expectantly. "Raven mentioned that Rowley has taken photographs of the footprints they noticed between the buildings. They've searched everywhere and can't find anything out of place." He pulled off his woolen cap, displaying a shock of white-blond hair. "It's hot in here. That's sure gonna mess with the time of death."

Shaking her head, Jenna met his gaze. "No, we've just arrived. We can start now."

"No, it's fine. Webber can do it." Wolfe smiled at them, seemingly oblivious to the stink in the room. "We'll record the scene and get this body out of the heat as soon as possible. Y'all go and interview your witnesses."

"We have a rough idea of the time of death." Kane moved to his friend's side. "One of the maintenance men delivered her here and then went back to check on her sometime later. I'll get the exact time from him and text it to you."

"That will make my job a whole lot easier." Wolfe turned to look at Emily. "We'll need to get her hands bagged."

"Not a problem." Emily dug into the forensics kit Wolfe had placed on the floor for evidence bags to cover the victim's hands.

"I'm concerned about her head and neck." Norrell moved closer to the body. "I figure for the perp to get that close to kill someone, she would have been pressed up against him at one time and have fibers in her hair." She glanced up at Wolfe. "Do you want me to cover her head?"

"Y'all don't need me here at all, do you?" Wolfe grinned at her, snapped on examination gloves and turned his attention back to Jenna. "My team is working as smoothly as yours now." He pulled on a face mask. "You can leave her with me now, Jenna. I'll call you later, after I've done a preliminary examination."

Knowing she'd left Ellie McBride in safe and caring hands, Jenna turned toward the door. "Thanks. We'll catch you later."

TWENTY-THREE

An overpowering sense of guilt hung over Jenna as she walked along the hallways back to the office. Ellie McBride had been her responsibility to keep safe and she'd let her down. She bit hard on her bottom lip and forced her mind to go through the list of procedures she needed to attend to. She needed to step up to the plate and make sure they caught the killer. By the time they had reached the office, she had jobs for her team already mapped out. She turned to Rio and Rowley. "I want you to take the principal to the media room and look over CCTV footage for the last twelve hours. Obtain a copy, if possible, and it will give you more time to check it out when we get back to the office." She looked at Raven. "I want you to speak to the administrator. Her name is Ms. Bell. She issues passes to anyone coming into the building who isn't part of the staff. Get a list of anyone, including students, who came to the office. I want to know about them. I also need a list of everyone who entered the building today. Everyone is logged in and out, so that shouldn't be a problem. It could be a crucial piece of evidence, so make sure that you insist that she gives you the information. Explain that anyone inside the building is in danger after what happened, which is in fact at least two breaches in their security system that we know about."

As she led the way out of the main building and into the foyer, she glanced at Kane. "We'll take Jesse Holland into one of the classrooms and interview him. As the last person to see Ellie alive, he becomes a suspect. Lean on him if need be. I want to know if he is involved in anyway whatsoever."

"Wait up just a minute." Kane placed his hand on her arm. "I've been thinking about the victims. Usually, serial killers have a type of woman they murder. They're usually around the same age and have some distinctive feature about them, and yet the two victims are almost complete opposites. One with dark hair, one with blonde; one in her early thirties and the other mid-forties." He met her gaze. "The only thing I can see that links them is children. They both work with children."

Allowing his words to percolate through her mind, Jenna nodded. "Yeah, so maybe the killer is one of her students, or has been through the system. That would put Holland in the right age group. He seemed so helpful, but then that's no guarantee he isn't a serial killer. Let's see what we can get out of him. He is young and would normally be quite vulnerable with law enforcement breathing down his neck. If he's not, we need to keep a very close eye on him."

"Copy that." A nerve in Kane's jaw twitched. "I'll turn up the heat and see how much he can take."

Leading the way into the office, Jenna stood to one side as her deputies moved to their various destinations. Jesse Holland sat in the administration area staring at his boots, his hands hanging loosely between his knees. She waited until he glanced up at her. "Jesse Holland? We spoke on the phone just before. We'd like to speak to you. Would you mind directing us to an empty classroom where we can have some privacy, please?"

"Yeah, sure." Holland pushed both hands through his hair and stood. "I just can't get Ms. McBride's face out of my head. It was a terrible shock finding her like that. Did you notice anyone else in the building?"

"Not yet." Kane folded his arms across his chest and looked at him. "We'll discuss this in the empty classroom. If you'll lead the way."

"All the classrooms are empty at the moment, so we can take the first one." Holland walked out of the office. He scanned his card to the staff entrance door and they walked inside, coming out in the hallway lined with classrooms. He stopped at the first one and pushed open the door, holding it open for Jenna to follow him through. He sat on one of the desks with one hand on each side and his legs dangling to the floor. "Fire away."

"As you're the last person to see Ellie McBride alive, we have to follow certain procedure." Kane stood in front of him, his face like granite. "First, I need to read you your rights. This isn't because we think you're involved with the murder. It's so you understand that anything you say will be taken down and may be used in evidence against you." He handed his phone to Jenna. "The sheriff is recording our conversation on my phone." He read him his rights. "The second thing I need from you today is your fingerprints and a DNA sample, to eliminate you as the killer." He pulled out his fingerprint scanner, followed by a DNA collection kit. "It's painless. All you need to do is open your mouth."

"I don't need legal representation because I didn't hurt anyone." Holland looked from one to the other. "Ms. McBride was one of my teachers. She has never been anything but kind toward me. Seeing her murdered like that will stay with me forever. I will do anything you require to assist you taking down this creep."

"Okay." Kane pulled on gloves and went to work.

Jenna took out her notebook and pen. If Holland decided to give up the names of the people he had been working with during the day and anyone else he'd seen, she wanted to get it down so she could act on it right away rather than waiting for the transcript of the interview. "That's good to know. I understand completely how you feel about finding the body. It is a terrible shock when it's someone that you know and respect."

"Can you recall where you were on Friday night between ten and midnight?" Kane moved Jenna's phone closer to Holland and rested one hip on the teacher's desk.

"I'm not one hundred percent sure." Holland rubbed the back of his neck and reluctance flashed across his face. "I drove around with the boys like we do every Friday night. So, I'm not sure of the time we went to different places. We went to a hockey match, left there, and went to get something warm to drink. I recall being in Aunt Betty's Café for a time. I figure I got home sometime around midnight. My folks were asleep and I crept into the house so as not to wake them."

After making a few notes, Jenna raised her gaze to him. "Have you been to the new convenience store on the corner of Pine and Stanton?"

"Macks?" Holland grinned at them. "It's a cool place. Yeah, we did swing by there one time over the weekend, but I don't figure it was Friday."

"I would like the names and contact details of everyone you were with that night." Kane glanced at Jenna. "The sheriff can take a photograph of your contacts list to save time. You just tell us which one of them went with you that night."

"Why exactly do you want to know where I went on Friday night?" Holland handed Jenna his phone and then looked at them suspiciously. "Ms. McBride was murdered today."

"An incident involving Ms. McBride occurred on Friday evening." Kane gave him a direct stare. "Like I said before, as you are the last person to see her alive, we need to make sure we've cleared you from any involvement with the attack on her on Friday night."

"Oh, I see." Holland nodded and pointed out the friends he'd been with on the contacts list.

Jenna made a note and then looked at Holland again. "What vehicle do you drive?"

"A Dodge pickup." Holland smiled. "The tricked out one in the parking lot. Cherry-apple red. I worked on it all last summer." He moved his attention to Kane. "The truck you drive is something else. It went flashing past me on the highway over the summer. Have you got nitro in that machine?"

"Yeah, but let's get back to Ms. McBride's murder." Kane's hard expression didn't alter as he stared at the man. "You work here every day?"

"Yeah." Holland shrugged. "I'm not a janitor. I've got my plumbing license, but I can run wire just fine. I'm part of the maintenance team, and we all go where we're needed."

"So you'd notice if someone new came along or shouldn't be hanging around the school?" Kane scratched his cheek. "Was there anyone?"

"Nope, not that I recall, but I'm involved in maintenance, so I can't say for all over the school." Holland frowned. "We do have people come by for specialist jobs, like IT, security, and audiovisual. Those interactive screens are going down all the time. The teachers have people in to do talks and there are others, to do with education, I guess. I'm not the person you should be speaking to about them."

During the conversation, Jenna scrolled through Holland's call log and hadn't noticed any calls around the time he'd supposedly taken a call to leave Ellie and go and fix a burst pipe. After taking an image of the call log, she handed the phone back to Holland, who looked at it stupidly for a few seconds as if not recalling he'd given it to her. She glanced at Kane. "You mentioned receiving a call. I don't see one on your phone around that time."

"We use a radio." Holland indicated to a small two-way attached to his belt.

That complicated matters and Jenna sighed. "Who contacted you?"

"One of the guys." Holland frowned. "It's noisy down there, you know, so I'm honestly not sure who called me." He moved around restlessly his eyes shifting back and forth. "The thing is, it couldn't have been the person who murdered Ms. McBride because they'd need a radio and everyone on duty was there fixing the pipe. They'd almost finished by the time I arrived."

Making a quick note in her book, Jenna considered his reply. "Who else carries radios?"

"All the maintenance staff, including the janitors, gardeners, cleaners." Holland scratched his head messing up his hair. "I'd say everyone apart from the teachers. The admin has them to contact us if they need something done, so does the principal. I figure that's all."

"Where were you on Saturday night and Sunday morning?" Kane leaned forward and narrowed his gaze. The move reminded Jenna of an eagle waiting to swoop down and capture its prey. "Tell me the truth because we can check the GPS on your phone."

"My folks went to see my grandma, and they stayed over." Holland lifted one shoulder in a half shrug. "They like me to stay home and feed the animals, so I watched TV. With all the snow and all, I didn't want to risk getting stuck somewhere."

"Were you alone?" Kane flicked a glance at Jenna and then continued his relentless stare at Holland. "If not, we'll need to corroborate your alibi."

The smell of fear rose up from the young man and Jenna noticed a sheen of sweat above the man's top lip. Why was he sweating?

"Dang." Holland shook his head. "My folks will kill me."

He gave Kane a remorseful stare. "My girlfriend stayed over with me. Do you need to tell them?"

"No." Kane slid from the desk. "I can be discreet. Give us her name and where we can find her. I suggest you don't contact her. You've already given us permission to look at your phone logs, so we'll check if you call her."

"Okay, okay." Holland gave them the details.

"One more thing." Kane cleared his throat. "Do you know Laney Prescott? She's a social worker."

"Can't say that I do." Holland wiped both hands down his face. "Is that all? Can I go now?"

Jenna handed him her card. "Yeah, thanks for your time. If you discover who called you about the burst pipe, call me."

"You can go." Kane picked up his phone and stopped the recording.

As Holland left the classroom, Jenna turned to Kane. "What do you think?"

"We'll check out the girlfriend, but I figure he's clean." His gaze followed Holland along the hallway and then he looked back at Jenna. "I checked out his gloves. I figure the killer wears black leather gloves similar to mine. I noticed dark particles under the victim's nails. His gloves are light brown, well used, and had no recent scratches. He is way too nervous for a serial killer who stalks women—and he showed remorse. He appears genuinely disturbed by finding the body."

Blowing out a sigh, Jenna stepped into the hallway. "Agreed, but I got two things from speaking to him. The killer has access to a radio and the school. It's a long shot, but if we can pair one of Laney Prescott's clients to one of the workers here at the school, we might just catch this guy before he kills again."

TWENTY-FOUR

Wednesday

The previous day, with so much information to digest, Jenna had sent everyone home at five after six, intending to start fresh in the morning. It had been a long day, with so many incidents happening at once that it had become difficult to keep them all separated. The snowplows usually went through town and to outlying areas between six and six-thirty each evening, so to make sure her deputies and herself and Kane got home without being stuck in the blizzard, they all left to follow the snowplows home. When they'd left the ranch, only a few snowflakes were falling and the road was recently cleared and covered with ice repellent. As they drove into town, the amount of people milling around surprised Jenna. It seemed everyone had taken advantage of the lessening snowfall to get out and grab supplies. Most of the stores in town opened at seven. Being a rural town, most of the ranchers were up and busy at daylight. People bundled up in bright colors and all of them moving round in a cloud of steam amused Jenna. In fact, the crowd of people lining up outside Aunt Betty's Café appeared to be cloaked in fog. She checked her watch. They'd made good time getting into town and arrived at the office a little after seven-thirty.

To her surprise, Maggie stood at the counter, and Rio, Rowley, and Raven sat at their desks hard at work. She gave Maggie a wave as she walked past the front counter to speak to her deputies. "You all look very busy. Do you have anything for me?"

"Yeah, Jesse Holland's alibi checks out. His girlfriend was with him as he told you." Rio glanced at Rowley. "We split up the CCTV footage between us and have been viewing it for the last hour or so." He leaned back in his seat and yawned. "It's not very interesting. Not many people came and went in the last twelve hours. Those we found we zoomed in and captured an image of them. Apart from Jesse Holland, Ms. Bell, Ms. McBride, and the principal, we haven't identified anyone yet."

"Ms. Bell cooperated and gave me a complete list of everyone who worked or entered the building over the last week or so, along with dates and times." Raven spun around in his chair to look at Jenna. "I've been trying to narrow it down to the times when we know someone stalked Ms. McBride."

Glad that everyone worked without supervision, Jenna nodded. "That's really good, Raven, but don't forget to include anyone who called in sick. It would be to pretend they weren't going to be at work and then slip in later. They all know where the CCTV cameras are situated and could easily avoid them, so it's imperative you check the logs to see who actually worked those days."

"Okay." Raven rubbed the back of his neck. "I'll call Ms. Bell and ask her for a list of anyone who called in sick over that time."

Turning to go, Jenna glanced over her deputies. "Keep me up to date. I'm going to get the search warrant for the social services department." She headed up the stairs to her office.

As she entered the office, Kane glanced up and smiled and

then went back to tapping away on his keyboard. The room smelled of freshly brewed coffee and she could hear the machine sizzling as the rich brown liquid plopped into the pot. She dropped her things on her desk, removed her coat and gloves, and went to sit down. Under her desk she could hear Duke snoring. They had intended to leave the bloodhound at home as he didn't like the cold weather and he wasn't getting any younger. They changed their minds when Duke followed them to the front door, his tail wagging with excitement to be going out, and they couldn't leave him behind. Kane had carried him to the truck and set him on the back seat and then carried him again from the truck and into the office. The dog had turned around three times and flopped down in his basket under her desk. As she bent down to rub Duke's ears, his tail thumped, and one eye opened to look at her. She tucked the blanket around him and gave his head a scratch. "You are such a good boy, Duke."

The dog gave a long, contented sigh, and Kane sniggered. She looked at him. "What's so funny?"

"I'm starting to believe that Duke prefers being here in the office in the quiet so he can sleep all day, rather than being home with the boys. I figure they're getting too noisy for him." Kane stood and walked over to the printer as paperwork started shooting out. "I've written up the request for a search warrant. I have everything covered. If you take a look at it, make sure I haven't forgotten anything, we'll walk it over to the judge before he starts court. Hopefully he'll sign it and we can head straight to the Department of Social Services before we need to be at the autopsy."

Jenna sat down at her desk and pulled out a legal pad. There were so many things to do that she needed to make a list. When they spoke to the director of the social services, she'd need to discover which of Laney Prescott's workmates were also her friends, or if any of them knew any of her friends. She needed her whereabouts before the night of her murder, her current cases, and also cases involving any children who went to Black Rock Falls Middle School in the last ten years or so. It would be a huge ask for the department and correlating information would take months unless she could convince Kalo and Beth Katz to get involved, as they had access to the type of software that gave them almost instant results. She glanced out of the window. The snow had finally stopped falling and maybe Styles and Carter would be able to fly into town. They would only need a break in the weather of two hours or so. As Kane correlated the paperwork for the search warrant, she pulled out her phone and called Agent Carter. "Good morning, Ty. It's stopped snowing here. Is there any chance you'll be able to fly over the next few hours? We really need your help right now. I will explain everything later, but we have another Christmas serial killer in town."

"We're all packed and ready to go." Carter's boots echoed on tile as he walked. *"I heard from Styles not fifteen minutes ago. They should be on their way shortly. We had planned to drop the birds down on your ranch, but will we have transportation to the office?"*

Jenna smiled. "Yeah, my department truck is there and Raya is at home with the boys. She'll give you the keys. You have the code to get into the cottage. You'll be sharing with Kalo, I hope you don't mind. Beth and Styles in the other rooms and Jo and Jaime in one of our spare rooms. Give me a call when you arrive. Tell Kalo and Beth to bring their laptops. I need them to run down a few things for me."

"Copy that. We can disable your security net from the choppers, so we'll be able to land without a problem." Carter chuckled. *"It sounds like I can look forward to another fun-filled Christmas in Black Rock Falls."*

Smiling, Jenna shook her head. Carter was certainly a character. His laid-back nature covered what lay beneath the surface. A Navy SEAL who'd suffered PTSD, he'd been dragged back into service as an FBI agent by his partner, Jo Wells. His two years off the grid had made him antisocial at first, but now he slid into the team and had become part of their family. "I'm sure you wouldn't have it any other way. We look forward to seeing you all again."

After disconnecting, Jenna made notes to organize the takedown of the drug distribution at the Withers ranch. The time had come for her to delegate responsibility. She had too many things to consider to take on any more burdens. Styles and Carter had experience in taking down drug cartels, and along with Kane as a backup sniper, they would work out a suitable plan. She needed to keep her mind on working with Kalo and Beth Katz on finding suspects for the murders. With her list of things to do sitting in front of her, she realized just how vast a task she had set herself. The leads to Ellie McBride being involved in Laney Prescott's murder had all fallen away to dust with the death of Ellie. Without any solid leads to find the murderer, she would need to gather herself and literally start the investigation again. She stood and exchanged her shoes for boots and then glanced at Kane as he carefully placed the paperwork inside a manila folder. "We desperately need this search warrant. I want to find a tie between the murders. If we follow the usual psychopath pattern, we'll be looking at someone who has problems with teachers and social workers. To me, this screams of a kid who has been placed in the system and maybe didn't get the help that they wanted. I'm going to play toward that angle and hope for the best, because right now it's all that I've got."

"It sounds like a fine plan, Jenna." Kane shrugged into his coat and, taking the gloves out of his pocket, pushed the folder under one arm and then pulled them on. "I figure we've got enough probable cause to sway the judge. He knows the severity of the problem we have in Black Rock Falls with serial killers. He also understands our methods. We might get a list of names but we will also treat them in a sensitive manner." He buttoned his coat. "One thing you haven't considered is if the person we're looking for isn't a child who went through the system. There is a possibility they could be a parent or someone who's had their child removed from their care and is carrying resentment toward the people who made it possible. If we get a bunch of names and Kalo and Beth can find matches with some of the other searches that we've been doing, we might strike gold." He pushed on his hat and glanced down at Duke, who snored in his sleep. "Let's go. Duke will be fine here."

Smiling broadly, Jenna slid her arm through Kane's as they left the judge's office. Happiness blocked out the blast of freezing wind that threatened to cut through her thick clothes. Under her arm she gripped the signed search warrant. Kane had been amazing, giving his genuine concern about any clients but stressing the need to prevent more murders. Between them they'd convinced the judge but it hadn't been easy. At last, they could move forward. The moment they were out of earshot, she planned to whoop and happy dance in the snow, but as she turned to look at Kane, she barely avoiding tripping over a woman pushing a stroller. Luckily, Kane had tightened his grip and she gathered herself and smiled at a red-nosed child peeking out from under a knitted blue bonnet and waving a teddy bear.

The toothless grin the little boy gave her shone out like a ray of sunshine. She suddenly missed Tauri and Jackson, although they would be thrilled with the arrival of the choppers. She'd made sure to call Raya to inform her they were coming and to tell Tauri about them right away as a chopper had landed in the yard previously and a notorious criminal had kidnapped him.

She hoped the arrival of the FBI agents, along with Jo's daughter, Jaime, would put a smile on his face.

"I miss them too." Kane leaned into her as they strolled along the sidewalk. "I liked being the rancher for a year as well. It was relaxing." He bent and kissed the top of her head. "I hate to admit it, but I loved the entire process. The late-night feeding, changing diapers. It was an experience I figured would never happen. I wish we'd had those important times with Tauri as well but just having him as our son and seeing him smile is enough."

Glad of him beside her blocking the chill, she smiled. "Yeah, it was exhausting—still is—but I loved every second. I'd have had ten kids, but the job got in the way. I love being sheriff. I need to be useful and I figure I can have both: my kids and my job. It's just as well. Most of the time, it's a peaceful town and we get to spend time at home. We should be grateful the mayor allows us the time we need."

"Talking about time"—Kane glanced at his watch—"we need to head to Wolfe's office, or we'll miss the autopsy."

Increasing her stride, Jenna headed for the office. She needed to keep moving forward on the murders as fast as possible. "I'll get Rio and Rowley to execute the search warrant. Raven will probably like to attend the autopsy. I'll meet you at the Beast."

TWENTY-FIVE

As they walked into the medical examiner's office, Kane's and Raven's voices dropped to just above a whisper. Jenna found it strange how the smell of the morgue had the same reaction on everyone, as if they had walked into church. Maybe it was respect. Although Wolfe had a ton of respect for the victims in his care, he was the complete opposite. Maybe because he spoke into a microphone for most of the day and needed to lift the volume of his voice to make sure the recording came out clear and precise. Jenna shook her head trying to imagine why she had contemplated the reason behind the volume of people's voices. Maybe she needed to squash the uneasy feeling of going to an autopsy to watch the dissection of two poor women. Jenna followed Kane and Raven to the alcove. She removed her coat, gloves, and hat and proceeded to pull on the scrubs and PPE. She looked at the others. "Ready?"

When they nodded, she led the way to the examination room with the red light outside, flashed her card over the scanner, and stepped inside. The terrible smell of decomposition crept through her face mask and crawled over her tongue like some alien being. She kept her mouth shut and breathed through her nose. Inside, bright lights shone on stainless steel gurneys and instrument trays set out alongside Wolfe and Emily. She immediately noticed a difference in the setup. Usually, Wolfe spoke into a microphone that he pulled down from an arm set above the gurney but this time they both wore headsets, the microphones tucked in underneath their face masks. The medical examiners had their backs turned to them, but the whoosh of the door caught their attention and they both turned at once to look at them.

The sight of the bodies made Jenna's breakfast solidify in her stomach. She would never get used to seeing a body cracked open for examination. After so many crime scenes and autopsies, she'd hoped that one day she would become hardened to the sights, but in truth, most times she became saddened and angry. Kane and Raven moved closer to the examination tables, but she leaned against the counter, positioning herself below the air-conditioning duct, hoping the flow of air would reduce some of the smell. She nodded to Wolfe. "Morning. I see you've already started. Have you discovered anything of significance?"

"It's good to see y'all." Wolfe's gaze moved from one to the other and settled on Raven. "How are the ribs?"

"Fine if I don't laugh, sneeze, or cough." Raven met his gaze. "Em is keeping an eye on me."

"So I see." Wolfe turned his attention back to Jenna. "We've conducted preliminary examinations as you know. Some interesting information came to light from Ellie McBride. Under her fingernails we discovered small traces from black leather gloves, but that's not all. We discovered samples of saliva, which carried DNA. I ran it through the sequencer right away and we got a match for Laney Prescott. As these women have never met, this is absolute proof that the same person murdered both women."

"I have something too." Emily placed instruments back on the tray and turned to look at her. "I found a few dog hairs on the back of Laney Prescott's clothes. She doesn't own a dog, as far as I'm aware. I can tell you that the dog is black and white, but I would need to go into further DNA analysis to pinpoint the breed, but likely it's a crossbred animal."

Intrigued, Jenna pushed away from the counter and moved closer to Emily's examination table. "That could be a very important clue."

"There's more." Wolfe winked at her. "The garrotes used on both victims are identical. The small pieces of wood came from a pine tree, which as we are surrounded by them, makes it a bit difficult to identify and the green twine used is exactly the same. I conducted research into the twine and it's a generic brand that's easily obtained in a wide variety of stores. So basically, the killer used untraceable items. I found no foreign DNA, trace evidence, or other particles on the garrotes."

"I assume that both victims were strangled from behind." Kane moved from one gurney to the next. "This is a very up-close and personal way to kill someone. Surely the killer left trace evidence behind, apart from a few dog hairs."

"We have more samples to examine." Wolfe crossed his arms. "It will take time to run them all through the DNA sequencer machine. Of course, there were other DNA samples, but most of them are likely to belong to the victims. We can't tell just by looking at them. The scrapings from the fingernails were a priority, so we did those right away. The others will take a little longer. The problem is, with all the information available about DNA and crime scenes, we're finding killers are being very particular about what evidence they leave behind. This makes our job a whole lot more difficult. It's the small pieces of evidence they miss that come to light that usually give us a lead."

"The injuries look identical." Raven walked around the gurneys examining the victims. "Did you find anything else?"

"They both have bruises between their shoulders." Emily

frowned above her face mask. "We both found this quite unusual, and we assumed that the perpetrator rendered the victims unconscious while he stood close to the body, and when they dropped, he used his knee between their shoulder blades to increase the pressure on their necks. As you can see, there are two main grooves in the flesh on the necks of both victims. This would indicate that the killer moved the twine during the attack. The first groove is lower and crushed the larynx and the second groove comes up under the chin." She indicated to one of two red welts on Laney Prescott's throat. "This I believe is the second attempt to suffocate her. It, in fact, crushed her hyoid bone."

"Normally I would say that this killer knew exactly what he was doing or he's done this before." Wolfe shrugged and his gray gaze moved over Jenna's face. "In this case, I can't be one-hundred-percent sure. One thing he does know: that it takes at least four minutes to strangle someone; and I have to assume that he knew breaking the hyoid bone would be an advantage. The problem is this information is readily available on the internet. The other thing: it takes a reasonable amount of strength to strangle someone, especially when they're kicking and gouging your hands. So we need to assume that the killer is bigger and stronger than the women involved. This makes me believe, the perpetrator in this case is male."

"Strangulation makes it personal." Kane stood hands on hips, feet apart, shaking his head. "I believe this guy has an ax to grind. He needed to feel the life leaving his victims' bodies."

The link between the victims would be crucial but Jenna needed a determination of cause of death to proceed. Jenna looked at Kane and nodded in agreement. "And he's escalating, so there may be more victims we haven't discovered yet." She moved her attention back to Wolfe. "So going on what you've discovered so far, what would you consider to be the cause of death?"

"The heart, lungs, and other organs are oxygen deprived in both victims." Wolfe cleared his throat. "Unless the drug analysis or further investigations prove otherwise, I'd say asphyxia due to strangulation, but I'll likely be adding anoxia due to the interruption of blood flow to the brain." He glanced at Jenna. "I'll send a preliminary report tonight and upload the complete doc in a few days."

Glad she didn't need to be present for the entire autopsy, Jenna nodded. "Thank you for not prolonging this examination for us. Currently, Rowley and Rio are collecting evidence from the Department of Social Services. Just before we left to come here, we managed to get a search warrant from the judge. We're hoping that we can link possible suspects with the victims. I'm eager to head on down there and see what's been found."

"Don't worry." Wolfe's eyes twinkled over the top of his mask. "If I find anything to help with the case, I will call you directly."

Smiling, Jenna gave him a wave. "I know you will. Thanks for everything, we'll catch you both later."

Once outside, she took a deep breath of fresh mountain air. The sudden cold burned her lungs, but she didn't care. The smell of pine trees with a hint of woodsmoke drifted across the town. Staring into the distance, she stood for a minute to absorb the snow-covered rooftops and the chimneys with lines of gray smoke wafting up into sky. Reluctantly, she followed Kane to the truck. As they drove along Main, Jenna looked out of the window. The town changed dramatically over the seasons, the townsfolk enjoying all the festivities in the calendar. Twinkling lights on Christmas trees glittered through the windows, and this year the council had placed tubs with live trees in them covered in bright colored balls all along Main. Stores had joined the festivities, all façades flashed with Christmas lights and brightly colored glittering garlands. Outside Aunt Betty's Café, a huge snowman had appeared overnight, complete with a red ski hat, a carrot for a nose, coal for the eyes, and a set of vampire teeth for the smile. In the window hung a huge MERRY CHRISTMAS sign.

Beside her, Kane's stomach rumbled. It wasn't lunchtime yet, but by now, he'd usually topped up his ferocious appetite with cookies and coffee or hot chocolate. She glanced over at Raven in the back seat. "When we're done with social services, we will head to Aunt Betty's Café and get some lunch. This cold weather really makes me hungry."

"Me too." Raven rubbed his middle. "Just the smell of the pie when we pass Aunt Betty's makes my mouth water. I figure if they rented out rooms, I'd live there." He grinned at her.

"Me too." Kane chuckled and flicked a glance at Jenna. "I'm joking—okay?"

TWENTY-SIX

The temperature had dropped again as Kane led the way along the salt-covered walkway into the social services building. Although, it didn't resemble a government building; it was more like a frosted gingerbread house. Snow eight inches deep sat on the rooftops and dagger-like icicles hung all around the gutters. He crunched through patches of ice before pushing his way through the front door and into a waiting area with a front counter with glass surrounds. The depressing foyer painted in magnolia offered no TV, magazines, or anything other than flyers about suicide and family problems. A few people sat in the waiting area. All held bleak expressions.

When they'd built the Her Broken Wings Foundation building, they'd made it like a family home: warm and inviting but with separate residences where people could have their privacy and dignity. The communal areas and kitchen were places to meet others, and more like a cozy home. They'd had enough land to expand and would be building another wing after the melt. Here, despair and resentment surrounded him. Kane ground his teeth. They needed to do more to help people in trouble. Raising money in their town had never been a problem. He'd speak to Jenna and they'd look into what else could be done. People deserved to be happy and most times they ended up here through no fault of their own.

A blast of warm air hit his face and he removed his gloves and pushed them into his pockets before unbuttoning his coat. Beside him, Jenna and Raven were doing the same. He followed Jenna to the front counter and waited as she asked the person in charge to direct them to her deputies. They were let inside and followed a woman to an office door with the name DIRECTOR embossed on a metal plaque.

After the woman knocked on the door and announced them, a man he assumed was Christopher Paul stood from behind his desk and waved them inside. Kane offered his hand. "Deputy Dave Kane. I'm sure you know Sheriff Alton and this is Deputy Raven."

"Yes, I spoke to Sheriff Alton on the phone." An expression of concern crossed Paul's face. "Is there a problem? The search warrant was very specific, saying that it needed names of anyone who had interacted with Laney Prescott during her time here. As it didn't specify individual cases or the reasons that they needed to see her, we were able to locate the list of names without any difficulty. I supplied your deputies with the list of names and the dates that they attended." He sighed. "I do understand the gravity of the situation. If there's anything else I can do to help, please ask. As long as it is legal for me to do so, I will help you any way I can."

"That's very helpful." Jenna stepped closer to his desk. "There are a couple of other things that we need to know, regarding Laney. We need the names of her workmates and any friends that you know she may have."

Kane nodded. "Can you recall anyone in particular that she became friends with at work? We're having difficulties finding out if she had any friends outside of work at all."

"I've given your deputies a list of everyone who works here

and added a couple of notes for anyone that she seemed to chat with, but you must understand, as director, I don't have the information you require. You may have better luck speaking to some of the other social workers." He opened his hands wide. "I'm really sorry but there's nothing much else I can tell you. Laney came to work, we had weekly meetings to discuss her clients, and that's about it. We never discussed her personal life at all. I didn't at any time see her meeting anyone at the door or anything like that. She never had any personal phone calls. It seems she divided her time between work and home." He frowned. "It's a quiet day today. If you have time, I'll find out if my social workers will be able to speak to you."

Kane nodded. "Yeah, that would be good. We can split up to save time. If that works for you?"

"Yes, of course." Paul picked up the phone and made a few calls. "I have three counselors who worked closely with Laney who can see you now."

"Thanks." Jenna nodded to Paul. "Point us in the right direction." She turned to Kane and Raven. "Record the meeting. It's better than notes."

Kane smiled. "Sure. We'll meet back in the foyer."

"If you go into the hallway, they'll call you into their offices." Paul stood. "I hope you find who killed Laney."

"We'll catch them." Jenna led the way into the hallway.

A woman with dark hair tied at the nape and a huge orange sweater over tight black leggings stepped out and beckoned to Kane. "Deputy Kane, isn't it? I'm Lucinda Bragg. It's terrible about Laney. She was such a sweet person." She waved him to a chair and closed the door before taking a seat behind the desk and looking at him expectantly.

Kane sat down in a low chair. It didn't worry him, but he could see how it would to someone else. It made Ms. Bragg appear to loom above him in an almost intimidating way. "What is your area of expertise?"

"I usually have clients who are coping with a marriage breakup or placement of a child into foster care." She leaned forward on the desk, resembling a huge pumpkin.

Nodding, Kane bit his tongue from commenting on the low chair and smiled. "I see. What clients did Laney usually work with?"

"Much the same as me." She linked her hands on the table and adopted a pious expression. "Does this have anything to do with her murder? Are we all in danger?" She grasped her throat.

Kane leaned forward in the chair and clasped his hands between his knees. "At this time, we don't know who may be in danger. Laney was the first victim in town, and we've had another since, but she has a different occupation to you, so the killer might be attacking random women." He met her gaze. "Do you recall Laney having any problems with any particular clients? Not necessarily recent clients, maybe ones over the time she worked here?"

"In this profession, we all have problem clients, Deputy Kane." She sighed and picked at her nails. "There are always two sides to a story, which means one side isn't going to be happy. Sometimes, no matter what we do to try and solve a problem, no one is happy."

After getting nowhere with this woman, Kane decided to change tack. "Do you know the names of her friends or acquaintances that she hung out with from time to time?"

"We went down to Aunt Betty's for lunch a few times." She gave him an inquiring stare. "Laney often went to lunch with different members of staff but I don't believe they got together after work at all. Laney never mentioned any close friends or relatives to me. She did mention she'd first moved to Black Rock Falls after ending a relationship with a very controlling man. She needed to get as far away from him as possible. I've worked here around the same time as she has and he's never shown up in town, so I couldn't imagine it would be him. She did mention his name, ah—Don something. I'm sure if you contacted her next of kin, they would remember his name, but as I said, he's never shown in town. In my experience men who are controlling like that would usually take to the hills once they realize their woman is gone for good."

Shaking his head, Kane wondered where this woman had received her training. "I wish that were the case. Both men and women who use coercive control over their partners often hunt them down and murder them, but it's usually within the first six months of them leaving. If they run into their ex-spouse or partner, they can become violent. They often stalk them over months, watching what they're doing. They would do anything to break up a relationship. They have the attitude of, *If I can't have her or him, nobody else can.*" He stood and towered over her. "If you could give me the names of anyone else that you know that Laney used to socialize with, I would appreciate it and then I can be out of your hair." He took out his notebook opened it and handed it to her.

Kane waited for her to write down the details of the other members of staff. He took the notebook from her, folded it shut, and pushed it back inside his pocket. The interview had been a complete waste of time. No doubt, Jenna and Raven were interviewing the two people that Laney went to lunch with most times. If she had any friends outside of work, it wasn't evident, and she hadn't mentioned any names to Lucinda Bragg. Seemed to him that Laney had been lying low. The thought of running into her ex could have been playing on her mind. He nodded to Lucinda. "Thanks for your time. If you recall anything else, call my office." He handed her a card and headed for the door.

Jenna and Raven waited for him in the foyer. By their expressions, he didn't have to ask if they'd discovered anything interesting. He followed them out of the door and turned to Jenna. "The only thing I discovered is that Lucinda Bragg had lunch occasionally with Laney and so did some of the others she worked with in the office. She wasn't able to give me any specific people who Laney had had trouble with over the years, actually saying that they all had trouble with people all the time." He rubbed his chin. "Lucinda did mention Laney ran away from a controlling relationship with a man she believes is named Don. It's a potential suspect we need to chase down. Maybe if we find any of her friends or relatives, they'll know his last name and where this occurred. I'll ask Kalo to look into it for us."

"That's the same info as Raven discovered. We were just talking about it before." Jenna pulled on her gloves as she walked. "That's a depressing place. I can't imagine anyone walking out of there and feeling better. When I spoke to one of the counselors, I sat in a little chair and felt like a child looking up at the principal over the top of his desk."

"Same." Raven shrugged. "It seems like a form of intimidation to me. Maybe you should speak to the director about it. After visiting Her Broken Wings Foundation, the counselors you have there are very good."

"That's because they're non-profit." Jenna smiled at him. "Of course they liaise with the department counselors, but everyone that we employ has a stellar track record. Most work at the Black Rock Falls County Hospital and go to the foundation when required, but we do have a live-in counselor anyone can go to if they need help or assistance. We use the money from our fundraisers to ensure that everyone who steps inside our front door gets the best possible support. Unfortunately, not everyone comes through our doors. I can see from the poor souls waiting that there needs to be a shake-up in the system here. If I'd stayed there any longer, I would have been so depressed I wouldn't have been able to shake off the black dog."

Kane slid an arm around her shoulders. "Yeah, we need to do something. We can raise funds and we have people willing to give their time for free to help out."

"I will." Raven fell into step beside them. "Anything you need, just ask."

"It's a plan we can look at, over our downtime." Jenna pulled open the door to the Beast. "Right now, we need to concentrate on finding suspects—but first we eat."

TWENTY-SEVEN

It was a little after two by the time Jenna had finished her lunch and headed for the door. Susie, the manager, came out from behind the counter carrying a large box. Jenna raised an eyebrow as she handed it to Kane. "Did you order more food?"

"Nope." Kane peered into the box. "There's enough here to feed an army."

"It's the order from your office. Apparently the FBI is in town." Susie looked from one to the other. "The instructions are to take it to the conference room, but as you're here, I'm sure you can deliver it for me?"

Glad to know that the agents had arrived, Jenna smiled. "That's fine, thank you. We're headed there now."

She opened the door for Kane as he stepped out into the snow. Behind her, Raven collected the bag of leftovers for the dogs. His dog, Ben, waited for them at the office. Jenna smiled and thanked Susie. Duke would know they'd been to Aunt Betty's without him and would sulk if he didn't get a snack. Carter's Doberman, Zorro, ignored everyone, but Carter could tempt him to eat the odd sausage now and then. Bear, Styles' Belgian Malinois, an overprotective K-9, guarded both Styles and Beth with a passion, but he'd eat if directed by Styles. With all the dogs staying at the ranch, the boys would be thrilled.

The wonderful aroma of the food filled the Beast's interior as they drove along Main. Outside, snowflakes fell in spirals, spinning away as they caught in the wind. The walls of snow from the snowplow had lost their white coating and resembled a gray wall made up of ice, sticks, and other debris. Jenna appreciated the beauty in a snowscape, but the aftermath became dirty piles of slush. Jenna sighed. More snow would be falling before long and she hoped they'd have the case sewn up before Christmas. She turned to Kane and Raven. "I hope the others have had more luck in finding suspects."

"I figure if you release a media report and set up the hotline again, we might find a few witnesses." Kane shrugged. "Someone out there might have seen something. The killer plans his kills. I figure he's a stalker, so he'd be close by to the victims. People in town are more suspicious nowadays. It's worth a try. Also, Rio's brother and sister are back from college on vacation. They'll be happy to man the phones. They love being involved."

Rio's twin siblings, Cade and Piper, had lived with Rio since his parents died. They'd become like part of the family. Jenna nodded. "Yeah, good idea. Right now, we're getting nowhere."

She climbed from the Beast in time to see Maggie returning with Duke and Ben. Both dogs shook themselves violently and Duke did a happy dance to see them. Jenna took Duke's leash and pushed through the door behind Kane. Behind her, Raven entered with Ben stuck to his leg like glue. That dog didn't like going anywhere without Raven and often howled like a wolf at the moon if left behind. Jenna smiled at Maggie. "Thanks for taking the dogs out."

"I don't mind two of them, but I don't figure I'd manage

four." Maggie pulled off her thick coat. "The FBI agents will need to care for their own dogs."

"I appreciate you taking Ben with you, Maggie." Raven smiled warmly at her. "I'm glad he went with you. He can be sticky with some people."

"He obeyed the signals you taught me and he needed to go outside." Maggie chuckled. "It was me or a puddle on the floor and he chose me. I figure having Duke along helped."

Jenna climbed the stairs, following Kane into the conference room. A cheer came from Carter as they arrived and Kane dropped the box of food on the table. Apparently, no one had stopped for lunch.

As everyone dove into the box for food, Jenna dropped into a chair and exchanged greetings with the agents. It was good to see Jo again. They'd been friends for a long time. Carter had become part of the family, and even Beth Katz and Styles seemed to be at home. Kalo sat at the end of the table, his concentration on his laptop, an unopened packet of sandwiches in one hand. She leaned back in her chair as everyone demolished the food. "Do you have anything for me?"

"Yeah, we do." Kalo smiled at her over the top of his laptop. "Three possible suspects."

"And we've planned out the takedown of the fentanyl distributor." Carter hummed over a spoonful of chili. "It will be like taking candy from a baby."

"Yeah." Kane frowned. "But these babies carry MK-47s. It's snowing and we'll be spotted unless we're very careful."

Jenna held up a hand. "Suspects first."

"Oh, you're no fun at all, Jenna." Carter tipped back his hat. "It's the holidays. Where's your 'ho ho ho' gone?"

Snorting, Jenna shook her head. "It will miraculously arrive when we've put these cases to bed. Now, what suspects?"

"Before we talk about suspects"—Jo waved a burger in one hand—"do you want to discuss the profile?"

Glad to have Jo's expertise as a behavioral analyst on the case, Jenna nodded. "Yeah, I would. Give me the rundown."

"We're talking about someone who carries a deep-set resentment. So I honestly don't believe it's someone who is young, for instance, under the age of twenty. This would negate any of the current children at the school. The reason I mentioned this is because a boy of fourteen is strong enough to strangle a woman." Jo placed her hamburger on a napkin. "In fact, this person could be any age from approximately twenty-five upward, which would again negate them being a student of Ellie McBride's past or present."

"What would make them stand out to us and what are we looking for?" Kane walked to the table and pushed a cup of coffee in front of Jenna and placed another down before taking his seat.

"Resentment could have come from during their childhood or anytime during their life. Maybe something happened recently that triggered them." Jo shrugged. "We're talking about a psychopathic brain. The need to kill could have lain dormant for many years before something triggered it. We all know that not every psychopath becomes a killer. This man, I believe, saw a resemblance between Ellie McBride and Laney Prescott that isn't evident to us. From the evidence that you've presented, the notes in particular tell me that he stalks his victims and plans every move prior to his attacks. He knew they would be alone and he likes to frighten them. This would tell us something terrifying happened to him as a child and this is payback."

Absorbing everything that Jo said, Jenna took a long sip of her coffee. "Yes, so are we looking at a classic abused child?"

"That would be the first avenue to investigate but when young people step out into the world, even if they've come from a stable background, they can be bullied. They might be pressured by people at work. They might have married someone who controls them. We could be talking about a married man who lost his children to the system through no fault of his own and maybe he blames a teacher and the social worker. These are points of reference that I added to the profile so that Kalo and Beth could work their magic and try and cross-reference people who could possibly be suspects."

"A couple of things happened while you were at the autopsy that you should be aware of." Rio stood and went to the whiteboard. "The principal called to inform us that the janitor, Caleb Dorsey, is often on the grounds after hours. He isn't sociable, especially since his divorce, and has become even more remote lately." He looked at Jenna. "I ran a background check on him. He has a minor criminal record for trespassing and a history of mental health issues. I'm wondering why he is employed at the school and near young children. All these things would put him in the right place at the right time to have murdered Ellie McBride. I looked into him a little more, and he and his wife went to Laney Prescott for marriage guidance." He sighed. "That was some time ago and another one of her roles as a social worker. She was qualified."

Impressed, Jenna nodded as Rio added Dorsey's name and the reasons for being a suspect to the whiteboard. "I guess if he's a little unbalanced and his wife divorced him, he might wonder what in the past caused all his problems. It seems to me psychopaths need an excuse to murder someone—as in, it wasn't their fault. They believe they're either doing someone a favor or the person made them do it."

"I'm interested in a man by the name of Ethan Rourke." Kalo met Jenna's gaze and smiled. "I've been centering my search on people who work with or are connected to local government facilities. Rourke is a freelance IT technician. He has the opportunity to work under the radar fixing systems in schools and other government buildings. This gives him access and anonymity. I dug a little deeper and discovered he attended the school, but they expelled him after a disturbing incident involving a teacher. He left the county and finished his time at Louan."

"Why does this make him a suspect?" Raven rested both hands on the table. "Being expelled doesn't make a serial killer."

"Kalo handed this over to me and I made some calls." Rowley smiled. "I wanted to find out a little about him. I asked the principal if he recalled him and he told me Rourke was quiet, intelligent, and socially awkward. The incident with his teacher involved him attacking her for taking his property. Apparently, Rourke carried a strand of his mother's hair. His mother passed when he was younger and his father had drunk himself to death. The kid had been sent to his old grandmother's house. He'd been playing with the hair during class and refused to put it away and when the teacher took it from him, he apparently went ballistic. The school expelled him after he refused to apologize." He cleared his throat. "The principal mentioned this was about fifteen years ago and times have changed. Now, he would have been suspended and offered counseling."

"This tells me the teacher involved embarrassed Rourke in front of the entire class." Jo sighed. "This would be enough for a person to carry resentment if they were inclined to be psychopathic."

"I found Rourke's name in the list of children who'd been involved with social services." Beth looked at Raven. "That makes him two for two. Not proof, by any means, that he's involved. He's kept his nose clean since leaving school, but we can't dismiss him as a possible."

Jenna waited for Rio to update the whiteboard and looked at the faces around the table. "Anyone else?"

"Yeah, I found a guy by the name of Sean Jones." Beth gave Styles a side-eye. "Over to Styles."

"Oh yeah." Styles gave her a lopsided smile. "I hunted down Sean Jones. He is a gardener who works for the local council, so he's frequently around schools, hospitals, and the social services department. He went to the school, but we found nothing bad there. He's another casualty of parents divorcing. He went through a long fight in court. He apparently wanted to live with his father, but his mother got custody of him. Not twelve months after the custody case, she died after a short illness. During this time, his father remarried and moved to another state. They placed Jones in foster care. He was bounced around and got into trouble. One report mentioned he'd hung a cat by the neck from a tree outside a teacher's house. He is one to watch. I figure he has an ax to grind with both teachers and social workers."

Listening with interest, Jenna nodded. "He fits the profile. They often start with animal cruelty. Anyone else?"

"There is one. It's a hunch really." Kalo shrugged. "Working beside Jo all the time, I'm starting to look at people from different angles. There is one person who showed up in my radar. He is known as Dr. Lionel Graves, although he is no longer a doctor of any description. He lost his license some years ago and is living on disability. He was once the local psychologist and former school counselor. I accessed some old files regarding him and discovered he treated several troubled students, including one who later died by suicide. He kept detailed notes that haven't been placed in any type of restricted files. It seems to me he has a fascination with criminal psychology and up until recent changes to the security system, still had access to school records."

"I discovered a number of complaints against him, from the teachers, the students, and the social workers that he came into contact with." Beth tapped on her keyboard. "There is also a complaint he lodged at the local hospital where he accused one of the nurses of writing a report about him to try and prevent him from getting disability."

"Yeah." Kalo nodded. "He seems crazy enough to kill."

Jenna stood and stared at the whiteboard. "We'll need to find these people and go and speak to them."

"We need an hour." Carter nibbled on a fry, dropped it back into the container, and brushed salt from his fingers. "Tonight, we plan to take down the fentanyl distributors out at the BW Ranch. Give us guys an hour to sort out what we need to do. I'll need Styles with me to organize our people to deal with the drugs. It's too dangerous for us to go near them and we have specialized teams to handle that part of the mission." He glanced at Kane. "I'm sure you'll have your deputies back real soon to hunt down suspects."

It was a reasonable request. She nodded. "Okay, you go and talk in my office. I'll be able to find these suspects with the help of Beth, Kalo, and Jo." She raised her gaze to Carter. "You'll never get a team from Helena here in time to deal with the drugs—not in this weather. Have you made other plans?"

"They're already here." Carter grinned around a toothpick. "The moment Kane alerted us to the mission, they hit the road. They're holed up at the motel waiting for the green light."

As the chairs scraped and leftover food vanished along with the men, Jenna looked at the others. "We've got this."

TWENTY-EIGHT

A warm glow surrounded Jenna's heart as she disconnected her call from Raya. She always called around lunchtime to see if the boys were okay and usually got to speak to Jackson before he went down for his nap. FaceTime calls were important and made leaving the boys at home bearable. Their good friend, Atohi Blackhawk, had just arrived to visit. Blackhawk had once been Tauri's guardian, and it was because of their friendship that Jenna and Kane had been able to adopt Tauri. His assistance in teaching her son about his Native American culture had been invaluable. Between him and Kane, they had taught Tauri his native tongue and made sure that his visits to the reservation were frequent. Jenna enjoyed visiting their extended family but Blackhawk had surprised her by arriving after the blizzard. The backroads were treacherous at this time of the year but her friend had organized an interesting afternoon for Tauri, which would give Raya a break. She sighed and hurried back to the conference room.

"Sean Jones, the gardener who works for the local council, is on vacation at the moment." Beth glanced up from her laptop. "I checked out his name against different traveling companies, airports, and bus stations and it looks like he spends his vacation time at home. With no commitments, this would give him ample time to commit the murders." She scrolled down her page. "Interesting. He lives at number seven on Fern, which is adjacent to Pine. All these roads are cleared by the snowplow regularly as they all run onto Stanton."

Jenna sat at the long desk. "Great, so we can see him this afternoon."

"I've found Ethan Rourke." Kalo popped his head up from behind his laptop screen. "It's difficult to locate him as he's a subcontractor, so I gave him a call to ask him about installing a security system. He said he was flat out at the moment installing a new computer system for the Cattleman's Hotel. He asked me to ring back in two weeks or he could give me a number of people to call. He seemed an okay guy, very helpful."

Making quick notes, Jenna nodded. "Two down."

"I found Dr. Lionel Graves." Jo stared at her tablet. "He lives on Maple, number seventy-six. I would assume he is at home as I can't find any type of employment, only disability."

Surprised everyone had made such progress, Jenna took a note of the details. "I'm a little concerned about Graves. From the reports, he sounds a little strange. I don't figure we should go there without backup. Maybe we should leave this one to Rio and Rowley this afternoon?"

"I have another one." Beth peered at her around the side of her screen. "Caleb Dorsey, the school janitor. His vacation doesn't begin until just before Christmas, so at this time of day he should still be at the school. I cross-checked the list of people at the school for around the time that Ellie McBride was murdered and he would have been there. As he has access to all areas of the school, he would have had ample opportunity to write on the whiteboard, plant the purse, and be there when Ellie came to collect it." She waved a hand toward the whiteboard. "The only problem I can see is that none of these men own a silver- or blue-colored SUV of the type or description that we've been given. I checked four members of their families as well and came up with a big fat zero." She met Jenna's gaze. "We could be wrong about all of them. The vehicle is a crucial part of the evidence surrounding Ellie McBride's kidnapping."

"All these people meet the criteria." Kalo raised his eyebrows and gestured with his hands. "People, especially criminals, obtain vehicles from anywhere so, if you're trying to hinge the case on using this one vehicle, you're making a mistake. The CCTV footage of the suspected vehicle isn't very clear. We assume it is an SUV, but it could be a number of brands and we have no idea what age, so we're flying blind. I figure if you forget that vehicle for the moment and listen to the algorithms, these four suspects are your best choice."

"I agree." Beth glanced at the office door as voices came from the hallway. "Good, it looks like the others have finished." She looked at Jenna. "How do you want to split the team between these four suspects for interviews this afternoon?"

"Unfortunately, I'll need to stay behind with Carter." Styles strolled into the room. "We'll be liaising with the DEA and the forensic teams that have come to assist with the takedown."

The air seemed to crackle with anticipation as the deputies and agents filed back into the room. They were looking forward to some action and the takedown of a fentanyl distributor had moved to the front of their minds right now, but she needed them out interviewing suspects without delay. "First up, I want everyone out there interviewing suspects to wear coms and Kevlar vests. We don't know which one of them is our killer—if any. Call for backup the moment anything looks wrong. We are all close by." She glanced down at her list of assignments. "Okay, Raven, I want you to go with Jo to hunt down and interview Sean Jones, the gardener who works for the local council. He should be at home at this time of the day and Jo will have his address."

"Copy." Raven grabbed his thick coat from the peg by the door and pulled it on. He motioned to his dog. "Ben, with me."

"Let me change my shoes." Jo hurried to push her feet into thick winter boots before dragging on her coat, hat, and gloves. "I'm ready."

Jenna looked at Rowley. "I want you to man the office and organize any calls that come in on the hotline." She smiled. "I'll also need you to grab the supplies for the team going out tonight. You know what everyone needs. Maybe check the rifles and make sure there's ammunition available for everyone."

He nodded and took his things from the desk before heading downstairs. She turned to Rio. "Rio, I want you and Beth to handle Ethan Rourke, the IT specialist. If he is a person of interest and using technology to bypass some of the security systems, Beth will know."

"That leaves us, and two suspects to interview." Kane rested one hip on the edge of the desk. "Give me a rundown on the men that we're going to speak to."

Jenna glanced down at her tablet. "Caleb Dorsey is the school janitor. He was on the premises during the time that Ellie McBride died, and at the same time as the messages appeared. His winter vacation hasn't begun yet, so he should be at the school. As we discussed this morning, he's recently divorced, known to be in the building after hours, and has a minor criminal record for trespassing. He also has a history of mental illness, but I'm assuming that he's on top of that or he wouldn't have been able to get the job in the school." She sighed. "The other one is Dr. Lionel Graves. He is an oddball and they can't find anything specific about him to tie him in with the murders. He was once the local psychologist and has been a school counselor, so he knows his way around the schools and likely the Department of Social Services."

"Why did you specifically select these two suspects for us to interview?" Kane stood slowly and went to fill two to-go cups with coffee.

Jenna grabbed her coat. "They are both in close proximity to each other, and from the reports, a little unhinged. I figured we could handle them."

"I like it best when you delegate and we get to stay in the office in the warm." Kane peered out of the window.

Jenna went to stand beside him and watch the snowflakes falling slowly. A brilliant white vista spread out in front of them. The pine forest climbed in an uneven moonscape of snow leading up to black mountains with whitecaps that spread almost all the way down to meet the forest. A single snowplow chugged by, a stream of vehicles following behind. She glanced at him. "We're in luck, the snowplow has just gone through and we should be able to get to our destinations without delay."

"Do you want to go out in the snow, Duke?" Kane peered into the basket and Duke opened one eye and then buried his head. "I figure the answer is no. He probably had his fill of the cold when he went out with Maggie. He knows to go down to the counter if he wants to go outside for a while."

Jenna chuckled. "I wish I had the option of snuggling under a blanket for the rest of the day. It seems to me that Duke has the best of both worlds."

TWENTY-NINE

As they drove along Stanton, Raven listened intently to Jo as she discussed the case. Happy for the opportunity to be beside one of the most talented behavioral analysts in the United States, he listened intently to every word she said. "I understand this suspect fits the profile almost too perfectly. What is your plan for the interview?"

"You should take the lead asking him his whereabouts at the time of the murders, and the note on the whiteboard." Jo flicked him a glance. "The main reason that I want you to take the lead in the interview is because if this is the type of serial killer I'm expecting, he won't like being questioned by a woman." She smiled at him. "I'll add my two cents' worth if necessary."

As they headed along Pine, Raven listened to the GPS to find the location of Fern. The snow had gotten heavier and built up on the wiper blades as he negotiated the tall piles of snow along each side of the road. "Every house looks exactly the same, more like igloos than cabins. There it is—the one on the left with the vehicle parked out front."

"It doesn't appear as if he's left the house today." Jo peered out of the window as they got closer to the house. "He has six inches of snow on his hood."

Raven pulled into the driveway and the snowplow attachment at the front of his vehicle cut a path in the snow. He glanced over the back seat to his dog. "Stay here, Ben."

The dog wagged his tail and it thumped on the seat, his mouth hung open in a doggy smile. Ben never worried about going out in the cold. His thick coat protected him, and often during winter he became the lead dog in Raven's sled. Making sure his deputy's badge sat on full display on his jacket, Raven pushed open the door and stepped out into the freezing cold. Snowflakes brushed his cheeks, and he pulled down his Stetson to prevent them from sticking to the front of his sunglasses. He looked over at Jo. She had dragged her FBI windbreaker over the top of her jacket. For anyone looking from inside the house there could be no doubt that they were both law enforcement officers. Even so, he approached the front door with caution. Along the pathway, Jo slipped and windmilled her arms. He stepped closer and grabbed her, setting her gently on her feet. He stepped back, waiting for a reaction, aware that some women were very specific about their boundaries and helping might have overstepped. He indicated to the snow-packed pathway. "Walk in the snow, the bare patches are usually iced-over footprints."

"Thanks. I appreciate your assistance." Jo scanned his face and smiled. "My dad had old-school values but I married an idiot and moved to DC. My husband would say how he valued my independence. He'd allow me to fall flat on my face and make it a lesson to be more self-reliant." She shrugged. "Self-reliant, in his mind, was leaving me to manage with a new baby while he cheated on me."

Frowning, Raven shook his head in disbelief. Jo had proved herself to the world in her expertise and countless bestselling books. "What an ass."

"Oh, it gets better." Jo smiled. "Divorcing me and moving me to Snakeskin Gully was his girlfriend's idea of punishing me for whatever reason, but it backfired on her. Working beside Ty Carter showed me what a real man is like. Yeah, he can run his mouth occasionally, but he holds the same values as you do, same with Kane, Styles, and Wolfe. It's nice to feel safe. A woman needs to feel safe."

Taken aback by her honesty, he glanced at the house and then back at her. "I wasn't aware you and Carter were an item."

"Me and Carter?" Jo grinned widely. "Oh, heavens no. I've had one woman chaser in my life, and I learn real fast. He's a great guy but I'd really like to find someone outside of law enforcement."

Raven nodded and stared back at the house. The long pathway ended in a small log cabin. Like all the others, it resembled a frosted gingerbread house, but this one didn't have any Christmas decorations or lights evident. He scanned the windows searching for a twitch of the curtain or any signs of life. No dog barked. "It looks deserted. Just be careful."

"That's my middle name." Jo unzipped her jacket to access her weapon and nodded to him as they stepped onto the porch.

They both slid to either side before Raven knocked hard. "Sheriff's department."

Boom.

The front door exploded, sending chunks of wood splinters and glass into the air. The debris scattered over the pristine white snow. Raven threw himself off the porch and onto the ground. He glanced over at Jo crawling carefully around the outside of the house. Rolling onto his stomach, he pulled his weapon and aimed it at the front door. He looked over at Jo. Glass fragments covered her woolen cap and she had a small cut under one eye that bled down over her cheek like a red teardrop. Her gun pointed at the front door and her hands were steady. He gave her a nod and tapped his com. "This is Raven. Shots fired at number seven Fern."

"This is Rio. We're on our way."

"This is Beth Katz. Give us details. Is anyone injured?"

Raven kept his attention fixed on the front door. "Shotgun blast through the front door. Jo has glass in her face but looks okay. No sign of the shooter."

Listening intently for footsteps, Raven belly-crawled closer to the front door. "Sheriff's department and the FBI. We just want to ask you a few questions. There is no need to draw down on us. We are no threat to you."

"You need to obey the sign, boy." A man's gruff voice echoed along the hallway. "We have laws in this state about people invading our property without permission. I have every right to protect my property. It don't matter if you're cops or FBI. I know the law."

"Sometimes a little bit of knowledge is a bad thing." Jo's voice came out clear and strong. "At no time could you have perceived that we were a threat to you. It's clear that we're law enforcement officers, and we announced ourselves. We didn't have weapons drawn or pose any threat to you. Using excessive force in this case would put you in the wrong. Adding the fact that you have injured a federal officer could mean that you could face criminal charges. No judge would believe that blasting a hole in your front door after we knocked wasn't excessive force. I would suggest that you put your weapon down and come to speak to us in a reasonable manner." She sighed. "We know you were at the school over the time that Ellie McBride was murdered. We want to know if you saw anyone hanging around or noticed any footprints in the snow while you were working. We're looking for witnesses, is all."

Sirens and flashing lights announced the arrival of Rio and Beth Katz. Raven moved slowly to the side of the house as Rio and Beth jumped from the vehicle and spread out coming in from both sides through the trees. "Mr. Jones, put down your weapon and come to the front door and speak to us."

Footsteps echoed along the hallway, and a burly man wearing a cowboy hat kicked open the door and surveyed the damage. He tipped back his hat and scratched his head, slightly bemused at what he'd done. Raven peered at him from around the edge of the house as Rio came up behind him. "Put your hands where I can see them and step out onto the porch."

"I don't have my shotgun." Jones turned to look at him as Beth bounded round the side of the house, grabbed him by the hands, and cuffed him. "What are you doing that for? I did what you asked me to do."

"I'm just making sure you haven't got a weapon tucked into your pants." Beth patted him down and peered around him to look at Raven. He's clean. You're a doctor, aren't you? Maybe you should take care of your partner?"

"It's a scratch, I'm fine. Raven can pull out the splinter of glass when we get back to the office." Jo raised a brow and glared at Beth. "I'd rather get the interview over and get out of the cold."

"Well, I figure this guy needs a few days in the sheriff's jail to think over why he tried to kill law enforcement officers." Beth stood her ground. "Castle law isn't an excuse in this case."

"I was protecting my property, is all." Jones gave Raven a pleading stare. "Get her off me. I'll tell you everything you need to know."

Raven noticed the flash of amusement in Beth's eyes as she peered at him over Jones' shoulder. He holstered his weapon and noticed that Jo had done the same. "Okay." He indicated toward Jo. "It will be up to Agent Wells if she intends to press charges against you." He read him his rights. "I will also add here that it is an offense to lie to a federal officer."

"I understand." Jones looked from one to the other. "I'll

cooperate. Can you remove the cuffs and step inside? It's freezing out here."

Rio, being Raven's superior, turned to look at him. He figured he had the situation under control but Rio was a stickler for the rules. "I want to make sure you have no further surprises for us first and then we'll interview you inside."

"We'll clear the house." Rio looked at Jones. "It will be in your best interest to tell me if anyone is waiting inside."

"Nope." Jones stared at his feet. "I'm all on my lonesome since my wife left me. She took my dog too."

As Rio and Beth disappeared down the hallway, Raven took in Jones' unkempt appearance. "Do you have anything you can use to replace the door?"

"I'll cover it with something and go to the reclamation yard." Jones kicked away a fragment of wood from the porch. "There'll be something I can use down there. Doors are pretty standard and I'm good at fixing things."

Moments later, Rio and Beth came out. Rio shook his head but it was evident that he had something to say. As Beth removed Jones' cuffs, Rio tilted his head toward Raven.

"Can I have a word?" Rio stepped off the porch and walked into the snow. "The inside of that place should be condemned. I understand the guy has divorced his wife but he's living in squalor. Maybe it would be healthier for you to interview him out here. You have everything under control. We'll get back to it."

Nodding, Raven waited for them to return to their truck. He went to the porch, taking out his notebook. "We'll talk out here." He thought through his questions. "We're looking for information on the recent deaths of Ellie McBride and Laney Prescott. Do you know either of the victims personally?"

"I know the victims by sight. Ms. McBride is one of the teachers at the school and Ms. Prescott is a social worker. I would have seen them frequently during my work. I might have interacted with them on occasion and would have been introduced to them when I started working in their buildings. It was the normal thing to do, so they would recognize me as a member of the staff rather than someone who just wandered in."

Raven made a few notes but noticed Jo stood close by holding out her phone and recording the interview. "Have you ever worked near their homes or the places they frequented?"

"I've no idea where they live." Jones scratched his stubble and shook his head. "Same goes with the places they frequented. I guess if they ever went to Aunt Betty's Café or any of the stores in town I would have gone there as well. I don't really know."

"Where were you on Friday night?" Jo hadn't brushed the glass from her hat and her mirror sunglasses reflected Jones' image, making him appear grotesque. "Say around the hours eleven to one?"

"Here in bed." Jones sighed. "It's too cold to sit up late and I'm running out of wood for the fire." He indicated to the smashed door. "At least I'll be able to use the door for fuel."

"What about Monday and Tuesday, early in the morning? Where exactly were you? Did you go to work?" Jo kept her attention on Jones.

"Yeah, I went to work." Jones gave his head a little shake. "I went to the school early Monday. I worked there on Tuesday as well."

Raven nodded. The records at the school already indicated that Jones had been there over that time. "Did you happen to go into Ellie McBride's classroom?"

"Nope." Jones gave them a bleak look. "I shoveled snow from walkways most of the morning on both days. On Tuesday morning when I'd finished, I had a job at the council offices. I had some time to spare, so I went to Stanton Forest and collected some wood for my fire. I didn't have time to collect very much and I'll need to go back and get some more. At this time of the year most of the dead fallen trees have already been taken."

"Just a couple of other things I need to ask you." Jo looked at Raven from over her glasses and raised one eyebrow. "I'm familiar with your childhood. What was your relationship with your mother before she died?"

"Great." Jones frowned. "I still miss her."

"How did you feel about your father remarrying and then placing you in foster care?" Jo cleared her throat. "It would have been a very painful time for you."

"At five years old, yeah, I guess so." Jones kicked at the debris on the porch. Agitation rolled off him in waves. "Before that, my father used to beat me. He hated me. I told my teacher at school, but I ended up getting into trouble for that. When I spoke to a social worker, they did nothing to help me. It was a relief when they placed me in foster care. I hated my father and still do."

"Do you blame the social workers and teachers for ignoring you?" Jo remained perfectly still.

"I blame my father." Jones screwed up his face. "Look at you, trying to twist everything to make out I had an ax to grind with the woman that sent me to foster care." He stared at Raven. "Arrest me or let me go into town so I can fix my door." He looked at Jo. "I didn't mean to hurt you."

"You don't point a gun at someone unless you intend to kill them, Mr. Jones." Jo stared at him. "I'll need to write a report on the incident. Any charges are pending the amount of damage you caused to my face."

Seeing the color drain from Jones' face, Jo had made her point loud and clear. Arresting him could go two ways in Montana, often a small fine would be all he'd get for supposedly feeling threatened in his own home and the time and paperwork wouldn't be worth the trouble. Figuring he had enough information, Raven nodded. "Okay, Mr. Jones. That's all for today. Don't leave town without notifying us."

"Fine." Jones shook his head slowly. "Can I go now?"

Raven nodded. "Yeah, but pull that shotgun on us again and you're going to jail." He stood and watched Jones go back inside.

His feet had frozen during the interview and he tried to stamp some life back into them. He looked at Jo. "You have glass in your face. I'll need to treat you when we get back to the office." He pulled off her hat and shook out the glass. "There, that's better. Don't touch your face."

"I feel fine." Jo climbed inside the truck and pulled down the mirror to peer at her reflection. "Oh, that's not good. My cheeks are so cold I didn't feel a thing."

Raven rubbed Ben's ears and then started the engine. He looked at Jo. "It will be fine. I'll have you fixed up in no time. What do you think about Jones?"

"Like I said before, he fits the profile." Jo fastened her seatbelt. "Add to that he gives in to streaks of violence. He knew darn well we were on the porch and yet he discharged his weapon with no thought or remorse for coming close to killing us. He has no witnesses to say he wasn't near Laney Prescott's house. He admitted being close by in the forest. He's on the list."

THIRTY

Listening intently to her deputies' reports, Jenna sucked in a relieved breath when Rio announced that everything was fine. They'd reached the school by the time Raven came over the com to give her a brief rundown on what happened. "Okay, Raven, thanks for letting me know. We'll definitely keep Jones on our suspects list. We've just arrived at the school and we're heading inside to speak to the janitor. Get on back to the office and patch up Jo and then write up your report." She tapped her com to close it and collected her things. She looked at Kane. "Maybe Jones is our man. The problem is not finding any prints at the crime scenes. We can't haul him into the office and lock him up without evidence."

"There have been many people convicted on circumstantial evidence. There are four possibles. All we can do is collect the evidence for the DA and let him decide." Kane pushed his Stetson down lower on his head and slid out from behind the wheel. "Watch your step, Jenna. It's very slippery. It seems that now the students are on vacation, the upkeep to the pathways is falling a little behind." He held out his hand for her. "Take my hand."

Jenna slid a few inches away from the Beast, and Kane gathered her up closer to his body. He just spread his feet and became stable. She clung to him. "Thanks."

As the icy wind buffeted them all the way to the front door, Jenna looked at him. "I hope this guy is close by. The school is massive, finding him if he doesn't want to be found will be difficult."

"Maybe not." Kane pushed open the front door and they stepped inside into blissful warm air. "They need to use their cards as they move around. We should be able to track him via the office."

Jenna's phone chimed. It was Maggie. "I'm just at the school now."

"A call came in on the hotline. I have all the details here. The main thing is that a college student driving his younger brother to school noticed the janitor hanging around the teacher's SUV over the week before she claimed to be abducted. He mentioned seeing him twice and figured it was unusual. The student knew Ellie McBride's vehicle as he'd helped her carry some things to her vehicle previously."

Nodding, Jenna met Kane's inquisitive stare. "Thanks, Maggie, that's very interesting." She disconnected. "I wonder what he was up to."

"Well, we know he's often in the building after hours." Kane shrugged. "He has a criminal record for trespassing and a history of mental health issues. I would imagine his mental health issues are resolved or the school would never have employed him."

Leading the way to the front counter, Jenna smiled at Ms. Bell. "We're here to interview Caleb Dorsey, the janitor. Can you point us in the direction where we might find him?"

"Yes, of course. Just let me get you a set of visitor cards." Ms. Bell opened a drawer and pulled out two lanyards with cards attached and pushed them under the glass partition at the front of the counter.

"Do you keep a record of who you give the visitor lanyards to?" Kane leaned on the counter peering at her through the glass.

"Not usually, because they're often contractors organized by the principal or expected visitors." Ms. Bell frowned. "We don't just give them out to anyone. I work from a list of approved people, but I don't keep a record of the dates and times they were here."

"It would be in the school's best interest if you did." Kane drummed his fingers on the counter. "Heaven forbid anything like this happens again, but if it did, the more people we can look at the better."

"That won't be a problem. I'll start a book today." Ms. Bell typed on her keyboard. "Mr. Dorsey has been moving around today. He mentioned something about checking for leaks in the classrooms. He used his card to enter section three about fifteen minutes ago. It's where his office is located, so he could have gone back there to take a break." She printed up a floor plan of the school and using a highlighter marked the areas where Dorsey had been working. She handed the map to Jenna. "Your cards are all access. You won't have a problem getting through doors."

Staring down at the map, Jenna nodded. "Thanks, that's good to know."

"Are you aware that Dorsey had a few mental issues prior to working here?" Kane gave her a long look. "I'm wondering how he obtained a job working close to children."

"I am aware that Caleb suffered PTSD after a traumatic incident in his childhood, but as far as I'm aware, that has been resolved over the years. He did discuss it with me but I'm not at liberty to divulge a private conversation to you. I hope you understand."

"I do indeed." Kane's lips curled slightly at the corners. "We'll get at it."

As they let themselves through the door into the main building, Kane's boots clattered on the tile. Jenna peered into the darkened classrooms. Without the chatter of students bustling through the hallways, an eerie quiet descended on the school as if all the life had been sucked out of it. She glanced up at Kane as they walked. "You used a very subtle way to extract information from her."

"I gathered if she'd been working here the same time as him, they would become comfortable with each other. My only reservation about Dorsey is, if his psychopathic tendencies have been lying dormant, what triggered him to kill? As far as we're aware, Dorsey hasn't been involved in any other murders—although he could have been running riot in any other county and we just don't know about it. We know darn well that often psychopaths keep their kills away from their homes."

Using the cards to obtain access, they easily found the way to the correct section. The heating had been turned off in most of the vacant parts of the school, and Jenna's breath came out in puffs of steam as they walked. She spotted an open door. "That's the janitor's room over there."

The door with JANITOR written on a metal plaque stood open. Inside, the shelves were packed with an assortment of items, including tools and cleaning products. A desk in the middle held a computer and behind the desk were shelves with small labeled boxes. A sink and a small kitchen area ran along one side. A coffee pot bubbled and hissed beside a crumpled brown paper bag that Jenna assumed held the remains of Dorsey's lunch. She approached the desk and two things immediately caught her attention. The first being copies of school photographs. She lifted the pile out and noted that they went back a long time. Beside her, Kane examined a box that contained old report cards and held them out for her. She frowned. "Images of kids and report cards from way back. Who keeps this type of thing?" She pulled out her phone and, spreading the images and report cards across the desk, took photographs.

"We have Dorsey in the building around the time Ellie discovered the message, and also when Ellie McBride was murdered." Kane scrolled through his phone. "According to the records, he didn't start work until ten on the day that Laney Prescott died."

Jenna opened her mouth to reply but the sound of footsteps in the hallway made her glance at Kane and raise both eyebrows. The next moment, Caleb Dorsey stopped in the doorway his eyes round with shock. "Ah, there you are, Mr. Dorsey. We were waiting for you. We'd like to ask you a few questions."

"I assume this is about Ms. McBride's murder?" He let out a long sigh and dropped into his office chair, making it moan. "Terrible thing, terrible thing. Have you found the person who hurt her?"

"Not yet but we're getting close." Kane pulled up a chair for Jenna and then one for himself before sitting in front of the desk. He set his phone on record and pushed it into the middle of the table. "We'll be recording this conversation so we don't have to come back and ask you the same questions again."

"Am I in trouble?" Dorsey moved around restlessly in his seat. "Do I need a lawyer present?"

Finding his defensive attitude a little unusual, Jenna stared at the man. "That needs to be determined and the reason why we're here to question you. My deputy will read you your rights. You are under no obligation to answer our questions, but if you refuse, we will take you to my office and hold you until your lawyer arrives."

"I didn't do anything wrong." Dorsey's eyes moved shiftily. "Okay, fine, ask me the questions."

Jenna waited for Kane to read him his rights and looked at Dorsey. "You've been working here for some time, I believe?"

"Yeah, about ten years." Dorsey blew out a long sigh and his shoulders relaxed.

"You'll be aware that we have a list of your movements during the time that Ellie McBride discovered a disturbing message on her whiteboard, and at the time she was murdered?" Kane leaned forward in his chair. "Why were you in her classroom before school started on both days?"

"I checked to see if there are any leaks. Often when we have heavy snowfall, the doors to the playground leak water over the floor and it's dangerous if anyone slips in it." Dorsey shrugged. "I know the classrooms prone to leakage and always check them before the teachers arrive."

Indicating toward boxes on his desk, Jenna lifted both eyebrows as she peered at him. "Why do you keep photographs of past students and old report cards?"

"Memories." Dorsey indicated to the boxes. "I'm not trying to hide anything, am I? They're out for everyone to see. I knew a lot of these kids from the time that I came here, is all. I often wonder what they're doing now and if they succeeded in life."

"You were seen hanging around Ellie McBride's vehicle on more than one occasion." Kane's eyes bored into him. "What reason did you have to be in the teachers' parking lot? You park your truck round back, don't you?"

"I don't recall being in the teachers' parking lot. You're mistaken." Agitated, Dorsey gripped his hands together tightly on the table in front of him. His eyes flashed with unmistakable anger. "Someone is telling lies about me. Who said that?"

Ignoring his outburst, Jenna leaned back in her chair. The hairs on the back of her neck prickled in warning. The man's sudden change of demeanor concerned her. He went from placid to aggressive in a split second and she'd seen the change in his eyes before in mentally disturbed people. "Can you confirm your whereabouts between the hours of eleven and one on Friday evening?"

"I was at home." Dorsey shook his head slowly. "Before you ask, no, I had no one there to verify that."

"What about Monday and Tuesday mornings?" Kane cleared his throat. "I can see on both these days you didn't arrive until eight. Yet some days you arrive at the school at seven. Is there any reason for the varied start times?"

"I don't recall what time I got to work on Monday and Tuesday mornings." Dorsey picked at his short dirty fingernails. "My shift is variable as I'm often needed to fix things early in the morning and sometimes needed to come back here late in the evening, after everyone has gone home. Sometimes clubs use the classrooms and they need to be cleaned, which means I need to be here at nine at night sometimes. It is part of the job. I don't mind because I have no one waiting for me at home and I'd rather keep busy."

The shift in the man's demeanor had changed again in seconds. Seeing this and knowing that this unstable man worked at a school sent shivers down Jenna's spine. "Do you know a woman by the name of Laney Prescott?"

"I don't know her personally, but I do know she has visited the school from time to time because I needed to have a room ready for her to interview students at one time." Dorsey opened his hands wide. "I also know she was murdered because it's been all over the news. Are you going to blame me for her murder as well? I figure next time we speak I want a lawyer present."

Unable to continue with the questioning, Jenna stood. "Very well, that's all for now, Mr. Dorsey. Thank you for your time."

Jenna waited until they'd moved through two doors and headed along the hallway back to the office, before she turned to

Kane. "That guy scares the hell out of me. I want to know why he's working close to children. If he is not involved in these murders, he needs to be investigated. It seems that right now we have two viable suspects on our list."

THIRTY-ONE

As Jenna picked her way through the snow and back to the Beast, exhaustion dragged at her. Cold crept through every crevice in her clothes and her numb fingers ached. She didn't ask Kane but could see by his frown that his head throbbed due to the steel plate. The cold played havoc with him and they'd been out for a long time. The day dragged on and on, and as she fully intended to go with Kane to the drug distribution takedown, it would be very late before they made it home. She checked her watch. "We can swing by and see if we can catch Dr. Lionel Graves. He is not a priority and we need to make sure we have time for everyone to get a decent meal and warm up before we head out to the BW Ranch."

"We?" Kane started the engine and turned to look at her. "I figured you'd be staying at the office and going over the files from the interviews. You didn't say you wanted to be there. Are you sure you want to go out for hours in the freezing cold, waiting for a delivery truck to arrive—or not?"

Jenna entered Graves' address into the GPS and then sat back in her seat and shook her head. "I know you'd like to run these types of things like a military mission and I'm happy for you to take the lead. This is what you do best and I'm sure you, Carter, and Styles have everything planned right down to the last second, but I'm the sheriff and this is my county, which makes me responsible for any missions going down. Why don't you bring me up to date with the plans you have? I'm happy to slip in anywhere you might need me."

"We have everything covered." Kane raised both eyebrows and then stared at her for a long moment. "We're parking Wolfe's van along the fire road in the forest opposite the ranch. I'll have Kalo positioned there. He will be flying a drone overhead to monitor the arrival of the delivery truck and to give us a heads-up of any potential problems ahead of time. Wolfe is fitting out the van with monitors so he can keep an eye on our bodycam footage during the raid. I would really appreciate your help as backup for Kalo as we'll be all out in the field, and honestly, I have no idea what to expect after someone shot at Raven when he collected data from the trail cams."

Clearly Kane had not wanted to include her in the raid. Deep down inside she understood his reasoning. He cared deeply for her and wouldn't put her in danger, but she had a dangerous job and being sheriff carried a responsibility she refused to ignore. "We're not sure if one of Withers' men shot at Raven." She sighed. "Two stray bullets are common at this time of the year, and he was wearing camouflage. I don't believe anyone from the ranch spotted him up a tree in the forest, but I also don't want to leave Kalo at risk. I would never forgive myself if anything happened to that young man."

"That's settled then." Kane's relieved expression spoke volumes. He checked his watch. "I figure we have half an hour to speak to Graves and get back to the office. I would say everyone is freezing by now and we'll all need time to recharge before we head out." He turned the Beast around and headed back to town.

Before Jenna could reply, Rio's voice came through her earpiece. "Copy. What's the problem?"

"We've been chasing all over town after Ethan Rourke. We just missed him at the Cattleman's Hotel, then at a computer supply place in town. I figure he's collecting items he needs for his job. The manager at the Cattleman's Hotel informed me that he's usually there before eight each morning and works late, so we could catch up with him then. As time is getting short, do you want us to keep on searching for him now or head back to the office?"

Three interviews were better than none and Rourke could wait for the morning. "I figure you should call it a day and meet at Aunt Betty's Café. If you could contact the others for me, we'll be along as soon as we've interviewed Graves. Can you ask Carter to take Duke with him?"

"Yeah, not a problem."

Ten minutes later they bumped along a dirt road that led to Dr. Graves' rundown house. Weeds had long ago taken over the garden alongside the house, leaving dead sticks protruding through the snow. Jenna surveyed the front of the house, surprised to see dead vegetation sticking out of the gutters. From what she could see of the house, the paint on the front door had peeled, leaving the bare wood to the elements. An old porch swing hung by one chain and the rest of it trailed on the floor. Animals had gotten into the cushion and torn it up. She eyed the floor of the front porch with concern. People that left their property in disrepair created a death trap for anyone visiting. She touched Kane's arm. "That doesn't look very safe. The floorboards could be rotten."

"You stand to one side and I'll go and knock on the door." He grimaced. "We don't want another incident like what happened to Raven and Jo."

Jenna noticed a twitch of a curtain at the front window. "They know we're here and I'm sure they can read the words

SHERIFF'S DEPARTMENT all across the front of our windbreakers."

The sound of footsteps running came clearly from inside the house, echoing as if the place were empty. She glanced at Kane as he crept up the front steps. "Be careful, someone is running toward us."

"I don't think so." Kane jumped down from the front porch and took off around the side of the house.

Tearing after him, Jenna lifted her knees to get through the thick snow alongside the house. Pain hit her lungs as she rushed forward, sucking in the freezing air. She struggled through deep snowdrifts as Kane sprinted toward the forest. As they reached the perimeter, Kane stopped and looked back at her, enclosed in a cloud of steam. "We're assuming that's Dr. Graves. What if it isn't? He might be back there in need of medical assistance. The idiot that ran away will be easy enough to follow if there is a problem, as he's left his footprints in the snow. I figure we should go back." He gave her a long look. "If it's Graves and he has something to hide, he's on foot and won't get far. When we leave, he'll come back. I'll stick a tracker on his truck, and if needs be, we can pick him up later."

Nodding, Jenna walked beside him treading in her own footprints. As they reached the back of the house, the door stood wide open and in the short while they had been away snow had formed a wet puddle inside the door. They pulled their weapons and Kane went high and she went low as they moved slowly inside the house. Heart pounding, she edged forward. "Sheriff's department. Dr. Graves, are you in there? Call out."

Keeping her back to the wall, Jenna moved slowly along the hallway checking each room as they went. The house seemed more like a cabin with two bedrooms, a family room, and kitchen all on one floor. As they reached what Jenna imagined to be the third bedroom, Kane held up his hand. Gripping the handle of her weapon, she waited in the hallway, as keeping low, he in moved inside. Moments later, his head came around the door and he beckoned her toward him. "Did you find him?"

"Nope." A nerve in Kane's cheek twitched and anger flashed in his eyes. "I figure Dr. Graves has a ton of things to answer to." He indicated to a computer screen alive on the desk. "Child porn."

Sickened by the site, but knowing they couldn't touch anything or the evidence would be inadmissible in court, she pulled out her phone and called the judge. Luckily, he'd finished court for the day and his secretary put her through to his office. "We came to interview Dr. Lionel Graves regarding the deaths of Ellie McBride and Laney Prescott. When we arrived, we heard someone inside the house. I called out but they ran out the back door. We gave chase but lost them in the forest. Concerned for Graves' wellbeing, we went back to the house to find the back door open and entered to do a welfare check. We didn't find him inside the house and when we went into his office, the computer displayed child porn. I need to arrest this guy and can't leave this evidence. I would like to request an immediate search warrant for the premises."

"Send me an image of what you've discovered. I'll only need the one. If it's as you say, I'll issue a search warrant immediately and text it to you. You can send one of your deputies to collect the original from my office."

"I'll do it." Kane took the photograph and sent it directly to the judge. He pulled a thumb drive from his pocket and pushed it into the computer to download the files. He shrugged. "Don't worry, we'll get the warrant."

Moments later Jenna's phone chimed. She followed the link and downloaded the file to her phone. "Should we take the computer?"

"In normal circumstances I would say yes, but Graves is out in the forest playing catch me if you can." Kane scratched his cheek. "I'm wondering if it would be better to leave everything as is. If he doesn't know we've been inside the house, it's likely he'll come back and carry on as usual. I'll look at what's on his computer. By the time I've finished, I'll have downloaded a copy of his entire hard drive. We take that to the DA, and the next time we come by it will be with an arrest warrant and backup."

Liking his style, Jenna smiled. "That sounds like a good plan. Make sure you check his emails. Get copies of his address book and any suspicious emails. While you're busy, I'll search the rest of the house. Make sure everything is back in its place when you're done."

"Not a problem." Kane wiggled his gloved fingers. "He'll never know I've been here."

Nodding, Jenna pulled on examination gloves and slowly went through the office drawers. She discovered files mostly on children the doctor had as clients. As she flicked through the files, she noticed some of names had small red hearts beside them. A sick feeling curled in her stomach. This man had been in a position of trust. If these files lined up with some of the sickening photographs, it would mean he'd been abusing his patients. Leaving Kane, she went along the hallway and found the doctor's bedroom. She meticulously searched through the drawers and went to the closet, pulling a shoebox from one of the shelves. She stepped back in disgust at finding the trophies that the sick freak had collected over the years. She took photographs and tipped half of the box into an evidence bag and then sealed and labeled it. As Kane had a complete copy of the hard drive, physical evidence like this might be important and she didn't plan on leaving it all behind. Evidence collecting would come later, but for now this would do especially if they could link the items or DNA to any of the photographs on the computer. Leaving the room exactly as she'd found it, she headed back to the office.

"I'm done here. We'll drop the evidence into the DA's office and then head to Aunt Betty's. Time is getting away from us." Kane removed the thumb drive, pushed it into his pocket, and then indicated for them to leave. "We'll leave by the front door. It's snowing heavily now, and by the time he gets back, our footsteps out back will be covered. I couldn't see more than a dark shape running through the trees. He obviously knows his way through the forest, and for all we know, has a vehicle parked on a fire road somewhere. I doubt he even noticed we were following him."

Distaste for Graves crawled over Jenna like a rash. She couldn't wait to get outside the house. From the notes she'd read about Graves, for many years he'd maintained his office inside his house. The thought of him abusing kids right where she'd been standing made her sick to her stomach. She watched as Kane collected a tracker from the Beast and attached it to the underside of Graves' truck. "You know I don't care what anyone says, but I'm not leaving our kids alone with anyone. If they need counseling, I'm gonna be right there. After what we have seen over the years, I don't trust anyone anymore."

"Same." Kane swung inside the Beast. "Let's get this over with and go and get something to eat. I'm tired and cold. I figure this day has forty-eight hours in it. Worst of all, we have to deal with criminals instead of eating dinner with our children. I know they understand but I always feel like I'm letting them down when I'm not there."

Jenna squeezed his arm. "Me too. Don't worry, this will be over soon. We have at least three solid suspects. With a little more digging, we'll be able to narrow it down and maybe this case will be solved by Christmas. It will be good to spend some time at home with the boys."

"You can say that again." Kane turned onto the highway.

THIRTY-TWO

After leaving the evidence with the DA, Kane drove Jenna to Aunt Betty's Café. They found a parking spot some ways away, and battered by the freezing wind, hurried along the sidewalk. In the windows of the stores, Christmas lights flashed in bright colors and festive music filtered into the street. Most had Christmas trees just inside the door adorned with brightly colored gifts. Head throbbing from the cold, Kane embraced the warmth in Aunt Betty's Café. The team had pushed tables together in their usual spot and everyone sat around chatting. Duke bounded over to see him, his thick tail windmilling. He nodded to Carter. Duke would go anywhere with him and Zorro, but Duke stressed out a little if Kane went missing for some time. He rubbed the dog's ears and, after removing his coat, slid into a seat beside Beth Katz. He didn't know her very well. Jenna had spent some time with her during his time away on a mission and found her to be a very experienced agent. He sat enjoying the warmth as Jenna brought everyone up to date about Graves. Beside him, Beth cleared her throat trying to get his attention. He swiveled his gaze toward her. "So, you weren't able to locate Ethan Rourke?"

"We'll catch up with him tomorrow. If you all survive taking down Bryce Withers." She rolled her eyes toward the ceiling. "Styles has insisted I remain at the office and bring the files up to date. As he is technically my boss, I agreed. He wants me to do in-depth searches on the suspects. He doesn't want the case to run over Christmas if possible. Styles takes Christmas very seriously and is looking forward to being part of your family's celebrations."

Kane smiled at her and slowly removed his gloves. "We'll enjoy having everyone along. Unfortunately, apart from the boys, Jenna and I don't have any family—I mean siblings or parents. We do call Atohi Blackhawk and his relatives family, due to our son Tauri. So we've made our team an extended family. We celebrate all the holidays together, and you and Styles are more than welcome to join us."

"Thanks. We're very much loners as well." Beth barked a laugh. "Unless you include my father in the state penitentiary. I'm not sure if anyone has told you but it's no secret that I'm the daughter of a serial killer by the name of Cutthroat Jack." She sighed. "Before you ask, no, I never saw him kill anyone and I didn't know he had murdered my mother until a long time after. The cops questioned me at the time and I didn't know what they were talking about. To me, he was just my dad. I've never visited him in jail. To be perfectly honest I couldn't look at him after knowing what he's done."

The conversation paused a while as everyone gave their orders to Wendy. Kane turned back to her. "Is that why you joined the FBI?"

"My first love is IT." Beth leaned back in her seat looking at him. "I became proficient very early. I discovered the dark web around the age of fourteen. By the time I got to college, the FBI approached me to join their cybercrime division. I admit I found it tough going. They were always waiting for the psychopath to break free in me. I ended up in Snakeskin Gully with Styles because they believed I didn't show enough empathy toward a child kidnapped by a predator. It's a long story. I arrived and took care of the child but found a man bleeding out from a cut throat. I made sure I had the kid safe and tried to save the man's life. Later we discovered I'd tried to save the perpetrator and the Tarot Killer had murdered him minutes before I arrived on scene."

Astonished, Kane looked at her. "You could have been killed."

"I don't think so." Beth took a sip from a cup of coffee. "Seems to me, everything I've read about him tells me he murders serial killers. I don't believe he's a threat to law enforcement. I figure he's just cleaning up the mess we leave behind."

Her theory made sense. "You've brought down many pedophile rings. Untouchable people." Kane explained the situation they'd stumbled on previously.

"The thing with pedophiles, Dave, is they're like cockroaches—there's never just one." A shadow crossed Beth's eyes. "I'd like to look at his computer when you're done. It's likely that he's connected to others. They use the dark web and have many disguises. They're in every walk of life and aren't 'the dirty old man' everyone believes. As a sexually deviant type of psychopath, they have no empathy for the children they destroy. Over the last ten years or so, I've made it my life's work to hunt them down and bring them to justice."

"I'm sure the DA will be more than willing to hand over the computer." Jenna leaned forward in her chair to look at Beth. "I agree with you. I've seen things over the last decade or so that keep me awake at night. The more we put behind bars the better."

The conversation became lighter as they all enjoyed their meal. Susie, the manager of Aunt Betty's Café, also provided large plates of leftovers for each of the dogs. Kane watched with interest as Duke, Ben, and Bear woofed into their plates of food, demolishing them in seconds while the Doberman, Zorro, ate daintily. With three dogs watching him, it didn't take long before Bear tried to sneak a sausage from his plate. Zorro, sitting like a sphynx with the plate between his front legs, gave a low growl. His top lip quivered over a set of formidable canines. Kane chuckled and looked at Carter. "Is he always like that with his food?"

"We don't have many other dogs around." Carter moved Zorro and his food beside him. "With Duke, it's mutual respect." He smiled. "Then again, he usually gets kibble. I don't spoil him with sausages. I guess he figures it's a onetime deal and he's gonna savor every bite."

Back at the office, Kane made sure everyone had the equipment they needed while Jenna uploaded files to the server. He assumed that the pedophile had returned to his home without knowing that he had been discovered as the tracker app on his phone indicated that the vehicle remained outside his house. A DMV check confirmed that the vehicle was his only form of transport. Convinced they would be able to arrest him easily enough the moment the DA issued an arrest warrant, he put Graves to the back of his mind and concentrated on the mission. When Jenna appeared at the door of her office, they all moved out but left a few minutes apart to avoid appearing like a convoy. They kept the vehicles to a minimum and left all the dogs in the office with Beth. She appeared to be quite happy to work in the office alone, even though Jo had offered to remain behind.

Night had fallen by the time they headed to the fire road in Stanton Forest. Kane dropped Jenna, Jo, and Kalo at Wolfe's van. He emerged from the front seat wearing combat gear and carrying an automatic rifle. He slid into the front seat and nodded to Carter.

"Do you know how to use that thing?" Carter's eyes widened.

"Marine." Wolfe faced front, his face frozen.

"Is there anyone in Black Rock Falls who is not ex-military?" Carter raised both eyebrows.

Kane glanced at him in his rearview mirror. "Rowley and Rio, as far as I know. I figure the rest of us all came here for a quiet life. You know, a nice peaceful backwoods town set in the mountains. Who could want for anything better?"

"Uh-huh." Carter smiled around his toothpick. "Y'all came looking for paradise and found Serial Killer Central."

Nodding, Kane slid the Beast into a small clearing on the edge of the fire road. The black vehicle would be totally hidden once the snow had coated its exterior. The other vehicles would be concealed in different positions. He checked his watch and then contacted the members of the team through his com. "The delivery is due in approximately ten minutes. Kalo will have a drone up by now and will feed information to us about the truck's location. I'm moving into position now. Move out." He slid out of the Beast with Wolfe and Carter at his side. He slapped Carter on the back. "Go get 'em, cowboy."

As Carter slipped away, Wolfe snorted beside him. He looked at him. "What?"

"I'd like to shoot that toothpick out of his mouth." Wolfe grinned at him, his teeth white in the dark. "Then he'd know I can handle a rifle."

Kane smiled back. "Come on, I have a nice ice-covered boulder to watch the action. It gives me a clear line of sight to the barn where the deliveries are unloaded."

"You've played this mission very close to the vest." Wolfe moved beside him, their boots hardly making a sound in the snow. "I drove past getting here and noticed the security cameras. How are the men going to get into position without being seen?"

Keeping to the edge of the fire road to avoid detection, Kane scanned ahead for any movement, but all appeared to be quiet. They reached the large boulder and climbed up the slippery surface until they reached the top. As he set up his sniper rifle, he glanced at Wolfe, who lay down peering at the BW Ranch through field glasses. "They'll be coming in from behind, apart from Carter and Styles. They'll be using the outbuildings for cover. Kalo hacked into Withers' CCTV setup and has looped footage running through the system on all cameras. The moment Carter sees proof of fentanyl tablets in the delivery, they'll move in. We were lucky and have six DEA agents working alongside us. Rio and Rowley are with them, coming in from behind. Five minutes away, we have enough prison buses to carry all these men to County. If luck goes our way, I'm hoping it will be a clean bust."

"Not with all the firepower I see. It's gonna be a bloodbath." Wolfe didn't lift his eyes from his field glasses. "The snow isn't helping but the deep shadows around the buildings are shielding Carter and Styles because I can't see them and I know they're there."

"Showtime." Kalo's voice came through the com.

Kane dropped into position. His sniper rifle had all the gadgets necessary not to need a spotter. He peered down the scope and moved it from one of Withers' men to the other. One move in the wrong direction and he'd be able to take them down before they pulled the trigger. Wolfe had insisted on coming along to watch his back. That's what Wolfe did and there would be no arguing with him.

"The truck's turning in now." Wolfe moved his field glasses across the view. He tapped his com. "I can confirm the flatbed contains horse pellets. It's heading along the driveway now.

Withers' men are in position. I can see men in hazmat suits just inside the barn."

Kane slowed his heartbeat as adrenaline pumped through his veins. Remaining calm meant he never missed his target. Right now, one mistake could cost a member of the team their life. He took a few deep breaths and dropped into the zone. As Withers' men unloaded the horse pellets from the truck and exposed the rainbow-colored fentanyl pills, men in hazmat suits came forward carrying large plastic containers. The shouts of "federal agents" and "sheriff's department" came through the night as the team moved forward to make arrests.

Without warning, one of Withers' men fired into the air, spraying the driveway with bullets. They weren't going down without a fight. Kane held his breath as the team shrank back and took cover, but Withers' men raised their rifles. Shots rang out and Withers' men scattered, using the truck for cover. All would be easy targets for Kane.

"Kane, we're directly in the line of fire with no escape." Carter's voice came through Kane's com. *"Have you got eyes on the targets?"*

Kane had expected they wouldn't go easy, considering the value of the shipment. The decision had been taken out of his hands. He tapped his com. "Copy. Keep your heads down."

If he didn't act right away, his team would be slaughtered. Carter and Styles would be the first to die. He took aim. A few seconds later, five men lay dead and the remaining members of Withers' team had laid down their weapons. Before he could blink, agents and deputies moved in to disarm them. Scanning the area and keeping vigilant, he remained in position until every last one of Withers' men had been secured. As Carter and Styles cuffed Withers, Kane rose to his knees, scooped up handfuls of snow, and rubbed them into his face. He didn't enjoy killing and wanted to wash away the memory.

"You've saved hundreds of thousands of lives tonight—not

to mention your friends." Wolfe sat beside him, his face chiseled in the moonlight. "The mission is a success. Your team looks up to you and Jenna. You lead by example and never take a life unless it's absolutely necessary." He slapped Kane on the back. "Put this behind you and hold your head high like you always do or I'm going to start believing that being a father is making you soft." He shouldered his rifle and slid off the boulder.

Kane dismantled his rifle and stared into the peaceful forest. He pushed away doubts and jumped down beside him. He smiled. "Come on, old man, I'll race you back to the Beast."

THIRTY-THREE

Thursday

A cold crisp morning greeted Beth and Rio as they headed toward the Cattleman's Hotel to interview Ethan Rourke. Beth had spent the night with everyone at Jenna's ranch and Styles had talked nonstop about the mission the previous night. The takedown had uncovered a massive hoard of fentanyl within the BW Ranch. The success of the mission had made the FBI director very happy. The agents had filed their reports and been given two weeks' vacation. They would, of course, be remaining on Jenna's ranch for Christmas, and she couldn't believe she would actually enjoy the company. Something strange had happened to her since she arrived at Rattlesnake Creek. Working with Styles had made her human again. It had started with his dog. She really loved Bear and found that she trusted Styles with her life, which had been something she'd never experienced before. Being the Tarot Killer, and using her own brand of justice to rid the world of serial killers that had escaped the net, meant she'd been a loner all her life. She still wanted to rid the world of unstoppable serial killers, but day by day she'd changed. She had friends and people who trusted her. This had become a phenomenon that took a lot of getting used to.

Meeting Rio at Jenna's office and heading out with him seemed surreal. Having Styles around all the time, she'd gotten used to him, but Rio had been totally different. She found him professional but way too observant. To keep her cover, she'd need to be very careful around him. She turned her mind to the current homicide cases. They had two solid suspects, and in her opinion, either of them could have murdered both women. Rio had asked her to take the lead in the Ethan Rourke interview. As the suspect's specialty involved working with anything to do with IT, he figured she would be able to understand any technical jargon he might come up with. Beth formed some questions in her mind to ask him. He moved around everywhere. From what she'd read about his qualifications, he could easily hack into security systems and CCTV cameras. This knowledge, if used correctly, caused no harm to anyone and was vital for anyone in the security business. It also provided a perfect cover for a serial killer. It meant they could move around under a cloak of invisibility. She would need to be very specific with her questions before deciding if he qualified as a viable suspect or just a hardworking Joe.

Snowflakes spiraled down around Beth as she led the way into the Cattleman's Hotel. A wave of warm air hit her cheeks as she stepped through the doors and into the reception. Astonished by the opulence, she gazed at the huge picture of stampeding cattle above the check-in counter. It dominated the room. Large open fireplaces blazed with wooden logs and the snapping and crackling of pine cones. Earlier, she'd spoken to the manager and arranged to meet Ethan Rourke in the staff break room. She followed Rio into the room and checked out the man seated at the table with one hand wrapped around a cup of coffee. When Rourke stood and looked from one to the other apprehensively, Beth met his gaze. "I'm Agent Katz and

I'm sure you know Chief Deputy Rio. We're interviewing possible witnesses in the timeline of two homicide victims. Laney Prescott and Ellie McBride." She took two photos from a folder and laid them on the table. "Do you know these women?" She placed her phone beside them, waited for him to drop into a chair, and sat down opposite him.

"I met Ms. McBride when I installed the interactive screen in her classroom." Rourke tapped at Ellie's photograph. "The name Laney Prescott rings a bell. Do you mind if I check my phone?"

"Go right ahead." Rio remained standing, one shoulder leaning against the doorframe. One hand rested on his weapon.

"Ah, yes, she has a place on the outskirts of town. She called me for a quote about home security. I'd planned to drop by and see her tomorrow." Rourke shook his head slowly. "It seems I didn't get there in time."

Beth narrowed her gaze. "I didn't mention that someone murdered Ms. Prescott in her home?"

"I assume that being stuck out there all alone, something must have happened to her." Rourke lifted his gaze from the photograph of Laney. "She mentioned hearing noises outside her house and was afraid that someone was stalking her. She told me she worked as a social worker and needed to deal with all different types of people." His attention lifted to Beth's face and then back to his cup. "Maybe you should be looking at one of her clients."

This man appeared to be socially awkward and not what she expected. Very average, clean-shaven, and tidy and nothing about him made him stand out in a crowd. He was one of those forgettable people. A badge with his name and company had been attached to his shirt—maybe because people forgot his name. Beth allowed his background to filter through her mind. "You seem to prefer to work alone. Is that by choice or necessity?"

"I get enough work to keep myself employed. I can't see any reason for hiring someone to work with me. It's expensive hiring someone, which means I would have to increase my rates, and then I would lose the competitive edge I have against other contractors in this county." Rourke shook his head slowly. "I don't like having to rely on someone else to do work for me. What if they made a mistake? I would be liable. The only person I can trust is myself."

The reply appeared to be truthful but Beth hadn't finished with him yet. "Let's walk through your week. Where were you on Friday night between eleven and one?"

"I grabbed a pizza around ten-thirty." Rourke scratched his head and stared into space. "So, I figure I would be driving home around that time. I'm sure you already know that I live alone, so I don't have anyone to corroborate my story. Although I know the pizzeria has CCTV cameras, so I'm sure you could check the feed to prove where I was at that time."

"Why were you out that late on Friday night?" Rio remained pinned to the wall. "Girlfriend?"

"Nope." Rourke leaned back in his chair and stared at him. "I got a call from Antlers. They were having trouble setting their security system and I dropped by to check it out. I discovered a small glitch, fixed it, and grabbed a pizza on the way home."

Everything he had mentioned could be easily verified, if he had told the truth. "So, I gather you logged into the Antlers system to gain access? Did you install the system?"

"Yeah, I did." Rourke shrugged. "That's the same answer to both your questions."

Beth nodded. "Good, we can check the time stamps." She checked her notes. "Now where were you on Monday and Tuesday mornings?"

"Here." Rourke leaned back in his chair. "Ask the manager. I moved back and forth all the time getting parts for the job.

Working on a place this size takes a lot of time and things happen that you don't expect."

Again, his answers were easy to check. Beth tried a different angle. This intelligent man knew his way around various systems, but could he be a killer? "You're able to access to systems most people wouldn't even know existed. Have you ever been tempted to use that access for something more personal?"

"What do you mean by that?" Rourke looked taken aback. "As in spying on people, you mean? No, it's never entered my mind." He glanced at his watch. "Is this going to take much longer? I need to get back to work."

"What vehicle do you drive?" Rio pushed away from the wall.

"A new GMC truck." Rourke narrowed his gaze. "Why?"

Clearing her throat, Beth smiled at him. "The one good thing about having a new truck is that we can track your movements with your GPS. It will be your alibi if it tells us that you drove straight home."

"Why would I need an alibi?" A confused expression crossed Rourke's face. "I didn't kill anyone." He shook his head slowly. "No, ma'am."

Standing, Beth picked up her phone. She had recorded the entire conversation. "Thank you for your time and the information. If you think of anything else you believe we need to know, call Deputy Rio." She waited for Rio to hand over his card and then headed for the door.

As they walked back to Rio's truck, she ran the interview back through her mind. Being familiar with the behavior of psychopaths, she could easily be seeing one in his passive state. Some psychopaths were really nice people until something triggered them.

"What do you think about that guy?" Rio swung open his

door and peered at her. "Is he one of those quiet killers? I figure we need to check his alibis."

Beth climbed into the truck and fastened her seat belt. She turned to look at Rio. "Although he looks harmless enough, I wouldn't discount him just yet. He might be innocent. He didn't try to evade any of our questions and I watched his body language very closely and didn't pick up anything unusual. The thing that worries me, is that he could know how to erase digital footprints. If so, he could manipulate data enough to cover his whereabouts if necessary. I've been able to do that since I turned fourteen. As he works in a variety of different IT areas, it's possible he could create his own alibi using a digital footprint."

"But you'd be able to see if he changed anything, wouldn't you?" Rio started the engine and flicked her a glance. "Styles told me you were the best in the business. I know Kalo is good, but you've been working in cybercrime for years, haven't you?"

Laughing, Beth nodded. "I don't have my supercomputer with me at the moment, but I figure we'll be able to get the files he mentioned. If there are changes to the data, I'll be able to find them, and if I do, he'll be going to the top of our suspects list."

THIRTY-FOUR

Excitement and anticipation shivered through Jenna as she waited with Kane in the outer room of the DA's office. She couldn't sit still and paced up and down, much to the annoyance of the secretary sitting behind the desk. They'd handed over all the evidence they'd collected from Dr. Lionel Graves' house, but they'd annoyed the DA by not seizing the computer and the trophies Jenna had discovered. When she'd explained that they'd left everything behind, apart from the samples of trophies she'd collected, to make sure Graves would be there when they went to arrest him, the DA reluctantly agreed with her plan. Moments later the office door opened and the county prosecutor waved them inside.

"You have no idea if Graves is still in his residence." The DA sat behind his desk, towering his fingers. "Why didn't you hunt him down after the welfare check?"

Jenna leaned both hands on his desk and stared at him. "It's a matter of priorities. He has an outside chance of being the killer, and we're only here as he falls into the person-of-interest category because he was working with kids and social workers at one time. We are aware Graves has child pornography on his computer. No child is at risk at this time. I have a serial killer in town and that is my priority. Two murders in the same number of days means that a third is on the way. My experience in psychopaths tells me we need to apprehend this man before he murders again. This is why we allowed Graves to escape, and by leaving his house untouched and placing a tracker on his vehicle, we can assume he returned to his house. At first, he likely figured we were there to question him about the pornography. If he believes that we didn't enter the house, he will likely think he is home free and we came by for another reason—which in fact we did. His vehicle hasn't moved since we went to see him. I have no reason to believe that he isn't at home right now."

"This is why we took a portion of his trophies and I downloaded a copy of his hard drive." Kane stood with feet apart and hands loose at his sides. "If he decided to destroy evidence, we have copies and many photographs. It doesn't matter what he decides to do, we have enough evidence to take him down." He heaved a sigh. "My question to you is, why the delay in the arrest warrant? We did everything by the book and I have FBI and deputies waiting to arrest him. All we need is the warrant from you, and Graves will be in County before supper."

"And if he's escaped"—the DA looked from one to the other —"we've allowed a predator to run free."

At the end of her rope, Jenna threw her hands in the air. "The longer we stand around discussing this, the more time he has to escape. Do we get the arrest warrant or should I get back to hunting down serial killers?"

"You may have your warrant." The DA signed a document on the desk in front of him. "Call me the moment you have him in custody. I have a van standing by to take him directly to County." He pointed a finger at Jenna. "Next time, collect all the evidence."

The DA's attitude toward her stung. She always insisted on following procedure to the letter. Someone like Graves wouldn't be able to disappear. From what she'd seen in his bathroom, his dependence on medication would take him back to the house. He wouldn't be able to walk miles in the snow, so the chances of him returning to the house once he'd seen they'd left were high. He had only one vehicle, so if he did return and decide to run, they would have been able to track him. Getting back to catching a serial killer had been her priority and she believed she'd made the right choice. They had the evidence and now an arrest warrant. Once they had Graves in custody, the FBI would be all over his house. Likely his computer would be given to Beth and she would dive deep and discover if he had any contacts and then they would take it from there. After today, the case would be out of her hands and she would be glad to be rid of it.

They hurried back to the office, and minutes later Beth, Styles, Carter, Raven, and Rio headed to Graves' home. The man's vehicle remained parked in the same position and hadn't moved since they were last there. Carter and Styles headed around the back. Kane and Raven went to the front door and knocked. Jenna stood to one side with Beth and Rio. "Sheriff's department."

Nothing.

Jenna pressed her com. "Anything happening round the back of the house, Carter?"

"Nope, the door is open. There is a wet puddle just inside. I figure snow has been getting in for a time."

Turning to Raven and Rio, Jenna indicated toward the front door. "Watch the door, we'll head round back."

Following Kane, Jenna waded through the thick snow to the back of the house, with Beth at her side. She stared at the open door. "I wonder if he came back. Maybe he froze to death in the snow."

"Now that would make my day." Carter grinned at her. "No paperwork."

"Let's check it out." Kane pulled his weapon and stepped inside.

Carter went next, followed by Styles and Jenna and Beth. They kept their backs to the wall. Ahead as they neared the office, she heard someone whistle. As she reached the office door, Carter looked at her shaking his head. No one said a word. As the men parted, her gaze rested on a man slumped in an office chair, with a tarot card stapled to his forehead. Staring in disbelief Jenna circled the desk. The handle of an ornate paper knife protruded from the man's neck, just below the skull. "Is he dead?"

"Oh, yeah." Styles shook his head. "I'd say the knife cut his brainstem. I suggest we all get out of here before we contaminate the scene."

"The Tarot Killer strikes again." Carter stared at the body with a look of incredulity on his face. "How did he know about this guy?"

"How does he know about any of the people he kills?" Beth folded her arms across her chest. "I'm going to request this creep's computer. This guy is a small cog in a big wheel. I figure he'll lead us to other creeps just like him. Let's get out of here. I can't stand looking at him for a moment longer." She turned on her heel and headed along the hallway.

Jenna looked at Kane. "I'll call the DA and give him the news. Can you call Wolfe? We'll wait for him to arrive."

"Sure." Kane gave Jenna a long look and then squeezed her shoulder. "He's not gonna hurt anyone anymore." He pulled out his phone and ushered her toward the door. "Come on, we can wait outside."

Outside a cold wind buffeted Jenna as she made the call to the DA to explain what had happened. "No, I don't have any idea what time this happened. The back door of the house is wide open and inside the temperature is close to freezing. I would say the time of death is going to be difficult to determine.

I'm sure Dr. Wolfe will contact you as soon as he is able to make a determination."

"*As this case concerns child pornography, the FBI will be taking over the investigation from this point in time. As you have agents on the ground, I will be contacting the local director to advise them to collect the evidence. I want you there to oversee everything. Unless you have someone to arrest in the homicide cases, make this your current priority.*" He disconnected.

Sighing, Jenna headed toward the Beast. Beth fell in step beside her and she glanced at her. "Why don't you climb into the back of our truck and give me a rundown on the interview with Ethan Rourke?" She pulled open the door and slipped into the passenger seat, turning to speak to Beth.

"I have the interview on my phone. Rourke knows both of the women. Well, let's say he's met Ellie McBride, when he worked at the school, and was contacted by Laney Prescott for a home security system but hasn't met her. He mentioned being snowed under with his current job but planned to swing by her place sometime this week." Beth shook her head. "I seem to see serial killers in everyone and for this reason I'll be checking his alibis for around the times of the murders."

A shiver slid down Jenna's back and she nodded. "Yeah, I understand. A serial killer could be sitting right next to you and you'd never know."

"Exactly." Beth removed her black wool hat, tidied her long blonde hair, and pulled it back into a ponytail at the nape of her neck before replacing her hat. "I don't plan to leave any stone unturned. Although after listening to the other two interviews, those suspects look more viable. When you look at someone like Sean Jones, the first thing that comes to mind is the fact that he wanted to live with his father but ended up with his mother, who died after a short illness. To me, this is a red flag because it's more likely he killed his mother or caused the illness. In his mind he would have been removing an obstacle that allowed him to be with his father. The huge trigger for him came when his father rejected him and put him in foster care. All that anger building up for years, he may have kept it contained while growing but maybe something triggered him recently. Bad memories can creep up on people even if they aren't psychopaths and cause mental issues."

Jenna agreed with everything she said. "Yeah, and the way he killed the cat is much the same as what's happening now." She thought for a beat. "I found Caleb Dorsey a little creepy. There's something about him sneaking around the school at night and hanging around Ellie McBride's vehicle. The fact he keeps old school photographs makes me wonder whether he has an ax to grind with someone. He's another one who's interacted with both of the victims recently." Jenna tapped her bottom lip. "The problem is it's all circumstantial evidence. Unlike here, where we walk in and discover enough evidence to send someone to prison for the rest of their lives, essentially we have nothing really to go on apart from our hunches. I'll be interested to know what you find on Ethan Rourke and if he has been manipulating any data to use as an alibi. To be honest, my money is on Jones. The moment I get back to the office I'm going to ask Kalo to do a more in-depth background check on him. There's something about him I just can't grasp. It's as if I know it's there and just can't reach it."

"The one thing I do know"—Beth leaned back in the seat and sighed—"he's going to kill again very soon. Interviewing him won't stop him. He believes he's gotten away with the first two. I'll be interested to see if he kills another professional. If he does, it will make it so much easier to discover our killer. People interacting with the same two murdered people in a town the size of Black Rock Falls wouldn't be too unusual, but three dead women isn't a coincidence. It's a big neon sign that points to the killer."

THIRTY-FIVE

Working night shift at the hospital in the middle of winter couldn't be any worse for Isla Monroe. With most of the lights switched off on her floor and the hallways as quiet as a tomb, being the only one there on the off chance someone would be admitted to the hospital and put into one of the wards overnight had been a waste of time. A few strange things had happened to her over the last few days. She'd arrived home twice in a row to a pool of melted snow inside her back door. Yesterday, after leaving work, she'd arrived at her vehicle and as usual went to work removing the snow from the front and back windows. Scrawled in the snow on the back window was a message: *Next time I'll be here.*

The message disturbed her, but she drove home and made sure her security alarm had been turned on before she went to bed. Inside her cozy little house, she should be safe and warm. She thought about the puddle inside her back door and figured it had been snowing so hard that melted snow had likely leaked under the door to form the puddle. She slept late as usual. Arriving home at two each morning meant her days started around noon, except on Thursdays, when she worked half a shift, which meant she worked from six through to ten. The day went along boring as usual. The old woman who had been in the ward she supervised had been discharged. She'd spent the day restocking everything just to pass the time.

Relieved when the clock struck ten, she headed down to her locker room. When she opened her door, a piece of yellow paper fluttered to the floor. She bent to pick it up and stared at it uncomprehending. *You kill people* had been scrawled across the note in red ink. Suddenly afraid, the note fell from her trembling fingers. She ran out into the empty hallway and stopped as footsteps echoed through the hospital. It would be unusual for anyone to be on this floor at night without patients, not even the cleaners came up here. Panic gripped her by the throat and she ran toward the elevator, pressing the button frantically. The numbers above the elevator didn't change, as if it had stuck on a floor below.

Clinging tight to her phone, she looked behind her, but nobody came along the passageway. The footsteps were getting louder. She bolted for the stairs and flung herself down the steps. If she could get to the ER, she'd be safe. There would always be somebody there. As she ran down the steps, she heard the unmistakable sound of the elevator grinding as it swayed its way down to the bottom floor. Heart pounding in her chest, she kept on going and, reaching the bottom floor, pushed open the door and rushed out into the hallway. Making her way to the ER, she relaxed a little under the bright lights and blended in with the people moving around inside. Trembling, she peered over one shoulder, but no one seemed to be following her.

Dragging in deep breaths to calm her shattered nerves, she made her way to the restroom. Inside she took a few minutes to compose herself. Someone in the hospital must be playing tricks on her and she'd fallen for it. She gave herself a little shake. She'd parked her truck just outside in the parking lot. After pulling on her coat and buttoning it up, she took a deep breath, scanned the parking lot, and then seeing no one, slipped and slid her way to her vehicle. She climbed inside, pushed her phone between her thighs, and started the engine. The next moment, something came over her head and around her neck. She glanced in the rearview mirror. Dark eyes peered at her through a balaclava. A strong smell of men's cologne wafted over her. As she opened her mouth to scream, the cord around her neck tightened.

"Drive."

THIRTY-SIX

Darkness had crept into Black Rock Falls by the time Jenna and Kane had left Dr. Graves' house. As a homicide, Wolfe had taken extra care to collect any shred of evidence available. Once he finished, they all went through the house with a fine-toothed comb. It hadn't surprised her to discover more disgusting literature that this man had stored in plastic bins in his basement. They hauled everything out of the house and packed it into one of the vans owned by the forensic department from Helena. Their interest had been in the takedown at the BW Ranch, but after arriving with three vans to collect the evidence, they had one spare. They had all staggered back to the office and, after writing up their reports, Jenna had insisted Jo and Kalo return to the ranch. She wanted to give Jo as much time as possible to spend with her daughter Jaime. The young girl enjoyed staying with Tauri and Jackson. When Jo had kindly offered to prepare a meal for the children, and Beth said she'd help as she wanted an early night, Jenna had agreed. Rio and Rowley had indicated they were needed at home, but Carter, Styles, and Raven wanted to head to Antlers for a steak dinner. After seeing the hungry look in Kane's eyes, she made plans to meet them there.

They'd dashed home to spend some time with their boys. She'd gone through the usual bedtime routine with Jackson, and he'd fallen asleep almost at once. After agreeing that Tauri could spend a little more time with Jaime decorating the house, she had slipped out with Kane to join the others.

The meal had been incredible, as usual. The twenty-ounce rib-eye steaks the men had ordered filled a sizzling plate of their own and another held all the sides. It didn't surprise her to see Raven arrive with Emily on his arm. The pair had been spending more time together lately. They were chatting over coffee when Jenna's phone chimed. She'd volunteered to take the 911 emergency calls this evening. A strangled voice came through her earbud. She held up a hand to the others to be quiet, muted her phone, and passed the other earpiece to Kane.

"Why are you kidnapping me?" A female voice filled with dread choked on her words.

"Shut up and drive or I'll strangle you." A man's raspy voice sent shivers down Jenna's back. *"I can take you to the brink of death and then let you survive."*

"Where are we heading? This road leads to the lake." The woman coughed.

"Go to the old boathouse."

Jenna stood. "There's a kidnapping in progress. They're heading toward the old boathouse by the lake."

"Go." Kane waved Raven away. "Take Em home."

"No way." Emily frowned at him. "You might need a doctor and you have two right here. We're going."

"And I have Ben." Raven shrugged into his coat. "Trained in taking down perps."

"Okay, get a move on." Kane dropped a wad of bills on the table and indicated to the others to head for the door.

With Carter and Styles riding in the back seat, Jenna gripped tight to the grab handle above the door as Kane backed out of the parking space, swung the Beast around, and accelerated along Main. Jenna gave a running commentary of what she could hear through her earpiece. The cold even tone of the kidnapper raised goosebumps on her flesh.

"Why are you doing this to me?" The woman forced out words as if she had something tight around her neck.

"I don't need an excuse."

"How long have you been stalking me? Did you leave that message on my window and in my locker?"

"Maybe I did and maybe I didn't. Did it scare you, Isla?" He chuckled. *"Did it make your heart race knowing that I could just pluck you off the sidewalk without anyone seeing?"*

Jenna glanced at Kane, who weaved around ice patches. His mouth set in a determined line as he listened to the same conversation through her other earbud.

"When we get to our destination"—Kane glanced in the mirror at Carter and Styles—"there is a pile of Kevlar vests in the back. The large ones are on the right. Grab one before we chase down this guy. We don't know if he's armed or not. There are flashlights in a wooden box, along with anything else you'll need." He looked at Jenna. "You'll need to convince Emily to remain inside the truck."

Jenna nodded as terrified screams and sobs came through her earpiece. It seems the poor woman had closed in on their destination. She stared at the map on the GPS. They were approximately five minutes away from the turning that led to the boathouse near the lake. Five minutes was four minutes too long to prevent murder. She wanted to tell the woman on the other end of the phone that they were close behind her but breaking the radio silence would mean her instant death. She looked at Kane. "We're going to be too late."

"She'll be dead the moment he sees us coming." Kane glanced in the rearview mirror. "Carter, contact Raven and tell him to kill his lights before we turn onto the driveway to the boathouse. It's a full moon and we'll be able to see where we're going, especially with everything covered in snow. Let's just hope this woman has the sense to slow down and give us time to get to her."

Listening intently to the conversation on the other end of the line, Jenna kept her attention on the way ahead. "If you recall, the forest surrounds the lake. We should be able to park in the trees and make our way on foot toward the boathouse without being seen. The driveway to the boathouse curves in and out of the trees."

"What are you hearing?" Styles leaned forward in his chair and looked at Jenna.

"He's making threats to her and she's terrified, but she had the presence of mind to dial 911 and leave her phone on. I figure she is pretty levelheaded."

"She doesn't seem to be mentioning a weapon." Carter waved his toothpick in the air. "I figure he has the garrote around her neck already, so he's likely sitting in the seat behind the driver. He could have been inside the vehicle waiting for her. Have you heard any names?"

Nodding, Jenna glanced over one shoulder at him. "He called her Isla. So, he knows her."

"If he's been following the same MO as the other murders, it's likely he's been stalking her for a while." Carter slid the toothpick between his lips. "If he's been leaving notes behind, why hasn't this woman contacted us before?"

Jenna swallowed hard as the woman's voice quivered through her earpiece.

"Why are you doing this to me? I don't kill people. I help people. Her voice cut off abruptly and she gasped for air. *"Stop doing that. Look, this is the turn to the boathouse. If you keep strangling me, I won't be able to drive."*

"Nurses—you're all the same. You don't help people; you just stand around and let them suffer until they die. So, I'm here to even things out. Now it's your turn. I figured the boathouse is a

nice, isolated spot where I could make my point and no one would be able to hear you scream."

"You're a monster." The woman's sobs came with long gasping breaths.

"That's what they all say."

THIRTY-SEVEN

To avoid the engine noise of the Beast, Kane drove at an agonizingly slow speed until he found a suitable place to leave the trucks. They climbed out and pulled on the Kevlar vests, grabbed a few items from the back of the truck, and leaving Emily inside the vehicle to notify everyone, waded through thick snowfall toward the forest. He'd formed a plan along the way; they would scatter through the forest and come out around the back of the boathouse. The building had an opening at both ends: one end allowing a boat to be unloaded and the another giving access to the boat ramp into the lake. Over one hundred years old, the building had belonged to an old settler who built fishing boats. The local council maintained it for its historical relevance. Cutting a path through the freezing drifts, Kane led the way into the forest and into the trees with Jenna close behind. Although snow piled high on the branches of the pine trees, the density of the forest protected the forest floor and made the way through easy. The fine dusting of snow beneath their boots muffled their footsteps on the crisp dead pine needles. He didn't need to know Carter's and Styles' positions.

His orders had been to surround the boathouse and he trusted their judgment implicitly. To his right, he just made out Raven and Ben, but only by the dog's eyes reflecting green in the moonlight.

From the boathouse the sound of struggling, screams, and thumps came toward them through the night. Against all odds, Isla fought for her life. Kane ran faster, bursting into the back of the boathouse weapon drawn but couldn't get a clear shot of the man grappling with the woman. Behind him, Jenna ran to his side. She indicated she intended to go around to the front of the boathouse to help the woman and sunk into the frozen white scenery before he had time to stop her. He raised his voice. "Sheriff's department. Get on your knees, with your hands on top of your head. Now!"

The man, dressed in all black and wearing a balaclava, rolled out of sight under the ancient boat, suspended in a cradle. A woman, her hair flying out behind her, dragged something from around her neck and threw it away before running full pelt out the back of the boathouse, down the ramp, and through the drifts and onto the frozen lake. Behind her, ran Jenna bounding through the thick snow, calling out for the woman to run her way to safety. Kane scanned the area. The boat offered the only protection from anyone with a weapon. A shadow moved on his right as Raven appeared out of the forest and took up position opposite him. The man, hiding under the boat, hadn't moved or uttered a word, but the woman still screamed and ran for her life.

"Sheriff's department. You're safe now. Stop running. The lake is beneath you. Stop now." Jenna's voice rang out across the lake. "Come this way."

Kane's gaze shifted, and his heart almost stopped beating when Jenna followed the woman across the frozen water. Pushing his mind onto detaining the kidnapper, he raised his voice again. "Come out with your hands up or we will send a K-9 to drag you out of there."

"Sure, you will." A raspy voice came out from under the boat. "And I'll blow its brains out before it gets here."

"FBI." Carter's voice rang out from the front of the boathouse. "We have you surrounded. Throw out your weapon. You can't escape. Right now, we've got you only for kidnapping. Shoot a police dog and you might as well be shooting a cop."

The screaming on the lake had stopped, and Kane took out his flashlight and aimed it at the boat. The man shrunk away, his hands out of sight. Did he have a gun? Taking no chances, he sent him a warning and aimed two shots just in front of his head into the boat's cradle. He didn't intend to kill him, but he wanted to make the threat real. Trash-talking would get his point across too and hopefully the man would come out before he injured him. "I figure another six inches to the left. What do you say, boys?"

"I can blow his head off his shoulders from here." Styles' voice came from the front right-hand side. "I have a clear shot. Although my revolver makes a ton of mess. It'll spread his brains all over."

Trying not to smile as the team followed his lead, he nodded to Styles. Figuring that if the man had a weapon, he'd have used it by now, Kane stepped out of cover and took two strides closer to the man. "Last chance. Come out from there and put your hands on your head if you plan on living until morning. I have no power over these FBI guys. They could take you out just for fun."

"Hold your fire. I'm coming out." The man crawled out from under the boat on his hands and knees and flattened himself on the ground with his fingers interlaced over the back of his neck.

Keeping his weapon aimed on the man, he waited for Raven

and Styles to go in and pat him down. The two agents dragged him to his feet, took him outside, and secured him with his arms wrapped around a pine tree. Before Kane could ask the kidnapper any questions, Jenna called his name. He turned to look at her. She stood perfectly still in the middle of the snow-covered lake. To her left a few yards away, the woman had dropped to her hands and knees, sobbing violently. He holstered his weapon and walked toward the edge of the lake when Jenna held up her hand.

"The ice is cracking." Jenna's face had drained of color. "What should I do?"

Wanting to run to her, Kane walked through the heavy snowdrifts and took in the shattering ice. He'd risk falling in to save her but right now it wasn't an option. One mistake now and they'd never get her out alive. "Don't move."

Kane pulled out his phone and called Emily. "There's rope in the back of the Beast, grab it and run as fast as you can to the lake. Jenna's on the ice and it's cracking. Stick to the forest as much as possible to avoid the deep snow."

"I'm on my way."

"Isla." Carter moved to the edge. "Take deep breaths. Try to stop sobbing. Any movement will make it worse. Can you move toward me and away from the cracks?"

Isla nodded and edged very slowly back toward the boathouse. "Good, keep going, but if you hear cracking, stretch out on the ice to spread your weight. We'll come and get you."

Kane stared at him. "How the heck do you plan on doing that? We'll go right through."

"She'll make it." Carter looked at him. "I've fished here and the lake is shallow where she is. Jenna is in the deepest part. The ice will be thinner there." He shrugged. "I'll get Isla, you need to help Jenna."

Walking up and down the edge of the lake, Kane searched

for a solution, but even if he belly-crawled, his weight would break the fragile surface and he'd lose any chance of rescuing Jenna. He turned to her and his heart sank. "Jenna, can you get down on hands and knees and move away from the cracking?"

"No, I'm surrounded." She bit her bottom lip. "It's only a matter of time before it opens up. It's cracking all around me."

The next moment, Emily burst from the forest carrying a coil of climbing rope. She dashed to Kane. He made a loop at one end and swung it around his head like a lasso intending to throw it to Jenna.

"Wait!" Raven came up beside him. He took the rope and slipped it over Ben's head. "Go to Jenna, stealth."

"Come on, Ben." Jenna dropped slowly to her hands and knees, holding out one hand to Ben.

Grinding his back teeth, Kane watched helpless as Ben belly-crawled across the frozen lake. As the dog got closer, water seeped around Jenna. "Loop the rope around your waist and hang onto Ben, we'll haul you both out."

Kane, Raven, and Styles grabbed hold of the rope and pulled it, moving hand over hand. Jenna and Ben flew across the cracking lake at high speed until they hit the snowy edge. The dog shook himself violently and bounded to Raven. Kane ran to Jenna and gathered her into his arms. She trembled against him, wet through. He stripped off her wet coat, took off his jacket, and wrapped it around her. "Are you hurt?"

"No, just cold. Remind me to buy a whole pound of sausages for Ben." Jenna's teeth chattered as she turned to look at Carter assisting Isla. "Is she okay?"

"That man tried to strangle me." Isla pointed at the man secured to a tree. She walked up to him and kicked him hard in the shins. "I hope they lock you up and throw away the key." She turned her gaze on Carter. "Thank you for saving me."

"My pleasure, ma'am." Carter smiled.

"What's your name?" Jenna stared at the prisoner.

She received a string of curse words. Kane stepped forward and ripped off his balaclava. "Anyone recognize him?" He shone a light into the man's face.

"I do." Jenna stepped a little closer and wrinkled her nose at the strong smell of cologne. Ellie McBride had mentioned her attacker wore a strong cologne. This man had to be their killer. "I spoke to Beth about him earlier and checked out his file. His name is Ethan Rourke. The guy who installed the new security system at the Cattleman's Hotel." She stared at him. "I can't wait to discover the reason you murdered two women in my town."

"It's good you caught me, Sheriff." A smirk crossed Rourke's lips. "I don't like women in authority. Maybe you would have been next." He laughed maniacally.

"Raven and Styles, please take the prisoner back to my office." Jenna leaned into Kane. "We'll be right behind you. Put him in interview room one. I'll need to get changed and then I'll be right along." She turned to look at Isla. "I want you to come back to my office. I have two doctors with me to assess your injuries. I need you to make a statement so we can get this man sent to County."

"I'd love to." Isla glared at Rourke and followed Carter and Emily to the Beast.

Kane wrapped his arm around Jenna and they headed back to the truck as fast as possible. The cold already bit into his flesh but he had a spare coat in the back of his truck. With Carter, Isla, and Emily safely inside the Beast, they headed back to town. No one said a word inside the truck, but when he escorted Jenna to the locker room, he pulled her close. "I came so close to losing you. I figure I used a lifetime of prayers out there tonight. How we managed to pull you from the ice before it broke open, I'll never know. I felt so utterly useless. If you'd fallen into the water, I'd have dived in to save you, but I'm not sure we'd have made it out alive."

"First up, prayers are infinite, and secondly, I figure surviving a frozen lake is a Christmas miracle." She went onto her toes to kiss him. "Isla and I both help people. This proves to me there is more work for us to do."

Kane smiled. "Amen to that."

THIRTY-EIGHT

Jenna took her time taking a long hot shower. She'd given instructions to Kane to contact the lawyer Sam Cross to have him standing by if Rourke requested a lawyer. She didn't want anything to jeopardize the interview. Emily and Raven would examine Isla and take photographs of her injuries, particularly those round her neck. Once Isla had signed a statement, they'd take her to the hospital and keep her under observation for a day or so. Styles had collected the garrote that Isla had ripped from her neck in the boathouse and secured it in an evidence bag on scene. It appeared to be exactly the same as the others that they'd discovered alongside the bodies of the previous victims. As she dried her hair in the bathroom, she heard voices and turned to see Jo walking into the locker room.

"I figured you might need me in the interview room." Jo smiled at her. "Don't worry, Raya is watching the kids. "This guy sounds complex. He might be an interesting addition to my next book."

Running a brush through her hair, Jenna breathed a sigh of relief. Psychopaths were complex people, and Jo had studied them for many years. She interviewed them in prison and discovered that the majority of them loved notoriety. The offer of being included in her "most notorious serial killers of the year" publication had often been the only encouragement they needed to give up their secrets. "Rourke has already threatened me. He told me he hates women in authority and maybe I'd have been next if we hadn't caught him. What do you consider would be the best way to approach him to get him to spill his story?"

"I figured we'd leave the men outside and speak to him ourselves." Jo turned and headed along the hallway. "Sam Cross, Rourke's lawyer, is here."

Jenna walked beside her. "I'll ask Dave to get the ball rolling. He can read Rourke his rights. It's good Cross is here. If you recall, Sam is defense all the way, and we need to make sure this scumbag isn't going to walk away from this."

"Yeah, I recall." Jo led the way to Jenna's office.

Jenna collected a legal pad from her drawer and slid the photographs of the victims into a folder. "Dave, I'll interview him with Jo. Head down and start the process, record everything."

"Okay but first read Isla's statement. He stalked her and likely stalked the others too." Kane frowned. "You sure you don't want me in there with you? He is a serial killer."

Jenna shook her head. "He won't get out of the cuffs attached to the table and you'll be right outside along with Carter and Styles."

They read the statement and discussed it before heading downstairs to the interview room. Jenna swiped her card and walked in with Jo. Inside, Kane leaned against the wall. He straightened and left. Jenna turned to Sam Cross. The lawyer, in a battered Stetson and snakeskin cowboy boots, gave her a curt nod. "Mr. Cross. Thank you for coming in at such short notice."

"It's what I do." Cross straightened his legal pad and clicked the top of his pen. "My client wants to speak to you. I've advised him not to incriminate himself, but he feels it's too late for that already. I will caution him if needs be as we proceed."

Jenna sat down and arranged her things on the desk. The recorder had been paused and she pressed the button to continue the recording. "Recording continued at five after twelve. In the room with Mr. Rourke are Sheriff Jenna Alton, Agent Jo Wells, and Mr. Rourke's lawyer, Mr. Sam Cross."

Jenna exchanged a look with Jo and then swung her attention back to Rourke. "When did you start stalking Isla Monroe? We're aware you were inside her house, left notes on the back of her vehicle, and inside her locker at the hospital. You intimidated her at the hospital and then climbed into her truck, placed a garrote around her neck, and made her drive to the boathouse near the lake." She kept her gaze fixed on him. "I'm sure you have a very logical explanation for why you behaved in this manner. Maybe you would like the chance to explain?"

"Yeah, I've been watching her." Rourke leaned on the table, his hands clasped together as if he didn't have a care in the world. "So what? It's what men do. Hasn't your husband told you that, or do you believe he's a saint?"

Surprised by his verbal attack, Jenna made a few unnecessary notes just to put him off guard. "Why were you watching her? Does she remind you of someone from your past? Because she doesn't know you and has never met you before."

"The thing is women like her—nurses—believe they have the power over life and death. They lie to people and tell them everything is going to be okay when it's not. They need to know it's me who has the power over life and death."

"Explain." Jo crossed her legs slowly. "What gave you this impression of nurses?"

"She reminds me of the nurse who cared for my mom." Rourke gave an agitated tug on his cuffs, making the metal clang against the loop on the table. "She told me to go home and everything would be okay, and the next morning my mom died alone. She lied to me."

"So you wanted her to pay for your mom's death?" Jo raised one eyebrow. "Although she is completely innocent."

"I wanted her to feel the fear I felt when Mom died and left me all alone." Rourke glared at Jo. "My pa didn't want me. He tossed me away like garbage."

Jenna leaned back in her chair. Sam Cross had allowed everything so far, so she'd move to the murders. "In your interview, you mentioned knowing Ellie McBride. You said you'd worked on equipment in her classroom recently."

"Yeah, I did, what of it?" Rourke rolled his eyes and stared at the wall.

Shrugging, Jenna inclined her head to observe him. "We know you attacked her in the parking lot of the convenience store at approximately eleven on Friday evening. We have you at the roadhouse shortly after. Ellie escaped and told us a lot about you. What were you planning to do with her?"

"I had planned to take her to the boathouse. She reminds me of the teacher who had me expelled for throwing a spitball at her. That incident caused problems for me at home. Soon after my pa left, my mother got sick and died. It was all her fault. If she hadn't had me expelled, none of this would have happened."

"Run through what happened that night with Ellie McBride." Jo looked at him expressionless. "What went wrong? You didn't try to strangle her, did you?"

"Nope. Not at the time." Rourke smiled at her. "I had been following her for a few days. I couldn't believe my luck when she went to the convenience store and parked along the pile of snow. I parked my truck out of view of the CCTV cameras—the ones I'd installed—and waited until I seen her coming out of the store. When she opened the back of her SUV to put her groceries inside, I had intended to strangle her, but I noticed someone heading toward the door, so when she bent over, I grabbed the jack in the back of her vehicle and smashed her in the head with it. I figured I'd killed her, so I pushed her inside the trunk of her SUV, grabbed her purse and keys and drove to the roadhouse. I noticed the vehicle had no gas, so I stopped to refill it using her credit card. I figured as I had her card, I might as well go inside and get myself a meal. I decided to dispose of her body in the lake and no one would find her because it would be frozen over until the melt."

"What did you do when you found her missing?" Jo kept her voice low and in control. "Did you go looking for her?"

"Nope." Rourke glanced at Sam Cross. "I know I'm making it difficult for you to defend me, but they've got me on the kidnapping charge anyway and as I've admitted to attempting to murder Isla Monroe, they can only keep me in prison for one life, can't they?"

"You've been given your Miranda rights. I can only advise you to remain silent. As you have chosen not to, I can only sit here and make sure your legal rights are protected." Cross blew out a breath. "I will explain why you committed the crimes. That's the best I can do."

"Like I told you, I figured I'd killed Ellie McBride. She climbed out of the vehicle and walked out into the night and then I heard she'd gone back to the school. I searched at her home for her and she was a no show. It took sheer genius to enter the school again without being seen and then get her to go to the boiler room." He chuckled. "No one else could have done that."

Jenna held up a hand. "Just back it up a little. So you went outside and found Ellie missing from the back of the SUV. What happened next?"

"I drove her car back to the convenience store. Dropped her keys under the back, climbed into my truck, and drove home." Rourke looked at her as if she'd lost her mind. "How do you figure I got back to the convenience store? It's too far to walk." He gave Jenna a long look. "Why are you here interviewing me and not at home with your kids? Do you leave them alone all night?"

The door to the interview room opened and Kane stepped in. He leaned casually against the wall, arms folded across his chest, but his expression had dropped into combat mode. Jenna ignored Rourke's question and allowed Jo to continue with the interview.

"So you left the messages on the whiteboard for Ellie McBride? How did you get into school without being noticed?" Jo cleared her throat. "I've had my people look over the CCTV footage. The school requires cards to come and go and everything is recorded. How did you manage to gain entry without being seen?"

"I made a copy of the janitor's card. I went to his house recently and he asked me to get something from the glovebox and there it was. I returned it once I'd made a copy." Rourke gave her a wide grin. "He moves around without anyone noticing him. They all figure he's crazy and let him be. Once I had the card, I could get inside the school at any time and change anything I wanted to on the computers and CCTV footage. You see I'm very smart. Smarter than you."

"So, it would seem." Jo nodded slowly as if agreeing with him. "How did you first come into contact with Laney Prescott?"

"I didn't lie to the federal officer during my interview." Rourke wet his lips as if he enjoyed reliving the moment. "I told her that Laney Prescott had contacted me for a home security system. I just left out the bit where I'd already gone to see her. She is one of these women that leaves a set of spare keys in a dish by the front door. I pocketed them as I walked around explaining where she needed to put her CCTV cameras. I had free access to her home anytime I wanted it."

"You left the note on her pillow using Ellie McBride's lipstick, didn't you?" Jo's lips turned up at the corners. "Were you trying to deflect the blame onto Ellie for murdering Laney?"

"Nope." Rourke barked a laugh. "Do you figure that anyone would believe that a schoolteacher murdered Laney Prescott? You are crazier than me. It was a trophy. I had it in my pocket at the time, is all. The thrill of chasing Laney through the house and then strangling her made me forget where I'd left it. Can I have it back?"

Jenna glanced at Jo. She wanted to wind up the interview, but Jo had one more question.

"Laney Prescott was a social worker." Jo uncrossed her legs and stared at him. "She helped people. What possible motive could you have for killing her?"

"If you'd ever been trapped in foster care, you'd know the answer to that question." Rourke turned his head away, disgust plastered across his face. "Do you know how many kids I've seen, who went to court on the hope they would get back with their parents and end up back in foster care because a social worker had given them a bad report. They don't care about the kids or their families. All they care about is keeping them apart. The world would be a better place without them. I'll make it my life's work, to take every one of them out."

"Oh, I figure that's enough for today." Sam Cross glared at his client.

"Can you get me out of here?" Rourke shot him a glance. "I need to feed my dog."

A dog? Jenna stared at Rourke and then looked at Cross. "One of my deputies has connections with Animal Rescue. I can send him to collect him." She looked at Rourke. She needed one last bit of information. "Can you describe your dog, and what's his name?"

"He's a black-and-white mixed breed." Rourke grinned.

"He's a big mean SOB and goes for the throat just like me. I call him Satan."

That was another nail in the coffin for Rourke. Thank the Lord they had taken this man off the streets. Jenna ignored him. "The interview concluded at twelve forty-five." She stood. "If you have finished with your client. We have a van ready to transport him to County, once he has signed a transcript of the interview. I will be handing all the information over to the DA and he will take it from there. You will be able to visit your client again in the morning once an arrest warrant has been issued."

"How long will that take?" Sam Cross checked his watch.

"It will be almost immediate." Kane straightened from against the wall. "AI produces a transcript of the interview. I'll go to the office and collect a copy for you now. I will also give you a copy of the video, should the need arise to check the transcript for any reason. The moment your client signs the document, we can all head home to our beds." He opened the door and stood to one side as Jo and Sam Cross left the room.

Jenna turned to look at Rourke. "Do you have any remorse for killing those innocent women?"

"They weren't innocent." Rourke shot a dark look at Kane. "You'll find out soon enough. I'll be free soon and I'll come looking for her. She's just the same as the others." He chuckled. "I can almost feel the life leaving her already."

"You'll never walk free, but if you do find a way to escape"—Kane slammed a fist on the table—"we'll meet again and next time I'll aim for your head. I won't miss. You have my word." He opened the door and waved Jenna through.

EPILOGUE

Christmas

On Christmas Eve the team spent the day bringing all the files up to date. The cases had all been taken out of her hands, and she had very little to do. Rourke had been arrested, charged, and awaited the court process before trial. The pedophile case had been turned over to the FBI and in the new year Beth would be investigating Graves' computer and hunting down any contacts he'd made. The forensics team had found no evidence to point to the identity of the Tarot Killer and the FBI case was ongoing.

The education department had started an investigation into Dorsey to ensure the children's safety, but as he hadn't done anything wrong, she doubted any action would be taken to move him somewhere else. This being the case, she would keep a file on him and check on him herself from time to time. The drug bust had been placed in the hands of the DEA, so Jenna's caseload had cleared.

At a little after two, Jenna decided to close the office. They'd all worked long hours for many days and it was time to celebrate Christmas. Raya had arrived in town with the children and they'd decided to spend an hour or so taking them to visit Santa Claus at the town hall. The townsfolk had decorated the hall with an abundance of flashing colored lights, Christmas trees, and sparkly things, so that the moment Jackson walked inside, he screeched with excitement. He ran around touching everything and it took both of them to make sure he didn't vanish in the crowd. Although Santa Claus didn't impress him. He wiggled and became upset when expected to sit on a stranger's lap. The small gift Santa Claus gave him didn't placate him either. His screams of "Dadeee" echoed through the hall, and Jenna giggled as Kane rushed to extract his son's grip from the poor man's white beard. Beside Jenna, Tauri and Jaime chuckled and Carter snorted with laughter.

"This is going to be the best Christmas ever." Carter grinned at Jenna. "The kids are so much fun."

"It's about time you settled down." Kane passed the wriggling Jackson to Carter. "Hold him for a moment. I need to find a wipe to get that sticky stuff off his hands." He searched his pockets.

"I never figured I'd live to see the day that Dave Kane carried a packet of wipes in his pocket." Carter held out Jackson as if he would explode.

"Yeah, well, that's what dads do." Kane grinned. "Kids are always sticky."

Jenna looked from one to the other. "Come on, we've got time to visit the stores. I need to buy a few extra gifts." She waited for Kane to clean up Jackson and then hoist the little boy on his shoulders. She took Tauri's hand and smiled at Jo. "Ready?"

Beth and Styles joined them and they all strolled along the cleared sidewalk enjoying the Christmas spirit. The townsfolk moved around with happy expressions, many stopping to wish them Merry Christmas. The town had turned into a Christmas card, with snowcapped storefronts and lights flashing. A beautiful happy place again. By the end of the afternoon, they all carried piles of gifts. No one had much time to think about Christmas before, with everything going on in the office.

The following morning, Jenna woke to the squeals and excitement of the three children. She grinned at Kane, already sitting on the edge of the bed and pulling on his clothes. "This is the best part of Christmas. I love watching the kids unwrap their gifts." She pulled on a robe and walked around the bed.

"Talking of gifts." Kane gathered her in his arms and pulled a small box out of his pocket. "I have something for you."

Jenna stared at the little blue leather-covered box. She had a wedding and an engagement ring, and the box would be too small for earrings or a bracelet. With his arms still wrapped around her she opened the lid. Inside sat an exquisite gold band set with small blue opals that matched her engagement ring. As she moved the box, colors in the stones sparkled like rainbows dancing across the night sky. "Oh, this is beautiful." A happy tear slid down her cheek.

"It's an eternity ring." Kane slipped it on her finger and stared into her eyes. "When I promised forever, I meant every word. Merry Christmas, Jenna."

A LETTER FROM D.K. HOOD

Dear Reader,

Thank you so much for choosing my novel and coming with me on another thrilling adventure with Kane and Alton in *Watch Over Me*.

If you'd like to keep up to date with all my latest releases, and get a free eBook, just sign up at the website link below. Your email will never be shared and you can unsubscribe at any time.

www.bookouture.com/dk-hood

It's wonderful to continue writing the stories of Jenna Alton and Dave Kane and having you along. I really appreciate all the wonderful comments and messages you have all sent me during this series.

If you enjoyed my story, I would be very grateful if you could leave a review and recommend my book to your friends and family. I really enjoy hearing from readers, so feel free to ask me questions at any time. You can get in touch on my Facebook page or join my Facebook Readers' Group for updates and giveaways.

Thank you so much for your support.

D.K. Hood

KEEP IN TOUCH WITH D.K. HOOD

www.dkhood.com

facebook.com/dkhoodauthor
x.com/DKHood_Author

ACKNOWLEDGMENTS

To my editor, superwoman Helen, the fabulous #TeamBookouture, and to the memory of my friend, Wendy Steenblok.

Also, to the fabulous reviewers and my followers on Facebook, BookBub, and all social media platforms.

PUBLISHING TEAM

Turning a manuscript into a book requires the efforts of many people. The publishing team at Bookouture would like to acknowledge everyone who contributed to this publication.

Audio
Alba Proko

Commercial
Lauren Morrissette
Hannah Richmond
Imogen Allport

Cover design
Blacksheep

Data and analysis
Mark Alder
Mohamed Bussuri

Editorial
Helen Jenner
Ria Clare

Copyeditor
Ian Hodder

Proofreader
Claire Rushbrook

Marketing
Alex Crow
Melanie Price
Occy Carr
Ciara Rosney
Martyna Młynarska

Operations and distribution
Marina Valles
Joe Morris

Production
Hannah Snetsinger
Mandy Kullar
Nadia Michael
Charlotte Hegley

Publicity
Kim Nash
Noelle Holten
Jess Readett
Sarah Hardy

Rights and contracts
Peta Nightingale
Richard King
Saidah Graham

Printed in Dunstable, United Kingdom